THEIR CONFESSIONS &
MY LIES

TJ MAKKAI

CONTENTS

Editing: Starr Waddell with Quiethouse Editing
Cover: Jason Van Winkle
Website: Scott Oine with LittleBox Social

Copyright © 2023 by TJ Makkai / Tracy Johnson
Email: info@makkaibooks.com
Website: makkaibooks.com

ISBN: 979-8-9864683-7-2

BOOKS BY TJ MAKKAI

Their Confessions & My Lies 2023

River Bend Series

Crow September 2020

Hawk October 2021

Pigeon September 2022

Next Book in River Bend Series Fall 2024

I dedicate this to
Helen, Robin, Lesley, Brad, Dean & KP
And from the M Section
Lori, John and Jen - (Jen, you were an M first)

We never moved a dead body but we did have fun.
Thanks for the memories past and future.

ONE

They called me Lou, but my name is Sarah Loudowski. My older brother, Matthew, was better known as Stew. Everyone we'd gone to school with had been called by some variation of their first or last name or whatever had happened in the moment we'd met them. No one picked out their own name, and often, it was done by third grade—even earlier if we had older siblings and were tossed in the mix of older kids at the playground who counted as babysitters back then. We were born in Dome, Wisconsin, in the late sixties and early seventies.

During that time in the Midwest, biblical names like Matthew, Mark, and John ruled the playground. Oddly enough, the name Luke never made it into the community until recently. I never understood why, especially since Luke precedes John in the Bible. The girls were Sarah, Rachel, or Mary. If we weren't one of those, then we're most likely to spend our days explaining what variation of Catherine or Christine we preferred until a name was bestowed upon us.

The girl who had disappeared from our town and who had haunted me for decades was named Claire Cosworth, but everyone called her Bo. Our community had had little to complain about—

and more importantly, I'd had little to complain or worry about—until Bo had shown up, or to be more precise, until she'd disappeared. Sadly, not for the right reasons. Give us a break, we had hardly known her.

Fast-forwarding many years, I now lived in Chicago. Depending on traffic, it was a two-hour ride back to Dome. Some months, I was here in Dome for two weekends, and then I might go for six months without coming back. My parents, my brother, and his family live in Dome, and a few friends were still in the area.

What had brought me back this week was the latest headline of another girl—Hannah "Gigi" Cunningham—gone missing. I was sure Gigi's disappearance had nothing to do with Bo's disappearance from thirty-four years ago, or at least I was pretty sure.

How could something like that repeat itself after so many years? When I'd read the statement online from the high school senior who stumbled upon the crime scene, he had echoed everything I'd witnessed all those years ago. The only difference was this kid had spoken to the police and the press, and I had done neither. I couldn't help wonder why Maz was insisting I come back to Dome. I needed to stay out of whatever was going on but something was drawing me back.

TWO

We'd never meant for the nicknames to be vicious or mean. Take, for example, Keith Harton, who everyone called John. In kindergarten, when the teacher would take roll call, Keith was always in the bathroom. Jackie, whose real name is Rachel Jackson, would tell the teacher Keith was in the john (she had four older brothers), and so keeping with Dome tradition, after the third day, everyone called him John. Being named after a toilet could scar a kid, but not John or anyone originally from our village. It was just the way things were in Dome. He was a star football kicker and an ok swimmer, had lots of friends, and had a girlfriend three out of four years of high school, so it seemed to have worked out for him.

Most of the teachers accepted everyone had nicknames, and it was best they learn them early on. Occasionally, a new teacher would show up and try to buck the system, but usually gave in before the winter break.

Mrs. Hartford, freshman English teacher, really dug in, refusing to learn the ways of Dome. She almost cracked after the great debacle of a *Romeo and Juliet* group assignment when kids were put in groups on the last day before Christmas break. Kids were in a panic because they didn't know who belonged in what group, and the assignment was due the day they returned from break. These were the days before cell phones and social media. Families kept phone numbers written on sheets of paper near the wall phone in the kitchen. The piece of paper might read Craw and a four-digit number because all the phone numbers had the same three-digit prefix, and an area code was never needed.

With the students unable to get together in groups, parents bombarded the school with complaints well into the month of February, a month after the assignment was due. The second week of break, kids took it upon themselves to figure it out, so one group had nine kids, several only had two, a few had all girls, and some were all boys. It was a lesson for new teachers, coaches, and interlopers to understand the ways of Dome. Mrs. Hartford was gone after two years.

If one were to look, they would not find Dome anywhere on a Wisconsin map. I wasn't sure when it'd happened or who had started calling our town—originally, Garden Creek—Dome, but the nickname was as old and as common as the oak and maple trees that lined the streets. A suburb of Milwaukee with fifteen thousand people was an idle place to grow up. Everything we needed to live and thrive could be found in Dome.

The north edge of town had a giant mall that took care of all our fashion shopping needs and provided lots of jobs for high school kids. Scattered around were two gas stations, grocery stores, a big chain pharmacy, a small industrial park that provided manufacturing jobs, two veterinary clinics, and even a pet cemetery. Of course, there was one bar.

The west side of Dome cozied up to a large county park that had golfing, a botanical garden, and some amazing sledding hills. The east and south side blended into neighboring towns, but everyone who crossed Cooks Ave. and Kurtz Rd. knew they're leaving the sheltered living of Dome, WI.

Dome was one of the many suburbs of Milwaukee and was

relatively small compared to other surrounding towns. If it weren't for the shopping mall, most folks would not even know where our town is located. It was crazy to think everything we needed from a big mall, grocery stores, all the schools, parks, and the village's main street fit in our town. That was the reason we never had to leave the confines of the Dome. We knew every corner of Dome so it was surprising when someone new had come in and even more surprising she had left without someone noticing.

Still, to this day, the center of Dome had one main commercial street with a city hall anchoring one end and, three-quarters of a mile down Main Street, the green grass of the football and baseball fields sidled up next to the high school. To keep up the full Americana look, along the street, was a play area for kids, sponsored by the local Garden Ladies Association, and two blocks away was a gazebo. The number of marriage proposals in the gazebo had gone from sweet to gag-me-with-a-spoon too many and back to sweet. The place was overrun with jazz concerts in the summer; in autumn, leaves sought refuge; it housed a twelve-foot Santa in December; and was the backdrop for one too many prom photos.

I didn't know if it was a village ordinance or not, but not one chain restaurant or store had ever set up shop on Main Street. The two banks were national names, but the residents let that slide. The library, with large windows, was more inviting than the high school library, so much so that the morning hours had been extended to accommodate the latchkey kids. I later found out that Mrs. Elizabeth had paid for those extended hours. I couldn't remember her full name; everyone had just known her as Mrs. Elizabeth, the eccentric, rich broad.

The family pizza place, Zsoka's, was the one mainstay. Most of the restaurants and shops had turned over a few times. Some had been for the better—like when Rodney the barber had retired. He could only use the electric clipper, so all the boys and men had a small buzz cut. It turned into a flower shop. That lasted a few years before becoming a travel agency and finally back to a barber shop, which had been there for eighteen years. The wedding dress shop and jewelry store were going on twenty years.

The Italian deli, turned video rental store, finally found its last tenant of an eye doctor. No one understood how the hardware store had stayed in business when all the mega chains had popped up in the late eighties and nineties, especially since we were never charged for two screws and a washer when our mothers sent us (by ourselves) ten blocks to the store. The drug and stationery stores had fallen to the big chains nearby, but something always replaced whatever had left.

My favorite place had always been Hattie's. Today, it was a coffee shop. When I was in high school in the eighties, it had been a bakery that sold bread, eastern European sweets, and a few breakfast-like items, which had been very progressive for the time. The lunch menu had had three sandwiches and two soups, sold only by the quart. It was mostly a place to grab a baked good and then leave. No one considered eating inside the shop back then, but thirty-plus years later, our lies revolved around places like that.

Back then, Hattie's dining room was a small space, originally created for customers waiting for their numbers to be called. Over the years, the dining space continued to expand with each renovation, evolving with customers' needs.

I worked there starting at age fourteen and continued on and off for years, through high school, college, and occasionally afterwards, I've picked up shifts. Even six years ago, when I came back for a weekend visit, I popped in for coffee and if the place was slammed. My friend Kit and I immediately put our stuff behind the counter, cleaned the dining room, unloaded the supply truck, and stocked the coffee bar supplies. An hour later, we grabbed two coffees, a bag of Hungarian baked goods called Kifli, paid our bill, and left. Some habits were hard to break, and some, I just didn't want to.

Today, I'd been summoned back because Maz had left a message with my former assistant yesterday, saying "We need to meet." No more, no less.

It wasn't that Maz was a man of few words, it was just that nothing more was needed. I hadn't thought I'd see him for another month. We had developed a pattern of seeing each other every year the weekend before the anniversary of the incident. This was a month early, but it was also the day after Gigi's disappearance. He was probably wondering if I'd noticed the similarities and if we could keep quiet after all this time.

THREE

Maz didn't know when or if I would show, and I parked behind the library, deciding if I really wanted to see him, which was ridiculous since I'd left after my final interview, had gone home, packed, and made the two-hour drive in only ninety minutes. Obviously, I should have thought about it before I'd done all that.

Our previous visits over the few decades had developed a comforting routine. The Saturday before the anniversary, we'd meet at Hattie's for lunch. Casual conversation to start—how have you been, family, divorces, work, and in the later years, we talked about our kids. Mostly benign conversation until our kids reached high school age, and genuine concern entered our exchanges. We shared the hope that our kids, my twins and his daughter, would have an ordinary high school experience of learning, growing, friendships, excelling in sports or academia and hopefully missing out on being witness to our town's forgotten disappearance.

Last year, something had shifted though, and I'd written it off as empty-nest syndrome because our kids had gone off to college. Last year, he was less willing to talk and quasi-suggested we could stop these annual coffee dates. He must have seen the look of sadness in my eyes and quickly retracted the suggestion.

I cut him off at the pass and said, "I don't need you doing me any favors. With or without you, I'll go to the spot and collect my sense of peace. I find solace in it, and more so because I can share it with someone who understands. I was letting that one moment, all those years ago, define my life, but therapy got me to understand I'm more than just one decision. It allowed the anchor that weighs me down to get lighter, but it'll forever be tied to me. If this isn't working for you, I get it. We deal with our stuff in different ways. Although it's only once a year, it's healthy to know I'm not alone."

With a solemn look, he replied, "You're right. We'll never be free of it."

Now, nearly eleven months later, his words from a year ago echoed in my head. *We'll never be free of it.*

Everything we'd done had been for the right reasons; however, the real crux for me was the heartache that no one had noticed. How could someone slip away, and no one take notice?

I sat there, staring at the back side of the library where the anniversary get-togethers had first taken place.

The incident had happened in April of our sophomore year in high school. The following year, on the anniversary, we had just sort of found each other in the library. Mr. Olsen, Leo, and Maz. Later, I came to believe we had been seeking each other out without realizing it.

The library was a kaleidoscope of high school social groups. It was the one place where we could mix with people outside of our normal clique, and no one would think twice about it. Of course, kids were there to supposedly study, but socializing took top billing. We had to talk in hushed tones though, and that got old after a while, so studying it was. When the middle school kids flooded in, their older siblings would run unless they had some real studying to do. Our high school was big on group assignments, and some brainiac nerds learned being seen with someone higher up the social ladder was good for them and quickly turned tutoring into a commodity.

Maz and I occasionally mixed socially. His friend group was higher on the social ladder. My social group included those with decent to high-achieving grades, some athletes, booze, but no hard drugs. Maz's circle of friends was similar, but some dabbled with drugs.

Mr. Edward Olsen, history teacher, was a favorite among the students for various reasons. He'd taught one year at the high school before moving to the middle school. He was also the advisor for the high school chess club. He could relate to anyone. It wasn't uncommon for him to drop a chessboard in front of a kid studying in the library and begin teaching him or her the game on the spot. He gained more members for the chess club this way, and it provided for a diverse group of members. Diverse as in different cliques: the smarts, the jocks, a glam girl or two, and even a few of the corners (aka smokers), who had to stand on the sidewalk before the morning bell because smoking wasn't permitted on school property. Present-day diversity did not exist in Dome thirty-four years ago.

Mr. Olsen was four years out of college, and this was his second teaching assignment. He was young and knew the music we listened to, understood our slang, and wasn't too far removed from student life. Teachers were never given nicknames, and this was as close as it got. Students in his first hour let everyone know what kind of day Mr. Olsen would have: JV, JM, or J2—just vodka, just mouthwash, or just too hungover. It was a measure of how the rest of his classes would go that day. The students knew long before the administration about his drinking habit.

Chess Club officially met every Thursday, but games and informal instructions happened almost every day. A year older Leo was a junior, chess member, and library regular.

Leo hung out with a few people but jumped from group to group, almost as if he was trying to figure out where he belonged. That's not abnormal for most kids in high school, but he seemed to know who he was and was looking for his match. He seemed comfortable sitting by himself in the library but could, at the same time, jump into any study group, invited or not. In middle school where the bullying was the strongest, he seemed he could have been the kid to get picked on or be a rat—the kid running to tell the teacher what was really going on in the locker room after gym class. But he turned out to be more of a wallflower, just taking notes and not getting noticed.

Things shifted for him in high school. He sat with the same three boys at lunch who were all-out nerds—school lunchtime was the highlight of their social lives. Yet Leo scored a prom date with one of the glam girls. He was on the golf team and gifted with computers and technology. He was a constant in the library. I never saw him enter or leave; he was just there. It was an odd thing to notice about someone.

The week of the first anniversary, everything seemed to be in slow motion. I figured—no, I hoped—everyone at school wouldn't remember the girl who had disappeared without them knowing.

I was one of the last students to leave school that day except those heading to the gym or pool. I slowly gathered my books from my last class and took my time heading to my locker. Friends talked to me, but later, I wouldn't remember what they'd said.

All day, I had been looking for Maz, Leo, and Mr. Olsen to give me some type of sign they recognized that day was different than the others. Before Bo had left, I hadn't understood why anniversaries were such a big thing. Maybe it was an anchor of three hundred sixty-five days' worth of memories that needed to be pulled to the surface so the memories wouldn't yank us down and drown us. Sometimes, the anchor could be so heavy, we needed someone to help pull it out.

Maz and I shared a class, and when I walked into the room, he was deep in conversation with Van—my mega crush—so I avoided that corner.

My footsteps echoed in the empty hallways. Outside, the crisp spring air felt heavy. I looked for storm clouds, but the sky was clear. I walked to the library, only looking towards the village and refusing to look towards the baseball diamond and the woods beyond it.

Just inside the front doors of the library stood the large square reception area. Wood paneling covered four sides, the countertop and the swinging half door that only employees used. After pulling the swinging door open, employees had to step up when entering the area—like the way pharmacies used to be. The employees had a bird's-eye view of the card catalog, the open seating area, then into the stacks. The reception/checkout area was set up like a guard tower in a theme park parking lot. A three-foot cutout on the left side with a lower counter allowed kids to check out books. This was long before everything was automated.

Once when I was in fourth grade, a new employee allowed me to go behind the counter to search the lost-and-found box for one of my mittens, not realizing she should have brought the box to the counter. I was in all my glory. Behind the sacred walls, I tried staying as long as I could. This was my one chance. But I didn't get much time because as soon as Mrs. Wilkes returned to the reception desk, I was immediately told to step out of the area. I couldn't hear Mrs. Wilkes talk to the new employee, but I watched the verbal reprimand with sheer joy in my heart because I'd gotten where no other schoolkid had ever been. I told everyone at school I'd made it behind the desk and was treated like royalty for a week until Kat2 showed the boys her bra strap.

On the first anniversary, I walked into the library wishing I was back in fourth grade and that I had the guts to swipe one of the new date stampers. Passing some friends, I told them I had to get some serious work done on a big English lit assignment. I skipped the open table gallery and headed for the left-side wall. Halfway down, I found a table with two chairs across from the biography section.

I threw open my book on the table and, pulling open a notebook, sat staring ahead.

I nearly jumped out of my skin when Maz and Van came up behind me. Maz tossed his backpack on my book. Van looked like he wanted to say something, but Maz pushed forward and grabbed the empty chair.

"See ya later, Van," he said.

I got a nod from Van and couldn't have been happier that I didn't have to try to form some coherent sentence to my mega crush.

"Rough day for you too?" Maz asked.

I shrugged.

"Your English lit book is upside-down." He lifted his backpack. "Van keeps asking me what's wrong, and I'm running out of answers."

We sat in a comfortable silence for a few minutes before a chessboard hitting the table interrupted it. Mr. Olsen pulled up a chair, and thirty seconds later, Leo dragged a fourth chair over to the table, which was designed for two. The four of us sat quietly, staring at a barren chessboard. Our silence united us more than any words could. They seemed to feel the weight of the first anniversary of Bo leaving as much as I did.

That day, we decided the open invite to meet at the library on the Saturday before the anniversary would always stand. I had never been able to figure out why the one-year anniversary had been more nerve-wracking than the day after Bo had disappeared. Had I been on some weeklong adrenaline kick, playing the role of just another high school student who hadn't noticed Bo had slipped out of our lives as quietly as she had entered?

For the first several years after Bo's disappearance, Leo joined us when he could. Mr. Olsen came the first two years, skipped a few, and then during the five year anniversary, he gave us permission to call him Edward. It was the last time he had joined us. At the ten-year meeting, Maz and I thought we had seen him lurking in the library parking lot, but he had never come in. Maz and I eventually moved our get-togethers to Hattie's.

FOUR

A blustery gust of wind beat the windshield, snapping me from my thoughts as I sat behind the library. My former assistant called with a second message from Maz that said "Meeting room 5 Library anytime."

No one was hanging around the six cars in the parking lot. Most of the Thursday afternoon shoppers would find spots in front of the stores and not be in the overflow lot with me.

The school bell would ring in thirty minutes, and if I didn't want to be the strange lady sitting in the car, I needed to exit the vehicle.

I slammed the door shut of my twelve-year old Land Rover and prayed I didn't rattle anything loose. Every day I expected some chunk of metal to drop from underneath the hood. I was balancing my expenses of helping pay my kids tuition's and my house expenses without asking for anything from my ex-husband. He is more than willing to pay more than what the divorce agreement states but it was my stubbornness that refused to accept anything extra. I just hoped I had enough left in my account to get me to a new job and my kids to their summer jobs so their requests for extra cash would slow down. I wrapped the scarf around my neck. March in Wisconsin can bring anything from snow, rain, to sunburn all in a seventy-two-hour period, but mostly a dampness that runs from your nose to your toes.

My daughter Maddie was in her second year at the University of Wisconsin-Madison and her twin brother, Jacob, attended Northwestern University north of Chicago. Spring break was next week for both of them. Maddie was headed to Florida with friends, and Jacob was staying around campus to work on his studies. As their mother, I should have been more proud of Jacob's choice, but walking around an old snow pile, I couldn't help thinking Maddie had made the right choice.

My eyes fixed on Hattie's across the street as I rounded the corner. All the storefronts were getting new signage and roofing. New sign but same old Hattie's. It was too early for the table and chairs to come out of storage, but that hadn't stopped someone from bringing a bench over from the park. Two moms sat with steaming drinks in one hand, and the other rocking their strollers.

I squinted my eyes, and my focus fell on the lady on the left. It was CoCo, she was a few years younger than me. At this stage in our lives, I didn't know if she was holding the stroller to her child or grandchild. I only knew she was still in Dome. Some people just never leave.

I pulled open the first set of doors to the library and unbuttoned my coat. The blast of hot air in the vestibule was almost overwhelming. I couldn't get my arm out of my coat and struggled with the second door.

Cold-weather states had arctic entryways to keep the cold out and a place for the snow and ice to fall from our boots. It was a strange sensation of extreme frigid wind at your face one second, then a blast of intense stale heat to the sanctuary of tepid seventy-two degrees.

As young children, we had honed the artful skill of navigating two sets of doors at shopping malls, removing our coats and scarves and not losing our mittens. Timing was crucial to balance the much-wanted blast of heat to avoid suffocation inside a hair dryer, opening the second door to keep up with our mothers who were on mission to find our new shoes and get home before *Dynasty* started at 8:00 p.m.

The lady behind the library help desk was drinking from a travel mug when I walked in. I didn't consider myself old at fifty-two, but sometimes I aged myself. Like now, seeing someone—especially an employee—drinking in a library seemed like a violation. I sometimes forgot coffee cups were no longer taboo in any establishment except church.

C'mon, people, you can go one hour without something in your hand.

I turned around and bolted across the street to Hattie's for something warm and heartwarming. Hattie's will always be a part of me—first and best job and the place I away missed when I was away. Since I'd stopped officially working full-time for Hattie's, there had been five owners, and I knew each of them except the current one, who had taken over eight months ago. Three of them were former residents of Dome looking for a temporary career change. The one before the current owner had been trying to be the next hot pastry chef. She had changed too many menu items, and villagers had had a hard time accepting her, but her greatest faux pas had been refusing to answer to the name Hattie. She insisted on Joanie, and like I said, we didn't get to name ourselves regardless of age.

Not everyone understood the ways of Dome.

Three years ago, I brought a friend to Dome from Chicago, and we stopped in the stationery store. I introduced her to the owner Ms. B, Beth Betrich, who had lived behind me growing up and had graduated high school two years after me. My friend thought it was strange to use the title of Ms. for someone our same age. I said, "Then you'd probably think it really strange my junior prom date's name was Grange, and we doubled with Jam and Ski."

My mother had told me the latest owner had gladly accepted her title of Hattie. I hadn't met her yet, but Mom also said the new Hattie had brought back the eastern European flavors to the menu, and the locals had returned.

I pushed opened the cafe door, and the sweet smell of pastry swept over me and instantly warmed my insides by ten degrees. Over the years, the dining room had grown in size, and the space behind the counter had shrunk. I liked the changes this owner had made. The current reigning Hattie had added vintage wall prints of Dome and of Milwaukee in metal frames, and she'd put in better lighting and more-comfortable furniture.

Four women in their midforties were in the process of ordering, and the lady at the register seemed to lose track of what they were saying. One lady repeated the order with a voice reserved for a kindergartener being disciplined by a teacher. I was ready to kick the woman out for her attitude, but then remembered I didn't work there anymore. I had *never* been allowed to kick anyone out, actually. As I waited at the back of the line, one of the women mouthed *Sorry* to the lady at the register, who was only partially visible to me. I assumed she was the new Hattie.

While I waited, I tried to evaluate her to figure out if I could continue to pick up shifts here. I didn't get the best look because she grabbed a worker by the sleeve and had her finish taking the order while she prepared their drinks.

I liked her gusto with the employee. It wasn't an angry gesture of throwing someone around; it was more *Let's take care of this now.*

I was finally able to get a quick look at her. My mother had said she was around my age. She had a sleek bob with a center part and bangs. I assumed jet-black wasn't her natural color. *Not one* gray hair on her head.

One thing stopped me from wanting to work with her—she had too many bracelets on her arms. The jingling would have driven me nuts, and wouldn't they get dirty while baking or reaching into the pastry display case? Also, the girl at the register had long nails. Long pointy nails. It kinda grossed me out. I thought about what would get under her nails as she worked with food. The thought of finding a long nail in a pastry made me shiver. Maybe I was finally done using Hattie's as my fallback career.

When I got to the register, I was still lost in thought about working here, and the girl at the counter had to repeat the special of the day. I ordered a chai latte and the donutlike pastry. The girl informed me it was koblihy, a Czech-style dessert.

I shot back across the street to the library and through the double doors. I shook off my coat and inhaled deeply. Hattie's was a regular visit for me, unlike this library. I had not been in here in over two decades. The card catalog had long been replaced by a computer station, and the library had doubled in size when it expanded into an old dental office and a cheese shop.

I'd always thought there needed to be an old-book candle scent. I loved the smell of a library and the old pages of a hardcover book.

I meandered down the hallway and pulled out an old book. Growing up, I would compare my blonde hair with the pages of old books. The best match I'd found was an old Agatha Christie book— until middle school. Then it was an old biography on Churchill. I was curious if those books were still around, and if the library still got the daily newspaper and put it in the wooden dowels.

I pushed myself towards room 5 and hoped I was alone so I could eat my koblihy before anyone showed up. I figured if the librarian could have coffee, I could eat in my former happy place.

The study rooms ran along the back exterior wall. Each had an interior window—probably to keep the high school kids in check. The rooms also had one table, and the number of chairs varied from one to six. With one fluorescent overhead light, it was the carpet and one framed picture on the wall that made it distinguishable from a police interrogation room, or so I guessed.

Five senior ladies were engaged in a heated debate in the first room. What they were arguing about, I'd never know because the door was shut. Rooms two through four were dark. The light was on in room five, and through the window, I spied the warm greeting of an empty space.

FIVE

I tucked away my phone in my purse and enjoyed each sprinkle of sugar. After I finished eating, I put the wrapper away in my purse and flipped through the old book I had taken from one of the stacks. After only a few minutes, its contents—the history of the Baltic countries—threatened to lull me to sleep.

The turn of the door handle jolted me from my history lesson. I flipped the book closed, inhaling the decades-old dust with delight.

In walked a wide-chested young man with wavy blond hair and blue eyes. The only problem was that he was probably a high school student, and I clearly was not.

"Sorry, this room is taken," I said.

"Room five." He tossed his backpack on the table and extended his hand. "Theo Van Dijk."

"She's local," Maz said, walking in behind Theo. "Or at least she was."

"Not a reporter?" Theo asked.

I shook my head, then stood and extended my hand. "Hi, I'm Lou."

"Dutch," he said, giving me his Dome name. He grabbed a soda from his backpack and dropped the latter on the floor before taking a seat opposite me. He had the confidence of a forty-year-old businessman. "Not a reporter? Then why—"

Maz cut Dutch off with a wave of his hand. I exchanged warm smiles with Maz, and he put his six-foot frame in the chair at the end of the table between Dutch and me.

I was comfortable in silence and never needed to fill the void. I had not always been like this, but the years of being a parent of two teenagers with active social lives, who had now gone away to college, I had gotten used to the quiet and sometimes sought solitude after a crazy day working at the radio station.

Here and now, I didn't need to say anything. It was more of wanting to know why Maz had invited Dutch to our reunion.

"Are we expecting more people?" I asked.

Maz tossed a familiar-looking waxy white bag on the table. "Help yourselves."

Dutch didn't hesitate to grab a Czech donut. I didn't want to be rude, so for the second time today, I enjoyed another koblihy. Neither man fared well with the jelly filling, and they used most of the napkins.

Maz spoke first. "I left messages with the other one, but as you know, we may not see him and there was no set time for us to get together."

Dutch seemed to interpret that to mean he was free to eat another pastry, but who was I to judge how many one should eat in a single sitting?

I looked from Maz to Dutch, curious about our newest club member.

Maz finally spoke again. "Have you read anything about what may have happened here?"

"Just the articles online. I haven't spoken to my mother yet. I'm surprised she hasn't called to divulge the latest details," I said.

"Dutch is the one who spoke to police," Maz said.

Dutch was leaning back in his chair with his foot resting on his knee like he was ready to do a drum solo on his shoe, relaxed as if this happened all the time. There was something oddly familiar about him.

I snapped my fingers. "That's how I know your name. From an article."

"That, or maybe my family," Dutch said.

He was too young and still living sheltered in Dome to realize family names didn't carry a lot of weight because people from Dome rarely associated last names with the nicknames that had been bestowed upon them.

When Facebook first came out, my old girlfriends and I had gotten together one night and tried finding out what had happened to all our old boyfriends or boys we'd had crushes on. We had to find a yearbook to figure out their real names. That was a long night of rum and Cokes and yearbook pictures we would like to forget.

I let my eyes drop to the drink in my hand and let my thoughts wander back to that fun-filled night with my girlfriends because looking at Dutch and knowing he had experienced what Maz and I had was too much for me. Maz and I had learned to live in our cocoon. We compartmentalized and rationalized our actions, using each other for support and telling each other we had done the right thing.

The sugar on my tongue turned sour when I looked at Dutch and thought of why we were sitting there. I'd known this reunion would not be like the others, but I hadn't expected to be fighting the urge to throw up within the first hour of being back in Dome.

Maz knows something he isn't telling me. He knows there's a connection. Why break our silence after three decades—especially to a kid. What about her family? Does Maz know the rest of MY story?

SIX

Sweat was trickling down my back. I looked between the two sitting in front of me. One man and one boy with too much in common. I willed my stomach to stay steady. I picked up my drink and faked taking a sip for fear of mixing my latte with the tinge of bile that hung on my tonsils.

Dutch swept his blond hair back off his face, exposing his crystal-blue eyes, high forehead, and high cheekbones. My common sense told me with a look like that and name like Dutch he was of Scandinavian descent.

"If she's not a reporter, why am I here? I'm not talking to cops without a lawyer." Dutch's eyes floated between me and Maz. His voice was confident. "You said there was someone I should talk to?"

"I said we would help you." Maz stood and walked behind his chair.

I noticed he had come in without a coat and was wearing only an untucked blue-and-white-striped button-down shirt with khakis and tennis shoes.

He leaned against the wall and crossed his arms against his chest. "You trust me?"

"Sure. I'm here," Dutch replied.

"No bullshit here. Either you trust us and we trust you, or this doesn't work." Maz didn't take his eyes off Dutch. "Can we trust each other?"

"I already said yes," Dutch said.

"Everyone says that when asked if they can be trusted. I want you to understand what I'm asking. Do we have an agreement that we can confide in each other? Whatever's said between the three of us isn't to be repeated or reported on."

Dutch didn't answer. He held the soda bottle in one hand and fiddled with the bottle cap in the other.

I wasn't sure where Maz was going with this, but if he was all-in, I had no choice but to join him and protect my secret.

The mom in me wanted to reach out to this kid, so I spoke up. "I only know what I read online. You witnessed something horrible, and there are only a few people who can help you."

"Thank you, ma'am. I'm fine. Nothing happened to me," Dutch said.

"First, never call me *ma'am* again. It's Lou."

His cheeks reddened. "Sorry."

"No need to apologize. Second thing is you're not fine. You're in a foggy haze. You don't even know you're walking on a tightrope, and you're one step away from falling off."

"All I, um, all I am is a witness." Dutch's voice cracked for the first time, and he sounded more like a whining teenager.

I sat upright, folded my hands on the table, and summoned the voice of mother/boss/principal and a bit of preacher; it didn't allow for interruption. "If I have to guess, you left out some information. Like why you were in the woods at that hour. Don't give me that line about an early study group. That's why you were headed here to the library, but not why you were in the woods at that hour. It's spring in Dome, and that means those woods are full of mud. Everyone knows to take the sidewalk behind the SMF Factory even if they have to smell the dumpsters. If I also had to guess, there was someone else in the area, but you didn't report that either. Here's the big one—you tampered with the scene. I'm not saying you were involved. Listen to me *closely* here, because I'm saying you were a witness who adjusted things or maybe you removed something. Just a minute before when I said I only know what I read online is the only lie I'll ever tell you. I know more than what was in the papers. So does Maz. I don't know what he's told you or how he got you here, but listen to me.

"You're going to need us more than we need you. Maybe not right now or next week, but let me tell you, as the years go by, you'll hope to always find someone in room five to talk to, so Maz is going to ask you a question again, and I want you to think about the answer this time."

Dutch listened, frozen in place, as the color slowly drained away from his pale face.

I kept my eyes on Dutch as Maz spoke.

"Can we trust each other? What's said between us stays with us. This is no joke."

"Who are you guys?" Dutch's voice was soft. He reminded me of my son who, when trying to solve a puzzle, would whisper his thoughts like he was thinking out loud. "So this was a setup? Is Gigi ok? Like, is this a hoax or one of those TV specials where they set up stupid scenarios to see how people react?"

I shook my head. "It's not a TV stunt, but we don't know about the rest. Were you asked . . . Did you know . . ."

"No!" Dutch said.

"Don't worry, we're on your side," I said. "We have to trust each other. At some point, you're going to have to tell us everything. The woods aren't your normal routine. Someone made sure you were there."

"Yeah, but I'm not part of some big plan," Dutch said.

"Not that you know of," Maz said. "Look, we're not accusing you of anything, but if you are just let us know. We can help."

"Part of a plan—are you guys crazy? You think I did something to Gigi?" Dutch's voice was soft. There was no forced or fake anger. He was using his energy to figure everything out.

"It's crappy to witness something you're not sure of and to have the press and Gigi's family after you for information," I said.

"Are you two some support system, counselors from the school?" Dutch asked.

Maz and I looked at each other. We'd known this moment would come. The time when we would have to verbalize what we had done. We had never before said it out loud. Our solace each anniversary came from being near each other. Saying the words now didn't mean freedom for us but accepting someone else into our shitty club.

"We helped a girl disappear, and we made sure the police stayed out of it," I said.

"How? What . . . Why have I never heard about that? It would be another great Dome legend. Why should I believe you?"

"You don't? That's up to you. If you don't, that's fine, and I walk out of here and you never have to talk to me again. But let me say this first, why would we make this up and tell you what we did? Second, why do I know the details about you being in the woods? We're asking you to trust us so we can help you and Gigi if she needs it," I said.

Maz said, "For the last time? Are you in?"

Dutch dropped his shoulders and lowered his head. His blond hair fell over his eyes. He reached inside his sweatshirt and pulled out his phone, punched a few buttons and tossed it on the table faceup. The screen went black as it shut off. "I'm in."

"If you were recording us, please delete it." I said. Dutch did as requested.

SEVEN

Two high school girls looked inside room five and slowly turned away once they saw it was Dutch. I could easily see girls his age being drawn to him for his looks and confidence. They probably would have lingered longer if it wasn't for me and Maz.

"Do we need to move somewhere else?" I asked.

"We're fine here, at least for a few more minutes. No one will think much of us using this room," Maz said to me. He turned to Dutch. "Are you good with Mrs. Neimeyer? Anything in the school paper?"

"I told her what you said, that I couldn't talk about the investigation, and implied I thought it would be tacky if I wrote anything. She's having someone else write a series about safety or something, and then she told me to finish the story Gigi and I had started as a team."

Maz turned to me. "Alice Neimeyer is the teacher for the school newspaper. She likes the sensational stories." He turned to Dutch. "Any other local reporters get in touch with you?"

"No. I haven't spoken to any reporters since the first day. My dad has gotten calls at work though. The school and Principal Hayes have been good at shielding me from those reporters hanging around the school. Today, I came here with Quinn just like yesterday. He'll drop me at home, or if we think someone is watching us, we're supposed to go to his house and his father will drive me home later. I can crash there anytime if I need to. The reporters can't figure out where we live."

"That's good. Is anyone else asking you to say anything? Your friends digging for information?" Maz asked.

"Not really. They asked some stuff the first day, and I told them to fu—well, I told them to back off." Dutch stood and stepped into the corner of the room. He shoved his hands into his pockets and dug the tip of his shoe into the carpet. "I don't get this! I don't get all this. Why do you two know so much? I said I would trust you, but why should I? Who cares about a girl from the last century." He instantly recoiled from his words. "I don't mean that about the girl but . . ."

"It's ok. I know you're confused and don't understand the connection. Thirty-four years ago, a girl named Clare Cosworth—Bo—disappeared exactly the same way, and I was the one who walked out of the woods that morning," I said.

We kept our eyes locked until Maz confirmed everything. "She's telling the truth. We know—"

A knock sounded at the door, and one of the girls who had walked by earlier stuck her head in. "Sorry to interrupt, but the computer froze again."

"I'll be right there. If anyone's checking out a book, just write the information down." Maz shut the door and turned to us. "I got to go."

"You work here?" I asked.

"Not really. Well, I guess just temporarily. We can get together anytime. You need to—"

"Wait, did you move back to Dome?" I asked.

This town just pulls you in, or maybe some piece of us never leaves.

"Maz," said a voice down the hall.

"Listen I have to go," Maz said.

Dutch held up a finger. "Can I stay in here? I heard some people at lunch talking about planning a vigil and to meet in the library. They want to stay away from Hattie's because that one reporter who's been bugging everyone has been hanging out there."

A reporter in Hattie's, damn. My happy place is gone. I can't be near a reporter if there is the slightest chance my name gets in the paper, even as a quote for a hometown story. I will lose everything.

"Stay as long as you need. The library isn't letting in reporters. I had the library make up some crazy residents-only hours. What channel is the reporter from?" Maz asked.

Dutch shrugged. "Some newspaper or magazine. I really don't know. Been avoiding most everyone."

"When is the vigil?" I asked.

"I'm not sure. Sunday maybe? Quinn will tell me everything later."

Maz pointed at me. "Lou, I'll walk you out. Dutch, we meant it when we said we're here to help. We're not some voodoo group; we have been where you are right now. I'll text you when we can get together, and you can reach us when you need to talk."

I looked at Dutch as if he were my own son and wanted to reach out and hug him. Isolation could grow while one felt themselves shrinking.

Just because I knew his secret didn't mean I understood him. He had talked to the police; he had done the right thing. That *was* the right thing to do, right? We had done so much of the same stuff, but I felt a world away. Would I have called the police if I'd had a phone in my hand when I witnessed what I had?

I was lost in my thoughts again and wasn't sure if Maz had had to repeat himself.

"Lou, I'll walk you out."

"That's my cue to leave," I said. "It'll get harder before it gets better, but it does get better."

I grabbed my purse and coat, and we left Dutch standing in the corner. Maz closed the door behind us and led the way down the hall.

"Poor kid, he's still in the middle of it all," I said.

"Do you think the vigil will be too much?" Maz asked.

"The community will expect him to be there in some form or another. Maybe being lost in a crowd is better than internalizing all the weird emotions about it alone at home like I did the first year."

Halfway down the hall, Maz pulled open a door. "Hold this open for me." He went over to a computer and hit a few keys. "Listen for the all-clear."

I didn't know what that meant, but twenty seconds later, someone yelled, "We're good." It was startling to hear someone yelling from the sanctuary of a library. I gave Maz a thumbs-up, and we quickly left the control room.

We stood in the hallway, looking at the main desk. "Seriously, you work here now?"

"A lot has happened, and I guess I should fill you in on it, but I have to get back. We'll catch up later. I suggest you stay away from Hattie's if the press is hanging around. Are you headed back tonight?"

"I'm headed to my parents' place. I don't know how long I'm staying, but I don't have to be back at work until Monday."

Maz did not need to know about my unemployment status. Standing there with my hands in my coat pockets with my purse slung across my body between the rows of books, I felt seventeen again. I was even worried about a boy, but this time, I was old enough to be his mother instead of his prom date. "Do you think we should have shared our story? I know you want to be there for him, but I just realized we said a whole lot, especially since we don't know if there's a connection."

"I'm almost certain there's a connection. He's a good kid, with a good family," Maz said, but his tone became slightly bitter. He seemed to have picked sides. As if it was him and Dutch, and he hoped I'd get on board.

I didn't understand the shift. "Family? Family does not make or break you as a good person. Wasn't that our point back then?"

Maz ignored my question. "We should do the right thing for the kid."

"I thought we did. Sorry if you didn't feel that way all these years. Or do you mean to say we have to do the right thing now because we didn't do it back then when we forged our own justice system?" I said and walked out on Maz.

EIGHT

I wanted to clear my head before I headed to my parents' house. They were not expecting me, and I didn't want to walk in all flustered. My mother had been overly concerned about me since the kids had gone off to college because I was usually alone in the house. She'd tried to set me up on dates before I'd finished signing the divorce papers. She liked my ex-husband well enough, but later, I learned it didn't surprise her when we divorced. She'd kept a list of eligible men for when the divorce finally happened. The real problem was her definition of *eligible*.

I don't know what she'll do when she finds out I'm single and jobless.

It was after 4 p.m., which was dinner-prep time for my mother and prime time for lots of direct and indirect comments about my dating life. She was less pushy during our phone conversations because she knew I could hang up on her.

I drove out of Dome, straight to a drive-thru window. I sat in the parking lot holding a waxy cup and twirling my key ring with my other hand. The warm paper bag sat on my lap. Cold fizz tickled my throat, and up rose a belch my son would have been proud of. I didn't drink much soda, but something about an ice-cold root beer could send me back to easier times. The burger barely filled me up, but the salty fries almost made me forget a girl had gone missing.

I sat in the car, reflecting yet again about some of the cornerstone moments that had changed my life.

Nothing was ever too big or something I couldn't handle. Sure, I got nervous taking exams, going on first dates, during job interviews and childbirth, but nothing could really rattle me.

No decision or challenge was worse than what I had faced thirty-four years ago. Sometimes it made me more bold because I didn't care about consequences. I'd talked back to bad bosses, had gone for jobs beyond my skills, and most oftentimes had gotten the promotion.

Not caring and not prioritizing outcomes wasn't always a good way to live. I'd thought love and safety were the foundation to having a good marriage for the long haul. When the passion had faded for me, so had the effort. When I was married to Joe, he'd thought suggesting divorce would scare me into seeing a marriage counselor. He said what hurt him the most at the end was that I didn't care enough to fight for our marriage, and an easy and amicable divorce wasn't something one should be proud of—that it was just a sad reflection of how easy it was for me to walk away from him. I told him all our effort had gone into his affair and then walked out of the room.

He'd failed to understand that I hadn't feared the challenge of being a divorcee and a single parent. I had gone into the marriage with love and hoped for a forever but had never quite believed in things lasting forever. I wasn't fatalistic, nor did I live in fear. Rather, I embraced whatever was next.

Right now, my next move was leaving the parking lot of this restaurant. The space next to me had filled up twice. If another car showed up, I probably would have been required to order more fries, not that that would be a problem.

I rambled back to Dome, still thinking about Bo. It hit me why I was there to begin with. These last two days, I had been reflecting so much about the past I had forgotten about Gigi, the girl who had disappeared. I wondered where she lived in Dome. Was she in the tree, lake, or maybe the constellation section of Dome?

When the village was founded in the late 1930s, each division of houses or sections had been given coordinating street names. The section where I'd grown up had streets named after rivers. My friend Jam lived in the bird section. Dome was pretty much middle class but had two bookend sections. The small homes and those subsidized by federal money, called Grant Homes in the thirties and forties, were in the tree section. The larger homes with bigger lot sizes were in the section with streets named after constellations.

Gigi had last been seen in the woods behind the high school baseball field in the early morning, so that most likely made it either the lake or the tree section. I drove around the lake section and then crossed over to the tree section until I saw a home with a large yellow ribbon tied around a tree. Two cars were in the driveway, and the curtains were closed. I guessed this to be her home. The news article had said she lived with her father and stepmother.

Lost in my thoughts, I didn't realize I was lost. Literally, lost. I had mindlessly driven to the rivers section, to my childhood home, only to remember my parents had moved into a condo in the mountain section a few years ago. Quickly I rerouted, and a minute later, I pulled into my parents' driveway and jumped out with my suitcase.

The front door was locked, and a light turned off down the hall. I rang the doorbell and got no response. I would have thought what happened with Bo and Gigi and getting lost in my old neighborhood would be the low point of my day, but getting shunned by my own parents was a real kick in the ass.

NINE

I pounded on the door then dug in my purse for my phone. Daylight faded, and the damp air clung to my face. I hadn't bothered bundling up for the seven seconds I'd expected to be outside. I hit the doorbell one more time. Was my parents' hearing really that bad? Couldn't they hear the doorbell? And since when had they started locking their door before going to bed?

A car pulled into the driveway across the street, and a person got out of the passenger side and walked up to a keypad near the garage and punched in some numbers. Tinted windows didn't allow me to see the driver, but from the thumping bass blasting from the slightly open window, I guessed a high school kid was driving. There was something sweet about a teenager waiting for another kid to get inside the garage before barreling out of the neighborhood. I wondered if it was a boyfriend/girlfriend scenario.

The garage door rose, and the person walked into the garage. The driver left, and the door was on the way down when it bounced back up.

"They're not home," the person said, gesturing to my parents' house.

I squinted to see if I recognized him. *Dutch.*

He stood at the entrance to the garage and seemed to notice me watching him. He looked up and down the street several times before walking to the end of the driveway. "They won't be back for a while."

I left my suitcase tucked into the corner of the porch and walked down my parents' driveway. "Meeting twice in one day what are the odds?"

Dutch seemed more nervous than before.

"This is my parents' place and for some reason, they seem to ignore the doorbell."

"That's your parents' place?" Dutch kept moving his head around and seemed to doubt me.

"Remember, I'm local," I said. Dutch remained quiet. "I used to live in the river section, and several years ago, they bought this condo."

Still nothing from Dutch. He took two steps back and finally said, "You would know they're not home if they're your parents."

I accepted his challenge with common sense. "I don't know what they do every minute. I saw lights go off in there."

His lip curled up slightly like the beginning of a smile, and he took another step back.

I had a strange feeling of déjà vu, as if I had a memory of us standing like this before, until his tiny smile faded. He took another step back.

"So, who's giving you a hard time? Is it my dad's gardening tips or Mother with her food drops? Don and Donna are well-intentioned, but don't always know when to pump the brakes."

As soon as I said their names, Dutch seemed to relax.

"Has she delivered her scones?" I asked.

"I like your mother's oatmeal cookies." He seemed to finally accept I was telling the truth. "You know they're in France."

"Oh, shit!" I felt like I was the teenager and Dutch was the adult. "It totally slipped my mind. I wasn't really thinking about them on the drive up here."

They'd left two days ago on a semi-spontaneous trip. The local high school had an exchange program with a French school outside of Paris. This summer a dozen kids would be going there for four weeks. The chaperone had suddenly backed out, and my mother's volunteer work with the high school's Foreign Language Club opened the door for her and my father to jump in as the new chaperones. Taking this role seriously, they'd booked this pre-planning trip. They wanted to understand where they were taking these twelve kids. They'd booked the tickets and hopped on the plane.

"I don't know if I even have their spare key with me. I guess I'll pick up stones for the next hour looking for the spare."

"We might have one," Dutch offered. "I think my dad exchanged keys with them." He turned back towards the garage.

He had seemed nervous talking to me, and I didn't want to push his comfort level, so I waited at the end of the driveway.

"You can follow me in," Dutch said, closing the garage door as I stepped inside.

It was a two-car garage with an older SUV parked on one side. Besides two garbage cans and some patio furniture stored for the winter, it was void of tools and garden items. From the garage, we walked in through the laundry room and into the hallway. A stairwell heading up blocked off the view of the living room I knew was on the other side. This condo unit appeared to be the mirror floor plan of my parents'. I stood in the hallway while he went into the office and turned on lights as he moved along.

Dutch searched the desk drawer. Coming up empty, he walked past me and headed down the hallway into the kitchen. No family photos or artwork hung on the hallway walls.

He tossed his backpack onto the table, just like my son.

"Do you mind if I ask you something?" I said.

"Go ahead." Dutch had his head in the junk drawer.

"So do boys just naturally throw their dirty bags on the table, or is it something your fathers teach you? My son has the same dirty, grungy habit."

"It actually takes great skill just to get it right. Too much power and you can send the pack flying off the end, hit the wall, and that is a whole new lecture I get, or used to get . . ."

His voice trailed off as I walked through the kitchen and stepped way left so I was standing near the foot of the staircase that separated the kitchen and living room. I could have said I was stepping away to give Dutch his space—or I was being nosy and wanted to check out how the place was decorated. Each of the rooms I had seen was sparse with furnishings. The little artwork hanging on the living room walls was dentist-office-level quality, and the furniture was as generic as a chain hotel. There was plenty of food on the kitchen counter. The only thing with personality was a ceramic cookie jar in the shape of a red British double-decker bus.

He turned triumphantly to me and held up a key ring fit for a janitor. "Good news, bad news. I found the key ring. Bad news, it's got about half a dozen keys."

"Ah, yes. Every neighbor has every neighbor's key. I forgot some of the ways of Dome. Do you mind if I take the set and return them in the morning after I make a copy so I don't have to bother you each time I want to leave the house this weekend?"

"Sure." His response was barely audible. Confident one minute and mild teenager the next.

I stood up straight and put my hands in my coat pockets. I was trying not to look confrontational but sincere. "Dutch, Maz, and I meant it when we said we're here for you. We didn't get into a lot back at the library and probably did a good job of freaking you out. We don't know why the girls disappeared in such a similar manner in the same spot all these years apart.

"Just know we'll figure this out together. We'll find a time to—"

Our phones beeped one right after the other. Maz had sent us each other's contact information, but little did he know, I had a direct communication with Dutch.

The garage/laundry room door opened and closed, and "Hola" came from the laundry room.

"We got company," Dutch shouted.

"Hey, Quinn. I didn't see your car," the voice responded.

Dutch said to me, "My dad."

"I might not be Quinn, but I like pizza. It smells great," I said.

Neither of us moved until the pizza box started to emerge through the hallway, then came the man holding it.

My world dropped.

It had not been déjà vu minutes ago on the driveway with Dutch. That memory coming back had been of his father.

Now the two men stood feet apart. Dutch's blond hair fell below his ears, and when he pushed it back, their high cheekbones and tall foreheads were identical. Van's hair was cut short around the ears and longer on top. I felt foolish for not connecting the dots sooner.

My crush from high school and a drunken make-out session in college stood in front of me.

"Van."

Not knowing if I'd said his name out loud, I ran my fingers through my hair nervously as if they were a magical comb that could fix the mop on my head. The massive key ring in my hand plowed into my forehead. The best I could hope for was no blood, continuing as if it was normal to comb your hair with keys. Keys that weren't mine, but even if they had been, nothing was cool about it.

"Hello." I knew I'd said that out loud, yet I got no response.

Van stopped one foot short of entering the kitchen. "Dutch, everything ok?" He didn't acknowledge me.

"Yeah." The kid had a solid poker face.

Van showed no recognition of me as I rattled the key ring. Thankfully, I saw no blood from my forehead.

"I was locked out, and Dutch was kind enough to find the key."

Van's eyes squinted. Dutch tilted his head. It was like watching a silent movie, and the usher was about to throw me out of the theater.

He didn't mince words. "You don't live on our street."

At least we were conversing, but I had not even received a hello. I guessed the people of Dome had changed their hospitality standards. The single bright overhead light in the kitchen, no TV background noise, and the thermostat set at a not-warm level elevated the sterile kitchen's inhospitable setting.

My insides melted with tears. My old crush was treating me like a trespasser and showed no sign of knowing who I was.

I could play that game too.

He didn't need to know he still occasionally popped into my dreams at night. I extended my hand. "Sarah."

He didn't extend his. I let the pizza box and briefcase explain away his rejection of my handshake, or I would have had to admit he'd grown up to be a dick.

"My parents, Don and Donna, do. I forgot my spare key, and Dutch saved me from having to go to my brother's house full of cats. Don't worry, he made sure I was who I said I was."

"You always exchange numbers with high school kids?" Van said.

Our phones flashed the information Maz had sent. Luckily, my fingers covered Maz's name, and only Dutch's displayed across the screen.

"He offered support. You can see from the key ring it might take me some time. I see you're not comfortable with this, so you can take the keys, and I'll delete your son's information." I placed the key ring on the counter and tapped my phone's screen several times, indicating I was deleting Dutch's phone number.

My kids had always accused me of mumbling "Woody" whenever I was flustered. They thought I was asking Woody from the movie *Toy Story* for help. They were four when they'd first seen the movie, and I wasn't about to correct them. It was really *worb* I said, or when things were really bad, I'd say *worby*. It had started in high school, and I had never lost the habit.

I struggled to open my purse to throw my phone in and realized I was mumbling. Today's iteration was simply *worb* with a deep inhalation.

Van raised an eyebrow, and his shoulders dropped. "Lou?"

This was my moment. Should I acknowledge dickhead with a cool indifferent shrug, a delighted I'm-so-honored-you-finally-remembered-me smile, or just drop everything and jump him in the kitchen? Dutch standing there prevented the latter, but the thought lingered.

"That's me. Now excuse me for taking up your time." I took two steps towards the hallway Van was blocking and I turned to Dutch and said, "Thank you for the assistance."

Van finally pushed his briefcase and pizza to Dutch, stepped around me, and said, "Wait."

I looked at Dutch. "Please don't bag-toss what's in your hands onto the table; you overshoot, and there's no dinner." I got a kind laugh in return along with a mock swing of the pizza box.

I had taken three steps down the hall when Van said, "Wait, please." He had the key ring in his hand and was unwinding the key with the green plastic cap on it. "Here you go."

"Are you sure it's the right one?" Now I was the one with an attitude, but I was ok with it.

"Green for Don because of his green thumb," Van said.

"Ok."

We stood in an awkward silence before he broke it with "Come out the front door. It's easier." He swung around and turned towards the front of the house.

I passed Dutch and said, "Nice to meet you."

He still stood there, holding the briefcase and pizza.

Van opened the door and stepped onto the small porch. He looked up and down the street, just as Dutch had done earlier. He was holding the screen door open for me. I stepped onto the porch and was ready to make my way past Van with nothing more than *Have a nice night*.

Dutch caught us both off guard. "Careful for the lights."

Van and I turned at the same time and stepped into each other. The smell of wood and lavender triggered my memory of our make-out session from college. Van seemed to hear me inhale and feel my exhale across his chest. I tried masking it with a cough. Not smooth.

"Don set up timers all over the house, but somehow, they're not on the right rotation," Dutch said.

I untangled myself from my woody lavender dreamsicle and stepped back inside. "Is that what I saw when I was banging on the door?"

Dutch nodded.

"The man can grow anything, but he's lost if he has to plug something in. Thanks for the heads-up."

Dutch smiled. "Something comes on during the night or the place is haunted."

"Gotcha" was the best I could come up with.

Thanks to Dutch, I had a second to compose myself. I calculated my next move and was determined to leave, this time with grace and cool detachment. I would not mumble *worb*, and I was most definitely not going to turn around with a fleeting look of please watch me go. Plan in place, hoping for a perfect exit game, and I went . . .

Pivot.

I gave them a nod, and with a voice of a queen, I said, "Gentlemen."

Point for me.

Step . . . step . . . not inhaling as I walked past Van.

Two points for that move.

Using my best earthy voice, I said, "Have a nice night."

Little heavy on the voice, so only half a point.

Head up, I had made it out the door without reaching for his chest. Reminding myself not to look back. Two steps, and I was almost off the porch. Another point. Three steps, and I was off the porch.

Four and a half points.

Not bad.

The door shut, the dead bolt locked, and the porch light switched off before my fourth step.

Dickhead.

TEN

Thankfully, the green key did its job.

I spent ten minutes looking for the timers on the first floor, and I adjusted the thermostat to a level that didn't require eight layers of clothes. I tossed my suitcase on the lower bunk and sat on the double bed kicking off my shoes. I threw on some sweats and an oversized T-shit, and went scrounging for food. My parents were on day two of their ten-day trip and no fresh food had been left behind. I stood in front of the open refrigerator door and opened the vegetable drawer twice, hoping something would magically appear. Between the Hattie's pastries and the fast food dinner, I was craving something green or anything with a stem from a garden or a tree.

If my kids had been standing there that long, I would have tossed out *We are not cooling the house with the fridge.* I settled on air-popped popcorn, heavy on the salt and butter, cozy sweats, a fluffy blanket, and hoped to find something on TV to take my mind away from the day. I plopped on the couch. My parents had two new sleek, modern, but comfortable reclining chairs, and even when they weren't home, the chairs were reserved for my mom and dad. Dad had his back pillow, and Mom's was closer to the lamp for better reading light.

A commercial for the upcoming season of *Deadliest Catch* came on. The show documented a fleet of crab fishermen in Alaska, and each season, my kids and I betted on which boats would lead the crab count. I had yet to win, but I had a feeling this was my year. I sent a text to my kiddos with my picks. Surprisingly, they sent theirs five minutes later. Maddie wanted to raise the bet to ten dollars each, and Jacob said twenty. I said I was fine at twenty if half the money went to charity. My daughter reminded me she was in college, and she *was* the charity, so after some banter, we settled on the original five-dollar bet.

I was lost in channel-surfing and in my thoughts when I got a text from Maz asking if we could meet again. We agreed to eight thirty tomorrow morning at the library. I barely touched the popcorn and was ready to throw the remote at the TV. I was looking for answers about Gigi and Bo, and not one show could tell me anything.

I thought about journaling my thoughts. I had listened to several TED Talks and always heard about people keeping a diary and how beneficial it was spiritually. My problem wasn't emotional; it was practical and possibly deadly. I had kept a diary once but stopped when it had become too real.

The doorbell rang twice before I registered what it was. I wasn't in the mood to chitchat with nosy neighbors. They all probably knew my parents were gone. I debated not getting up and wished I hadn't. I went into the kitchen to the front entryway, and through the long narrow window on the door, I spotted Van. He saw me and waved.

I turned around and was actually disappointed it wasn't Mrs. Bein, the neighborhood busybody reminding me to keep my car locked if I wasn't going to put it in the garage.

Van rang the bell again, and I turned back. He held up a bottle of copper-colored liquor. He held my attention, but I didn't budge until he flipped the bottle up. On the bottom was a Post-it note that read

"I'm sorry." His bright smile oozed confidence and got me to open the door.

"Peace offering," he said.

I reached out for the bottle, and he pulled it back.

"This is to be shared."

"Fine." I left the door open and retreated towards the living room. "It's pretty bold bringing that here. In case you forgot, the last time we saw each other, we were throwing up in the stairwell of some dorm after drinking that."

I think I saw a slight pause in his step in his otherwise confident demeanor.

"You're mistaken. That rotgut was nine dollars a bottle, and some would call it moonshine. This is on the other end of the spectrum."

I pointed to the cabinet near the sink and returned to my position on the couch. I looked down and realized I had been talking to him wearing no bra, a white vintage New Kids on the Block T-shirt, and sweats so big three people could have fit in them. He, on the other hand, had on black jogging pants and a long-sleeve shirt that subtly reflected his toned body. He projected the image of a guy on the cover of a ski magazine laughing while walking into a ski chalet with a tall blond model next to him.

I heard him rooting around the freezer for some ice, and I covered myself up with the blanket while I waited for him to play bartender.

Van joined me in the living room. He handed me the glass and went to my dad's recliner.

"Not there please," I said.

He moved to my mother's chair, and I shook my head. He moved to the love seat to my left.

"You know your parents are in France and will not be sitting in Statler and Waldorf tonight."

"Thanks for the family update," I said. "How do you know about Statler and Waldorf?"

"Dutch and I were here a few months ago, and your father explained his daughter named the chairs after two judges from an old TV show—*The Muppets*. I laughed and explained to your father that it wasn't very flattering because they were not judges but cranky hecklers. Don called his daughter, and she explained they were rather critical of all the contestants on *American Idol* and *The Voice*. Don loved the names even more after that."

"I remember that call. You're the bus duo from London?" I said.

"I don't know about that, but we moved back from London about eight months ago."

"My mother said two people from London—who she calls the Bus Duo—moved into the neighborhood, and she said she invited you guys over to dinner. I wonder if she's using bus instead of Van and thinks she's being funny."

"It could be that, or I think she has a mission to fatten us up. Each week, we get something for our cookie jar—the red bus. Sometimes more often if Dutch is shoveling their driveway. They're friendly folks, and your mom is a hell of a baker."

"She's a great baker and a generous cook," I said.

"So you're the available daughter in Chicago, and the story about Donna's son getting a flat tire outside the basketball arena after the playoff game is Stew, and the new-model Ford truck I often see here belongs to him?"

"I guess that is me, and yes, that infamous flat tire story belongs to my brother, and I can only guess about the make and model of the truck," I said, ignoring the fact my mother had been trying to set me up behind my back.

"I wanted to come by and say I'm sorry about earlier. I was less than civil. Sorry."

"That's two sorries. One more and it might be enough," I said.

"The third one is in your glass. If you haven't noticed, this is pretty smooth." He took a sip. "To be fair, I wasn't that bad if you understand what's been going on."

Oh crap, I was the insensitive one. "Yes. I read about it and didn't put it together until after I left your house," I lied. "Dutch been getting lot of reporters after him?"

"The press has been unbelievable. Gigi's parents too, which is understandable at first. Them wanting to know everything he saw is one thing, but Patty, Gigi's stepmom, attaching herself to him like he's a supernatural extension of her stepdaughter is where I draw the line."

I just nodded and listened.

He stood up and paced back and forth. "The school counselor and someone from the police department said it's best for him to stay in school and keep his routine. He wasn't involved and was just a witness. Some kids at school have been saying stuff like he was involved, and there are other crazy rumors out there. Thankfully, his close friends have been great, especially Quinn and his family. His mother, Justine, keeps me updated if there's something I need to know. She hears things from other mothers, so that helps since his mom is . . . isn't here."

Not here? What does that mean? Not alive? Not in the marriage? On a business trip? Jeez, I need to focus.

Van continued, "There are no leads on finding Gigi or the person who took her, and the reporters are begging for an interview."

"So a stranger being in your house was a cause for concern. I get that," I said.

"Still, it does not excuse all my behavior. Sorry."

"Well, there's the third sorry I was looking for. We're good. I appreciate the sincere apology and the Scotch. This is pretty good. What's the label? I don't recognize it."

"You know Scotch?" Van asked.

"A fair amount. I was over the wine kick everyone's been on. I belong to a Scotch club in Chicago."

He stretched his arm out for my glass. "May I?"

"I don't need any more. I'm slowly enjoying this glass."

He stood with his hands on his hips. Some of his blond hair fell forward, but I could still see his blue eyes. Although my heart skipped two beats, I didn't flinch.

"I was asking for some popcorn."

"Good. Because we know what happened last time." I handed him the bowl and sat back down on the love seat.

"That's the second time you've brought up that evening. Is there something you want to say to me?"

Damn, he called me out.

"Don't say that unless you're ready. I don't back down," I said.

He continued to munch. "Fair," Van said with a nod.

"New subject. How is Dutch doing? I only met him for a minute"—*lie*—"but he seems like a decent kid."

"I'm proud of how he's handling everything. This past year would be rough on anyone, much less a seventeen-year-old. A move to London and a move back, minus one parent, and now this. The kid is keeping up with his grades and has a group of decent friends."

"Are you sure about the friends? It's so hard these days with all the social media. I think kids confuse followers for friends."

"I'm blind to most of the social media, but my niece, who's eight years older than him, is all over that stuff, and we worked out a deal for her to keep tabs on him."

"Not to dive into family dynamics, but are you sure she's loyal to you?"

"Good point. I trust her enough, and at this point, I have no other option. She has his best interests at heart. We have a pretty good relationship, Dutch and me. He was open about his feelings about the move and other stuff."

"It's the stuff they don't tell you that you need to worry about. Just wait until he goes away to college."

"Thanks. I'll add that to my list of priorities this week," Van said.

"Give me back my popcorn if you're going to be that way. We're just talking here."

I reached over and grabbed the big bowl, but he held on. It bewildered me how I still wanted him all these years later since I barely knew him. I was determined to play it cool despite my adolescent outfit and behavior.

I yanked the bowl away. "How is he really handling being the star witness?"

"Fine. We both laugh at the fact that all he did was take Gigi's backpack she dropped to the school office and saw her getting into a car. You know, high school and rumors. I'm not sure and would never confront him, but I think Gigi's dad stuck the reporter on Dutch the day after because the police were not giving it the right attention. He's convinced his daughter isn't a teenage runaway."

"You're not so sure?" I asked.

"I don't know, and it's not for me to speak about someone I don't know."

"But?" I pushed him because I wanted more details about how Gigi and Bo were connected.

"If you want more out of me, you'll have to wait while I get a refill."

"It's your bottle. Top mine off as well."

I didn't want to interrogate him, and I had to let him lead the conversation. I wanted to be a friendly ear for him to vent to. I needed more information from Dutch, and if I had to get it through his father, I would do that too.

Van returned with our drinks and settled back into his position on the love seat. A large pour, which I had no hesitation in drinking like it was water. He failed to return to our last topic of conversation, so it was up to me. I held out the popcorn bowl, struggling to find something relevant to talk about, and he took it back.

I turned up the volume of the HGTV show *House Hunters* and mindlessly laughed at the couple and their expectations for their first home. He devoured what was left of the popcorn as we quietly watched the show.

"Need more popcorn? This is better than decent Scotch, so I'd offer to make another bowl if you leave the bottle."

"Popcorn is a weak offer for that Scotch. To be honest, I know that's your only offer because I checked the fridge when I was getting ice. Your parents didn't leave you much. What are you doing in town?"

Oh shit, what am I supposed to say?

Honesty didn't seem fitting. I didn't want to tell him I had more in common with his son this time. My phone beeped with a message, and seconds later, it beeped again, giving me extra time as I looked at the screen. It was my daughter changing her picks for the bet.

"Ah, I'm on my way up to Fish Creek to meet a girlfriend and stopped to surprise my parents for the night, but I really didn't think it through."

"Their loss is my gain." Van had said it with a well-mixed combination of sarcasm and a goofy grin, so I couldn't really read it too well. "Well, I should probably head out. It's getting late and I have to work in the morning and I've already apologized and spoke too—"

"Damn, Van. If you want to leave, just leave. You don't need fifty excuses to leave someone." I stood up, remembered to wrap the blanket around my bra-less body, and headed to the front of the house.

He stood too but stayed in front of the TV.

"Thinking of another excuse to leave?" I said.

"No, I want to know what house these people pick."

"It has to be house one," I said.

"No way, it has to be two. Loser buys the next drink," Van said.

"Deal."

We stood side by side, quietly watching TV. I was slightly wobbly. The Scotch seemed to have hit me.

The couple chose option three, and I said, "We're both losers."

"At least I'm in good company," Van said and headed to the front door.

Worb! Was he flirting with me?

We exchanged one more *goodnight*, and he was gone.

I left the kitchen light on but shut everything else off downstairs. If Van looked across the street to my parents' condo, I didn't want him thinking my evening ended as if I had been waiting for him to leave.

I texted my brother and made breakfast plans for the morning. I almost backed out when he said it had to be at seven so he could get to work before an early meeting. The Scotch was empowering me so I agreed to meet at seven, and then I ran to the guest room and pulled out my high school diary. I figured while I still had the courage and/or was slightly tipsy was the time to finally read it.

I had not looked at it since I'd stopped writing in it six months after the incident, and I wished I hadn't started it.

ELEVEN

I hadn't wanted to write anything the night of the incident. I'd thought if I put it on paper, it would be real and could be traced back to me.

The next night I wrote:

W

O

R

B

And at the very back of the journal I'd added a *Y*, because as we learned when we were young, sometimes *Y*. That *Y* is the reason I'm back. Maz, Dutch, and whoever else could think it was because of Gigi, but that was my lie.

The following night after the incident, I had written some crap about school, trying to mirror what I usually wrote. For years, my brother had tried to find my diary. He had never been successful, but he still worried me. For a few weeks, I wrote other lists and even tried poetry as a cover to the first list. My poetry failed miserably. Six months later, I stopped writing all together.

I knew I could never throw the book out or destroy it, so I wrapped it up in a T-shirt and put it in a paper bag. When everybody was out of the house (my childhood home), I went down to the finished basement and removed a drop ceiling tile. When my mother had told me they're going to sell the house, my first thought had been the diary.

At the time, I used retrieving the diary as a coping mechanism so I wouldn't have to confront my issues with my parents selling my childhood memories. Maybe I was being overdramatic, but few people talked about this milestone. There was high school and college graduation, marriage, childbirth, death, but no one talked about the last time we leave our childhood home.

I reached into my overnight bag and pulled out the bag the diary was in and threw myself on the bed, under the covers. The bedside lamp was bright enough to light the entire upper floor. I turned it off and grabbed my phone for light, holding onto the red bag.

When I'd retrieved the diary four years ago, I had thrown out the paper bag, but I hadn't unfolded the shirt; I'd just thrown it in a nylon drawstring bag my daughter had received at soccer camp and put it behind a pile of sweaters my daughter would never wear.

My hands clasped the shirt, and my fingers pressed into the spine of the diary. Instantly, memories flooded back to me as a girl writing nightly. I didn't need to look through it because I knew what I had written. I'd been reciting it for years: *WORBy*

The worry and the Scotch hit like a lightning bolt, and I fell asleep leaning against the headboard clutching the bag. I woke up at four a.m. to a bright light and a quiet house. My neck and back were stiff, my head pounded, and my eyes couldn't focus because of the lamp on the other nightstand.

This four a.m. light was on the nightstand next to the bunk bed. I only cleared the downstairs rooms of the timers and had failed to check the upstairs lamps and alarm clocks. I contemplated getting up and turning it off, but I slid into the fetal position, still clutching the bag, and tossed the blanket over my head and fell back asleep for another hour.

It was my parents' alarm clock going off at 5 a.m. that I could not ignore. Their room was on the other side of the stairs, but the buzzing echoed throughout the second floor. I had no choice, so I stumbled out of bed, turned off their alarm, and went to the kitchen and brewed some coffee.

I heard a thump on the window next to the door, and I jumped ten feet. Too tired/scared to investigate, I stayed put, and a minute later, I heard a dog yipping and a lady shushing it.

I walked up to the window. Mrs. Bein was walking away with the newspaper. She walked right past my car and over to her condo. I grabbed a mug of coffee and went to the couch and promptly fell asleep again.

At six forty-five, I woke up to my phone ringing. It was my brother asking if I was planning on being on time. Just for the record, I was always on time—early actually, well, except once. It happened to be his wedding, and he had never let me forget that. Since then, he called to confirm anytime we were getting together. He thought it was funny. I didn't. There wasn't much chance of being on time this morning, but I wouldn't let him win.

I hung up the phone, ran upstairs, and threw on my jeans from last night, a bra, a sweater, and socks that didn't match. I grabbed my makeup bag and hairbrush, ran downstairs, scooped up my boots and purse, and flew out the door. My breath was hideous, and I had nothing to combat it. Our restaurant of choice was a family-run diner next to the freeway a couple of blocks outside Dome. The frisky wind hit my face and blew through my sweater.

During the drive, I got my boots on, pulled my hair into a ponytail, and put on mascara. Ladies who put on makeup while driving drove me nuts, but I gave myself an exception this morning if it meant being on time and beating my brother.

I arrived two minutes before seven, ran to the last available booth, and started chugging coffee. I had the server pour Stew's cup, and it allowed me twenty extra seconds to drink mine and get an immediate refill.

Stew walked in at seven on the dot in a crisp suit and polished shoes. "Hey, Monica," he said to our server as he took the seat opposite me. Without looking at the menu, he said, "Let me get a sausage burrito please."

She shook her head. "No. No way, you're going to have sauce dripping down your tie after the first bite." She took my breakfast burrito order and left without getting Stew's.

"So how are you doing? You're looking a little rough," he said.

"Lots of love back to you too."

"Just being honest. You still have crease marks on your cheek."

"I had a rough night at the condo. Dad set up these crazy timers, lights were turning on at odd hours, and he left his alarm set for five a.m."

"Mrs. Bein calls me each day to complain and insists I go over and fix it. I guess their bedrooms share a common wall."

"I'm sure she has a key. Why doesn't *she* go turn the alarm off?" I said.

"According to her, Don and Donna didn't give her permission to enter, so she thinks it's my responsibility."

"And because you think she called the police when you parked four inches over her driveway and got a ticket, I bet you're waiting until the day before Mom and Dad come home to do anything about the five a.m. alarm."

My head had a slight buzz from the Scotch and multiple sleep interruptions, but hearing Stew's laugh made everything better.

"I think Mrs. Bein is stealing Dad's morning newspaper if that makes you feel better for not getting over there sooner," I said. "You're not even going to ask what I'm doing here?"

He waited a second before answering. "I'm surprised you weren't here earlier."

I held the coffee cup like an anchor between my hands on the table. "What do you mean?"

"Oh, come off it," Stew said. "Even though I want to hear whatever cockamamie story you've concocted, please don't play me for a fool. I let it go all those years ago in high school because I was a dumb teenager. I know you were friends with the girl that disappeared, and you tried so hard to pretend you were ok with it."

"Friends?" I said. "No one was friends with Bo. She started school after the January break and was gone four months later."

"You sat with her at lunch, and don't pretend you didn't."

"Once, but that does not mean we were friends. What do you mean I pretended to be ok with it?"

Monica dropped my breakfast as I had ordered it in front of me, and Stew received a bowl of oatmeal.

"Can I at least get some raisins?" he asked.

Changing the subject, I said, "She was quick with the food."

"At this hour, they have everything nearly ready to go. Trying to get people in and out as fast as possible. Now, stop changing the subject, why deny being friends with her?"

We waited for Monica to return with raisins and refill our coffee before we spoke again.

My knees were locked together and my shoulders pulled up to my ears because every time the door opened, cold air swept in and the air went through my body. I tried to relax but I couldn't fake it, so I tried to change the conversation again. The diner noise rose around us, but I was conscious of the level of my voice.

"Is that Farmer Ted, the guy with the roadside corn stand, sitting at the end of the counter?"

"No."

"You didn't even look."

Stewed poured the last of the raisins into the oatmeal. "Yet again, you're changing the subject."

"Well, at least answer the question."

"I already did," Stew replied and continued to slurp the oatmeal. "Farmer Ted died last year. So if you're seeing him sitting at the counter, you got bigger issues to worry about." His phone buzzed, and he stood to take the call in the corner.

I was dumbstruck. Had I not been as smooth as I'd thought I was at covering it up all those years ago?

Irritated he knew my secret, I did the only thing a sister could do: I would make him pay.

He returned with a sour look on his face. "Sorry, I have to cut and run. We're not done with this. Kay and I have tickets for the basketball game tonight, but I'm assuming you're here for another night, so let's do lunch tomorrow. Kay will be out with friends in Madison, and the kids are not home for break yet. Come to the house."

"Your wife is headed to Lake Geneva with some friends from Madison. Pay attention to things at home, and don't worry about me."

Monica swung over to the table and dropped the check.

He stood and pulled on his suit jacket. "Stop changing the subject. Oh, and thanks for breakfast."

I had tossed a twenty and a five-dollar bill on the table.

"That's more than enough to cover breakfast and a decent tip. Not bad, little sis. Now don't skip out on lunch."

"Not so fast," I snapped a little too loud, and some diners turned to look. "You didn't finish breakfast."

Stew never cared what others thought, but he lowered his voice to keep the conversation between the two of us. "I have to go. We have to rework this presentation before the meeting. I have a job that needs me."

"Just because I have a flexible office schedule does not mean I don't work as hard as you do." *He doesn't know how flexible my schedule is right now.*

"I beg to differ. You work for public radio. How stressful can that be?"

"I work as hard as you, but I manage the stress better. Work smarter, not harder."

I felt like we were teenagers fighting for control of the television.

Stew clearly thought he'd won. "Is that why you have pillow marks on your face?"

He was two booths away when I yelled his name, and he waited a second before he turned around in time to see his wallet come flying at him.

"Thanks for breakfast." I stood and went behind the counter to refill my coffee mug.

I said I would make him pay.

TWELVE

I returned to my seat and finished my burrito at a leisurely pace with two Advils, grapefruit, and Stew's bowl of oatmeal. The caffeine I guzzled sent my head spinning; however, the oatmeal helped ground me overall. I had a feeling the burrito would wreak havoc on my stomach. It was now less than an hour until I was to meet Maz. A proper shower and a decent outfit were now high priority.

Walking out of the diner, I saw a flyer taped to the glass door. Friends of Gigi were hosting a candlelight vigil at the gazebo Sunday evening. Next to it was a missing person flyer with another picture featuring Gigi. No one had thought to do any of that for Bo.

"Interesting reading?" A gentleman walked in and had to squeeze past me.

"Ah, just reading here. Terrible situation," I mumbled.

"We should know," the man said.

He was inches from me, but I got whiplash spinning to get a look at him.

We? What does he mean WE?

THIRTEEN

Mystery man walked past me, gave a nod to Monica as she pointed to an empty stool at the end of the counter. He declined her offer and went to the dirty booth I'd just vacated, sat down, and looked at me, extending his arm to the seat across from him.

When he walked past, I had seen his dark well-worn jeans, work boots, his arm muscles bulging out from under his navy T-shirt. He looked like the guy in my dreams that built the ski chalet Van and I would rent on the weekends—*a girl can dream!*

Monica cleared the table and set it for two. He was still looking at me for an answer to his invitation.

Slowly, I walked over, and each step erased the years and decades away from the Leo I remember from thirty years ago.

His brown wavy hair was peppered with gray, and his smile was still accented by his dimples. He was as much a part of the story as I was, sort of, and every time I recalled what we had done, I saw him as the teenager he had been. Just like Van, I always thought of them as I had last seen them several decades ago. Each anniversary, I'd hoped to see Leo, and I had expected high school Leo and not grown-up Leo.

I eased myself down into Stew's vacated seat. "Leo?"

"Is that a question?" he asked.

I couldn't help but laugh. "I was just surprised to see you. After all these years, to finally see you again is crazy." I corrected myself, "Good crazy."

Monica returned with two orange juices and asked Leo for his order.

"I guess I'm done with coffee," I said, laughing.

"Monica takes it upon herself to monitor everyone's diet. I only get coffee when I'm here at six. She knows if I'm in this late, I've already had my fill of coffee. The annoying part of her wielding her powers is she's usually right about what everyone should be eating and drinking. So, from the orange juice you received, you must have been on your way out and not in when we crossed paths in the entryway."

"I just had breakfast with my brother. You're a regular here? So everyone but me moved back to Dome?"

"Is that another question, or are you just thinking out loud? I don't know if I'm supposed to respond," Leo asked.

He put a smile on my face. He called it as he saw it. No bullshit.

I drummed my fingers on the table. "I've been back here for less than twenty-four hours, and I'm running into a lot of old faces. It's getting a little overwhelming."

"The people or what they represent?" Leo said without judgment in his voice.

I sat on my hands and leaned back in the booth. "Direct hit. Nicely done."

"Take no offense. I know why you're here, and you must have seen Maz already. I got the same message, or least I'm assuming the same message, about meeting room five."

"Maz! You made me almost forget I was on my way to see him now. Join us," I said the words, but I didn't know if I meant them.

It had felt good to be part of a tribe—me, Maz, Edward Olsen, and Leo. As the years had gone by, I was ok with it just being Maz and me. I needed someone to remind me of my actions. People tended to sugarcoat memories, and I needed a reality check of what we had done and how I had let her go. Inviting Dutch to our group seemed to have changed everything.

Monica delivered scrambled eggs, bacon, and toast to Leo and hung around for an extra second, almost waiting to join our conversation.

"Thank you kindly," Leo said, using a strong but polite tone, telling Monica this wasn't the time to chitchat.

She dropped the check and left.

I raised my eyebrow.

Without me asking a question, this time Leo answered, "There is nothing to tell except she's trying to bed every guy that comes in here, and if you give her an extra minute of attention, she latches onto you like a vulture."

"I doubt it's every guy. You just know how to put on the charm," I said.

"Every guy." He scooped up a forkful of eggs.

"She wasn't like that with my brother."

"Maybe she already shagged him." More eggs were piled onto the fork and then consumed.

"He's been happily married for years, and that isn't Stew's style."

He was eating fast but not inhaling. He'd come for food and was completing his mission.

Munching on the dry toast, Leo said nothing, but I needed to fill the silence somehow.

"So if she's after you, that doesn't clear up if you're single, married—happily or not—gay, or a lifelong virgin. I'll let you fill in the answer."

He gave me no answer. Again, I didn't know why now I was talking over his silence when I was usually comfortable in a void.

"No wedding ring, so that takes out married. That leaves single, dating, gay, or a virgin."

After he consumed more eggs, I let the silence hang in the air until he finally spoke.

"This time, I know there was no question asked. Things were assumed, but nothing was asked."

I drank some orange juice and felt my stomach twinge. The sun was finally past the clouds, and the rays were streaking over the table. The temperature inside the diner shifted. I leaned back and let out a sigh. "WORB," I mumbled. "It may be thirty years later and some gray hair for both of us, but I see the same ol' Leo. The one with cool detachment and a comment for everything."

"Good to see you too, Lou. Or do you go by Sarah these days?"

"I guess to some I'll always be Lou. How about you, ever leave the area?"

"After college in Madison, I came back to the Milwaukee area. A few years ago, I got a place just outside Dome."

"Thank you," I said.

"For what?"

"You finally answered a question," I said.

He laughed. It was a deep, genuine belly laugh. It melted my heart.

"Come with me to see Maz. Don't stay away this time. It would be good for all of us," I begged.

He took a sip of orange juice and leaned back. He was challenging me to the quiet game. I'd lost last time and didn't intend to break this time.

"Do you know why I stopped attending these anniversary get-togethers?" Leo asked.

I wasn't breaking my silence.

He leaned forward and spoke softly but directly. "Do you know why I stopped coming to the damn anniversary roundups?"

I didn't even shrug my shoulders to indicate any type of answer.

Leo continued, "It was always about *us*. How are *WE* doing? No one ever spoke about Bo and all of it. How messed up was that? I didn't need the three of you in my head. I was as confused as any of you guys."

He was right. Just a minute ago, I'd thought about us as a tribe, and I hadn't even listed Bo. My stomach turned over. I wished it was last night's Scotch, the breakfast burrito, all the coffee, fruit, oatmeal, and orange juice, but I had to admit it was probably my conscience hitting rock bottom. I'd always thought about my actions because I'd been the one to choose the plan: W-O-R-B. We had always talked about how WE were doing. But, really, how much can you talk about the absent? The dead?

"Lou, are you there?" Leo was waving his hand in front of me.

"Sorry, I left the conversation for a second," I said.

I waited for him to repeat what I'd missed, but he just sat there.

"I got to go meet Maz at the library. Join us if you want. I understand if you don't, but you know this year is different." I stood up and turned to leave but looked back at him. "Now there's a second girl who's disappeared. How is it not a copycat? Actually, we need to know how *is* it a copycat."

FOURTEEN

Bo and Gigi. Bo and Gigi. Bo and Gigi.

I just kept repeating their names on the way back to my parents' place. I parked in the driveway and ran up the stairs, peeling my clothes off and hoping nothing had dropped from my hands. The water was barely lukewarm when I jumped in the shower. Combining shampoo and conditioner in my hand and lathering up only once saved time but probably didn't allow for proper washing and conditioning. I also used the rinsing suds as bodywash. I thought combining three steps into one was ingenious. The water temperature had never reached hot by the time I stepped out of the shower less than three minutes later.

Like most ladies, I rejoiced in the fact that leisure wear is trendy, comfortable, easy to pack, and could be thrown on in seconds. Hair in a ponytail under a baseball hat. I was rocking fashion without appearing lazy or rushed. A quick reapply of mascara and eyeliner, and I was out the door.

I arrived six minutes early, but the overflow parking lot was reserved for the crew working on installing the new facade and signage, so I circled around and found a spot in front of Hattie's.

Being raised in Dome made it mandatory that I go into Hattie's despite already having breakfast and way too much caffeine.

Chamomile tea was the best option to keep me warm, and the lack of caffeine was best for keeping me from rattling off the earth. Disappointment dropped on me like someone who was just stood up on a blind date when the current Hattie wasn't at the register. My second time here since the newest Hattie had taken over the place, and I couldn't introduce myself as a former employee.

This was the only place in the world I got to say: *Do you know who I am? I'm one of you. I know how the thermostat works and how to freeze out the old ladies who linger too long. I know you have to hold the handle down on the second toilet for seven seconds, but it works just fine."*

I didn't need or want fame—for Pete's sake, I worked behind the scenes for public radio, but I wanted to have one place that gave me a large when I ordered a medium or gave me six scones when I ordered five or how about a knowing smile when the previous customer in line was being rude and a day-old pastry somehow got mixed into their order.

Maybe Hattie's is hiring?

The lady taking my order assumed I wanted the pastry after I inquired about the featured special of the day, and I didn't fight it and happily paid for it. She said it was a Serbian meat burek with beef, lamb, and pork in phyllo dough, not necessarily a breakfast item, but it was good and best eaten warm. It was never a good idea to waste anything from Hattie's, so I sipped and chewed my way across the street to the library, arriving one minute before eight thirty.

The sign on the door read something like "Dome residents only," but I blew past it without a second thought. I hadn't lived here for decades, but I would also consider myself home here.

The place was virtually empty. Most libraries across the country didn't open their doors at seven, but here, it gave students a place to go before school that didn't cost them a cup of coffee to sit. I usually visited Hattie's when I visited my family, but walking in here again after all these years for a second time in two days actually made me miss being in high school.

Back in my day, mornings at the library had held a different vibe than the afternoons. In some ways, mornings at the library had been my favorite part of high school. I'd felt like we were the island of misfit toys from *Rudolf the Red Nose Reindeer*. No one knew why we chose to seek refuge in the town library some mornings, and no one cared. I guessed it was mostly a sanctuary for latchkey kids who didn't want to be alone at home or at school an hour before the first bell. Voices were louder, and conversations crossed from table to table. It didn't matter what social group we belonged to or what grade we were in. We could see freshman and seniors debating Monday night football or the latest movie.

There was an understanding that if anyone was sitting along the wall at the small tables with a book open, it meant they were racing to finish that day's assignment and should be left alone. My favorite part was when an upperclassman would offer to help a freshman— we were a community in the mornings.

Occasionally, a nonregular morning student would pop in, thus shifting the community vibe I had grown to love, but it was back the next day when the interlopers were gone. I was there probably three mornings a week, and I now felt the void of my house with kids away at school, husband gone, and no place like this for me at home. I was truly homesick for the first time.

It was good to know the library still had the early hours to accommodate everyone. I was curious if it was still home to the favorite community I ever had. Did the mornings still rock at the library?

This morning, one lone employee was realigning tables and

straightening chairs. The middle school and high school bell had rung over thirty minutes ago, and any prekindergarten reading times wouldn't start for at least another hour.

On some tables and taped to the door were the flyers about Sunday's vigil in Gazebo Park.

Oh, *Gigi. The reason I'm here—Gigi. I'm not here to reminisce but to tie her and Bo together.*

The senior ladies from yesterday were in room one again. I hoped they were discussing a lighter topic than room five. The lights were off in our designated room, but I flipped the switch and set down my purse and tea and tossed the empty white pastry bag into the small trash can in the corner. I was about to sit when my stomach flipped and swooshed like a water balloon rolling in the grass and while I prayed it wouldn't snap wide-open. That meat-filled pastry might have been the straw that broke the camel's back. The balloon tossed again. My stomach was moving fast, and the balloon was rolling.

This was bad. I couldn't get home. I couldn't do it here—a public place, a quiet place. I could not!

Oh no, another swoosh followed up with a cramp. My stomach was like that water balloon expanding with each flip, and that wasn't a good situation. Sweat dripped down from under my baseball hat. I held onto the back of the chair for balance, but my hand nearly slipped off because of my sweaty palms.

There was nowhere to go. What else was open at this hour? Was there a bathroom at the hardware store, and why would that be better than the library?

I was losing time. My stomach was losing control, and all the clinching farther south was losing tight control.

There was no other option. Why had I fought it for so long?

Where the hell is the bathroom? Did they move it after the expansion? Why would they move a bathroom? Maybe it would be faster to find a group of trees or shrubs and hope for the best.

Think!

I had to think. I duck-waddled past the study rooms and stacks to the open table area and finally saw the sign for the restrooms. Knees pressed together, I continued my march. I could barely push the heavy door open and even thought to lock it behind me, but someone in a stall coughed. Beige polyester pants and thick-soled, sensible black shoes and a lime-green purse were visible under the stall. I didn't think it could get worse.

I lost my grip on all things that mattered in the moment. Disbelief swept over me as the last stomach flip cruised south so fast I couldn't maintain tight control. I thought again of that water balloon that someone tossed but the person catching it had missed. It didn't break when it hit the ground, but it was riding the edge of the sidewalk, ready to burst. The yoga leggings were mocking me now. At least if I were in real pants I would have some type of air-buffer zone.

I pushed the stall door so hard it bounced back and smacked the bill of my hat. I looked at the toilet paper. I'd learned the hard way many years ago that that should be the first thing one checked when entering a stall and deciding to stay or go. The stall door knocked my cap back, but I couldn't worry about it until it sprung forward again, and this time, it hit my forehead. I pivoted and threw my yoga leggings down and made sure I was centered on the toilet seat.

It was as much a relief as it was a horror that descended from me. I had the right frame of mind to reach behind me and activate the flush sensor to drown out most of the noise. It had to be flushed twice before I could even wipe. My hands dropped to the side of the toilet bowl and let the cold porcelain touch my wrist and send a cool relief to my body in shock.

When thoroughly drained of everything, new panic set in. I thought about how a balloon filled with water and then tied off would sometimes get a tiny bubble at the knot and sometimes that little bubble when pressed would squirt a thin shot of water—I looked at my underwear and saw I had not had as tight of control as I had previously thought. There were no words to match this newfound horror.

During my two flushes, the lady in the next stall shuffled herself to the sink and, finally, out of the bathroom. I quickly kicked off my shoes, stripped off my leggings and underwear, then dropped them to the floor and stood up. I unzipped my sweat jacket and tied it around my waist. I shoved my feet halfway back into my shoes and clopped out of the stall to lock the bathroom door.

I returned to the stall and dipped part of my underwear in the fresh toilet water, then I went to the garbage can and removed the large plastic dome cover. The current bag only held the paper towel from my previous stall-mate. I pulled it out and placed my soiled underwear inside and knotted the bag as if I had just picked up after a dog. There was a roll of fresh bags on the bottom of the trash barrel, and I pulled up a new one and set the old bag with my underwear in it, covered the top with paper towels so no one would be the wiser, and replaced the lid.

I did a spot wash on my leggings and pulled them back on. My sleeveless top was long enough to drop below my waist, but not long enough to cover all of my butt. I hoped the blue-and-white-swirl pattern camouflaged the wet spot in the crotch of the pants. My jacket wrapped around my waist would have to do the rest to protect what was left of my dignity.

In the bathroom mirror, I straightened my baseball hat. My cheeks were rosy pink as if I actually had done some yoga, and it gave me hope I could escape without further embarrassment. The hat rubbed the bump on my forehead from the double door bounce, but it also hid the bruise that was forming. My leggings felt damp in the ass and I was a little shaky, but overall I thought I could pull off looking like that nightmare hadn't just happened.

The goal was to avoid everyone, speed-walk to the car, and get to my parents' place and bury my head under a pillow.

The front doors were six feet away when I realized I didn't have my purse and keys. That was going to add another fifty seconds to my escape plan.

Maz greeted me walking down the hall, and I was trying to come up with an excuse to leave when he nodded to someone behind me.

Leo said, "Morning."

My morning just got longer.

I had no choice and followed them into room five. I picked up my warm tea and stood in the corner of the room, using the two walls to keep me warm and pretending I was comfortable since my sweatshirt was acting as an ass guard.

Leo pulled a chair so far away from the table he looked like a room monitor sitting next to the door.

Maz tossed a waxy white bag on the table and gestured to us both. Again, men tossing food on a table. I raised the cup to my mouth to cover my gag reflex. The smell of meat-filled pastries filled the room.

Leo jumped back up to the table and extended the bag to me.

"Thanks, but no thanks," I said.

"How can you decline Hattie's?" Maz said with a mouthful of water balloon.

Leo jumped in. "She probably forgot her Dome roots."

"I'm taking the healthy route"—lie—"I can resist temptation unlike you savages," I said.

"BS. You were probably there when they opened," Leo said.

With the weakest response ever, I said, "Wrong!" (Not really a lie since I wasn't there at six thirty.)

Leo's response was throwing a napkin towards me, but it only flew two feet—nowhere near close. He tried kicking it but with less success.

For a brief moment, I felt like we were all back in high school, and it was a regular morning at the library. The feeling of nostalgia was so intimate, it was both sad and sweet.

I did the only thing I knew to do in a moment like that. I went on the attack. "Wrong for the second time today."

"Second time?" Leo asked.

"I do think about her. About Bo," I said.

"I thought we all did," Maz said.

FIFTEEN

Silence clung to the walls of room five. The three of us collectively thinking about Bo made it ten times more real, as if it had all happened last week.

They were both looking at me.

"She was always there in the back of my head. I finally saw the movie where the guy was dead the whole time. It was the biggest spoiler in movie history. My first thought was Bo. I wanted to ruin the movie for her. The movie credits were rolling, and I thought back to high school English class. Our entire class had to read a book about a teenage girl dealing with real struggles we could never imagine in Dome. Everybody was into it—well, almost everybody. But we were having great discussions and actually enjoying reading it. Probably not because it was a great book, but we were just happy to be done with Shakespeare. Anyway, I've never known someone to raise their hand so much and dominate every topic. Bo was grating on everyone's nerves. Then she read ahead and spoiled the ending, and half the class was ready to throw their books at her. I wanted to find her and spoil the movie like she spoiled that book for everyone."

The guys said nothing. This time the silence was too much so I continued.

"I thought about her until I couldn't. What we did and didn't do haunted me for years. One day when I dropped off my kids at daycare, a child who had only been there two days didn't show up. The facility called the parents, their work, and finally the police to check on the welfare of the child. It turned out the child had a doctor's appointment and showed up two hours late. It was then I realized what haunted me the most wasn't our actions, but what happened the day after and the next day and the next that followed. No one noticed, or if they noticed, they didn't care she was gone. That was sad."

"What about Olsen?" Leo looked down as he spoke. The angry tone wasn't directed at me as it was at the three of us thirty years ago.

"He's living in Idaho," Maz said.

An icy shiver went down my spine. I pushed myself farther into the cinder-block walls for warmth and support.

"You found him after all these years? How? Since when? How long have you known?"

Maz's gaze bounced between Leo and me, but he never made eye contact with me. "As I said, he's living in Idaho. Teaching and runs a summer camp for troubled teens."

"How did you find him? You talk to him?"

As I was firing questions, he inhaled and slowly exhaled, then stepped forward to take a seat. His face was turning pink, and he wiped sweat off his forehead.

God, I wish I was that warm. Not that uncomfortable but that warm. My ass is still damp, and I just have to leave my sweat jacket wrapped around my waist.

Maz fumbled for the right words. He was shifting in his seat, trying to pull his phone out of his pocket, when his key chain dropped to the floor.

"What are you, the janitor? How many keys do you need, man?" Leo asked.

Maz put his phone facedown on the table before answering. "I work for Glen and Nindle Architecture and Construction Firm in the historical preservation division. We got the contract for the middle school being built next to the high school. Part of my job is to determine the best use for the current middle school building and land and the old historic police building."

Maz stopped talking. I was numb because Leo and I knew where this was headed. We caught each other's eye, and it only broke when I squeezed my tea cup too hard and the plastic lid popped up. I fumbled with the lid as calmly as one could when their hands were shaking from the cold and unsteady nerves.

Maz took a deep breath and continued in a robotic voice, one that would suggest continued repetition of this answer—or from what Leo and I knew—emotional detachment from the subject.

"Including the old underground steam tunnels that connect the aforementioned buildings to this one and the others on this side of Main Street."

Looking at the wall in front of him, he answered the question neither Leo nor I would ask but had immediately thought. "The tunnels were clear."

We let out a breath.

"Well, let me be straight. For what you two are thinking about, the tunnels were clear. They always were. We were careful. It was a walking path that many have been in over the years." Maz leaned back and talked more confidently. "Now, however, it's a different story. After we graduated and sometime in the nineties, the schools went fully computerized. Old paper records were transferred into the school's database and then were supposed to be destroyed. Not sure what really happened, but all those files and more were sent to the tunnels and never destroyed. When the village board found out, they had a fit—rightfully so. A deep investigation went into the tunnels—like what is in the tunnels and the tunnels themselves. Most people still to this day don't know about them.

"I work with a village historian to review the files and all the boxes down there. We verify the files are old school records or if they have historical significance to the village. We are tasked with shredding or preserving the materials. Believe it or not, part of my job is to give a full report on the operation, purpose, any historical significance that would prevent them from permanently sealing the tunnels off and if any building structure that sits above them is at risk ."

"You're shitting me?" Leo said.

I laughed like you do when someone falls. You know you shouldn't, but you can't help it. Leo shook his head in disbelief.

Even Maz kinda smiled and continued. "I've been spending so much time in the library basement accessing the tunnels and going through the boxes of material we found. Martha, the village historian, and I use the library basement as our basecamp and workroom. These days, it's easier than the old police station entrance point and less weird than going through the middle school."

Leo raised an eyebrow. "That's less weird than the school?"

"Honestly, not at first. Things quickly shifted. An adult male who isn't a teacher or an administrator or a parent tends to get strange looks and whispers behind your back when moving through a school of that size where everyone knows everyone. Yes, I understand the irony of that. Believe me, I've been living this for a while now.

"So, as I said, I was spending a lot of time accessing the tunnels and shredding documents in the basement with Martha. I got to know the employees. Allison, the main IT support person, went out on bedrest and eventually took maternity leave several months ago. Brian is the only other one that can handle the computer system, but he's part-time. The system here is old, and the new one won't be installed until fourth quarter. At some point, I volunteered to help reboot it one day when it crashed. I was spending so much time here, some employees and a few students thought I worked for the library. Now I'm the go-to guy when the library computer has issues."

My head was swirling like my stomach had been ten minutes ago. At least nothing could spew out of my head. I could barely step into this place after I'd heard the news about Gigi, and here was Maz retracing our steps.

There were so many questions I couldn't get one out. "Is there . . . has there . . . any connection?"

Leo remained as frozen as I was but had the comfort of a chair. His arms were folded across his chest and his feet flat on the floor with no expression, but he was listening to every word Maz spoke.

He didn't keep us in suspense. "I don't know. Not the tunnels anyway. The only people who have access to the tunnels are me and Martha. Because of the sensitive documents with people's personal information on them, I have to be down there when the engineers are looking at the structure of the tunnels. I've been diligent about locking all access points."

"I'm not sure all the details were in the newspaper or online, but it seems like Dutch may have told you more," I said.

"Dutch?" Leo asked.

"The paper used his full name, Theo Van Dijk. The kid that last saw Gigi. He's one of the after-school regulars here in the library."

"What do we know about this kid?" Leo asked.

"Get this one—you won't believe it—but he's Van's son. Remember him?" I said.

"Holy shit. This kid has family roots to Dome. Some people never leave this place," Leo said.

"Maybe this place never leaves us—for good or bad," I said.

"He and Gigi were doing a story for the school newspaper, and I helped them with some research."

"Jesus Christ, how many jobs do you have here?" Leo asked.

"Again, it all goes back to those files in the tunnels. After Gigi went missing, the reporters were vicious. They tried chasing him down in the building, and I helped him hide out in the office until they left. I got him talking until his friend came and drove him home. He claims he last saw her get into a car. She never made it to the library morning on Tuesday."

"So that's it. The two cases are not the same. You two are freaking out for no reason," Leo said.

"A girl is missing!" I said.

Leo stood up and walked behind his chair, placing his hands on the back of it. "Girls go missing every day. It's a sad fact of life. Why does this have to mean something to us?"

"You read the article? He was walking in through the woods! In spring! In Dome! And it's what he didn't say to the police and reporters that matters."

"What are you talking about? You talked to him?" Leo asked.

"Yesterday when I came here, I met Maz in this room, and he brought Dutch along and introduced us. I told him I knew there was more to the story, like he took something from where he saw Gigi, and he didn't tell the police. I told him we knew his little secret but stopped short of telling him everything, mostly because we got interrupted and our time was cut short."

"I get it. Two similar incidents, so that means everything is fine," Leo said.

"How can you . . . you say that?" My words were as slow as my thoughts. "You're right. Bo being gone was good for everyone. Well, I'm not sure *good* is the best choice of words. But it was the best option for everyone. That's what we decided. How do we know it's the same thing now?"

No one spoke. The hum of the overhead lights was the only pulse in the room.

"There's more." Maz's voice was unsteady. "I have to tell you more."

Leo and I exchanged looks.

Maz was pale and not meeting our eye contact.

I took a long sip of the hot tea so I could feel something to let me know I was still breathing.

"She's back. Bo is back."

SIXTEEN

"You spoke to her?" Disbelief suffused my whispered words.

Maz shook his head and ran his fingers through the air.

"When? Is she coming here?" I said.

Maz shook his head. "Last January."

"You're kidding me."

His stoic face and frozen body told us this was no joke.

"So, when we met last year, you had spoken to her? Is that why you suggested we don't need to have our anniversary get-togethers? You got your closure, and to hell with the rest of us!"

"Let me explain . . ." Maz said.

"Explain what?" I practically threw my paper cup on the table, then raised my arms in the air like I was reaching for an answer from the heavens. "What can you explain? I don't know if I can trust you. We're supposed to be supporting this kid and figure out if Gigi is really in danger, and you've been holding this back for months. My great comfort in all this was that it was something *we* did. Now I find out not only did you figure out where Olsen's living, you spoke to Bo. I guess it's every man for himself. Fine by me." I grabbed my purse, walked past Leo and out of room five.

I zipped past the stacks and out the front door. The sun broke the clouds and lit up Main Street like Times Square, adding a bit of warmth to my bare shoulders. The words coming from Maz's mouth should have surprised me more, but I'd always felt like an island.

Walking three blocks away from the library, I also found myself three blocks from my car. Without admitting it, I knew where I was headed. Four more blocks, and I would be at the high school baseball field and the woods.

Two local news vans were parked on Main Street, and a police cruiser was circling the high school. Another was going up and down Main Street. I guess when a popular girl goes missing, the town and police get nervous and reporters get a story.

I made my way to the baseball field. A reporter and a cameraman came out of the woods. Four minutes ago, Maz telling me Bo was back had rocked me to the core, but seeing a reporter come charging for me, put me in the depths of a nightmare.

The brunette woman with big hair and heavy makeup saw me watching and started trotting my way while yelling at the cameraman to keep up. "I would love to get an interview with someone local."

"No, thank you," I said.

Last month, I had applied for a promotion and had told them if I didn't get I was quitting. My boss didn't bite, and I stood my ground on principle and gave my notice. I needed more money. As amicable as our divorce had been, we were still hammering out financial stuff with two kids in college. I wanted to shove my ex out of the picture just to prove I'd won at something. He'd had the affair—hot new girlfriend and cool place in the city. I wanted to pay for our kids' education without him. In a week, I was supposed to start a job with a church. It was one of those megachurches that was more about franchising than evangelism. Their image was everything. My background check had been more thorough than if I had applied to the CIA. If my name was linked in any way to a missing person, I would be out of a job before I even started it. No job, no money, no tuition, and no telling my husband to kiss off.

"A quote from a local would be great. It would be beneficial . . ."

Tires screeched behind me, and someone yelled, "Get in."

With sheer relief, I turned to the *Local Focus On your Side* reporter and said, "Bad timing for you. My ride is here." I gladly hopped into Leo's truck.

"Don't I get a thank-you after rescuing you from that reporter?" Leo asked after I'd buckled in.

"Do you think you're my white knight in shining armor? It was just a reporter. I could have easily declined an interview," I said.

"Because you're so cool with your temper now. I wasn't asking to be your superhero, but I would welcome a thank-you for the ride."

"Ride? We are barely going ten miles an hour. What kind of ride is this?"

"It's the kind where you tell me where I'm taking you."

I flashed back to my high school days. The freedom of riding around with your friends. I was tempted to say let's swing by Jam's house and then head to the budget movie theater. "Oh. I'm staying at my parents' house."

"Rivers section," Leo said and finally pressed it to thirty miles an hour.

"Wow, you remember where I lived?"

"Maybe I kept tabs on you back then?" He turned and looked directly at me and smiled. "Not that you ever noticed."

His attention was back on the road.

"What are you saying? We were friends. We talked almost every day. You were probably even at my house. Of course I noticed you."

Leo made a left turn. "Yes, but you never really noticed . . ."

"What are you saying? You had a thing for me?" I said, blushing three decades later and at the age of fifty years old.

"Maybe. But that was then, and this is now. Where am I going?" Leo asked.

"Well, this is slightly embarrassing," I said.

"More embarrassing than admitting an old crush?"

"I won't compare the two, but you need to turn around. I just remembered my parents moved to the condos in the mountain section."

I caught his eye, and we both laughed. His throaty chuckle made his body shift and the blue flannel shirt swayed. It looked so soft, and I wanted to slide my fingers down his arm—I mean, his sleeve. Well, maybe across his whole body. Wow, those thoughts were a surprise to me, especially when I'd thought nothing would make me smile today.

We rode quietly for two minutes as I pointed out the turns. One block from my parents' condo, I remembered my car was parked in front of Hattie's, but I was so mortified that my thoughts had turned from Bo and Gigi to running my hand across his body, I had to just get out of the truck and not admit where my car was. It was looking to be a beautiful day. Maybe the walk back to my car would do me some good after I showered.

Oh my god, clean myself up.

I wondered if I smelled. Was my underwear still neatly buried in the bathroom garbage can?

Leo pulled into the driveway. "Look, I don't know much about anything, but I think we should hear what Maz has to say. I don't know what your little anniversary get-togethers were about, but if he withheld information, that would be pretty crappy. If Bo's back and another girl just vanished, we have to figure out what that means. Did she orchestrate some weird plan? I told Maz I would meet him tomorrow at eleven, and he better come with lots of answers."

At that moment, my head snapped, thankfully not my stomach again. "I'm done."

"What do you mean done? You came back to Dome and twenty minutes ago you were fighting for justice for Gigi, and now you're done?"

"I just realized it's not my problem. I feel bad for Gigi and her family, but not my problem. If Olsen is thriving on a ranch out West and Bo is back, then all is good. Over and out." I opened the truck door and slid out.

"This isn't you. What just happened to you?" Leo snapped.

I stood with the sun on my shoulders and smiled. "I don't know. Maybe I just realized, all these years, it was the unknown of their futures that drove me crazy. The craziness morphed into who I am and how I reacted to obstacles in my life, living on the edge, making risky decisions with a devil-may-care attitude. It's a bullshit way to live. It served me fairly well in my career but probably cost me my marriage. I fought so hard to keep it out of parenting so my kids could have a normal mother and childhood. I probably have spent five thousand dollars on parenting books just so I would know the choices I made as a mother were not reactions to a choice I made at sixteen.

"Now that Bo and Olsen have a happy ending, let someone else live with a festering nugget of a migraine for a few decades." I shut the passenger-side door and walked around the truck.

Leo yelled, "Eleven a.m. tomorrow."

I promptly walked into my parents' condo and to the bathroom on the first floor and threw up. I didn't know what was left in my stomach, but something came up. If Bo was really back, then where does that leave our secret? Not the secret I share with the boys, but the other one.

Is someone getting closure by repeating the past?

SEVENTEEN

I took a shower for the second time and put on my third outfit of the day. The weather had warmed significantly since I had run out the door to meet Stew, but nothing beat a flannel shirt and an old pair of comfy jeans to help settle me.

My email showed several job openings in the Chicago area. I figured I'd better start applying because, the way the day was shaping up, that reporter would probably track me down and I would confess everything just to let it all out and let it stop running my life. I pulled out my laptop and began searching for a new career and a new life. I sat at the kitchen table, figuring I might slouch down into a nap if I returned to the couch.

At three o'clock, my stomach rumbling prevented further job searching from being done. The entire drive up here yesterday, I had been uncertain if it was the right choice to come back, but I was certain I wanted some of my mother's cooking.

I laughed at the irony of it all and almost called Joe, my ex. It irked me that he still popped into my head as someone to share a funny story with. Sitting in my parents' house hungry was punishable by law, according to my mother. If I told Joe I was hungry, sitting in my parents' kitchen, he would immediately express sympathy because that could only mean my mom was dead. I wouldn't have said my mom traipsing through Paris qualified as dead, but it was a sad moment for me.

It suddenly hit me how my mother never allowed anyone to go hungry. She was more prepared than a troop of Boy Scouts.

I pushed my laptop aside and threw myself down the stairs. The unfinished basement was good for storing wrapping paper and extra Crock-Pots, and it functioned as a place to sit while tornado sirens blasted, and housed the extra refrigerator. The freezer held all sorts of goodies. I had a choice of potpie, stew (my brother's namesake), casseroles, and cherry pie. The thought of warm beef stew made me melt.

I ran back up, found a pot and let the frozen stew slide out of the Tupperware, waiting for the steam and aroma to slide me into my happy place. I picked at the pieces of beef and carrots as they melted off. The carrots could be frozen and, at the same time, burn my tongue.

I had nearly eaten half of it standing at the stove when someone knocked on the front door.

I debated if I wanted to talk to whoever was there. Either they're looking for my parents and would get the point when no one came to the door, or they were looking for me.

The latter was the least appealing, and still not in the mood to talk, I ignored it.

The person shouted. "You know I can see you?"

Leo. God, what is he doing here?

He stood in the tall narrow window beside the front door where Van had stood just last night. I turned off the stove, opened the door, and waited for him to speak first.

"Just wanted to check how you're doing."

"Fine."

The third shower had distanced me from the shock of it all, job hunting and resume building had distracted my brain, and food had taken away some of my anger, but I felt as if I had suddenly built walls up around me like I had thirty years ago.

I glared at him. "I'm fine."

"Really? I'm not fine," Leo said.

"Thanks for the update." I reached for the door.

"Come with me, and we can—"

"I'm not getting in your truck. I don't need you rescuing me again."

"Good. Because I walked here. The weather is nice, so let's go. We can talk, not talk. I think I would feel less insane if I knew someone else was having the same thoughts I am."

I nodded for a full ten seconds before I finally spoke. "Give me a minute." I kept the door open but didn't invite him in.

He waited patiently with his hands in the front pockets of his jeans, leaning on the doorframe while I went to the bathroom and grabbed my keys.

A moment of panic set in when I exited the first-floor bathroom and came out to find a light on in the office. I thought Leo had breached the doorway, but when I went to investigate, it was a light I had missed last night. My father had set the timer for the light to be on for forty-three minutes.

Leo was in front of the condo walking along the flower garden and jumped when I walked up next to him. "Didn't expect you so soon. I thought you went to change." He gestured towards the garden. "Who has the green thumb? Lots of tulips are getting ready to pop, and I'm assuming some daffodils. The side of the condo has a nice assortment of things to come this summer. I need to remember to check back in a few weeks."

"It's my father's hobby. Kinda surprised he left for ten days this time of year when the tulips will be peaking. Come back during summer, and my dad will be happy to show off his work, and if you time it right, you can get some tomatoes."

I found myself in a better mood just being outside, or maybe it was standing so close to Leo. A wave of nostalgia rolled over me as I inhaled his scent. I could never pinpoint it. It was a cross between a fresh shower and cedar.

I thought he'd caught me smelling him because he looked at me funny.

I quickly charged forward with the afternoon. "If it's not going to rain, I'm good unless you have a strange standard for what people wear when they go for a walk with you."

"The weather should hold. Tell your dad he has a fan; it all looks great. I wish I had the time," Leo said.

"We all have the time. It's just what we choose to do with it," I said.

"Ok, Ms. Philosophical." Leo led me towards the rear of the condo complex.

"Not so much philosophical as much as smart-ass." I grinned at him.

"I agree. I was just being polite."

I couldn't help but laugh. Whatever angst I had been carrying with me since I arrived yesterday was slowly dissolving away. The stew, the sunshine, and Leo's smile almost made it a good afternoon, except—well, you know—the missing girl. The angst would still probably always be with me, but right now, it was manageable. I couldn't help but wonder how long it would last.

EIGHTEEN

"If we turn the other way, we'll end up at the park with the nice walking paths," I said.

Leo gave me a sideways glance. "I didn't come get you to just go for a walk. Follow me."

My steps slowed. "If you're taking me back to the muddy trail for some kind of let's-reenact-the-crime therapy session, you can count me out. I've done it one too many times in my head, and I need to let it rest."

"Easy does it. This isn't a challenge," Leo said.

We continued walking farther into the condo complex in a quasi-comfortable silence. Only comfortable because no one was talking. Three blocks later, we reach a small green space between the last two condos. The tall grass had a well-worn path down the middle that pulled us in.

"Not to be challenging, but where are we going? Do I need to send my last-known-location alert to my kids?"

"Don't you know where you are? How long have you been gone from Dome?"

"I know enough to know this backs up to office-slash-industrial parks and then out to Sherman Township."

"Exactly," Leo said.

Sometimes, all I needed was a one-word answer. This wasn't one of those times. I followed him anyway.

We passed a beige brick warehouse, which could be spotted when driving on Simool Road. I had once been told they produced the blue chemical used in airplane toilets. I had never been sure if it was true and had been too embarrassed to ask because I'd thought Stew was screwing with me. We didn't have Google back then, and now if I drove past it, I enjoyed thinking that was the sole purpose of that building.

I was impressed my tennis shoes were only wet near the toes and not covered in mud when we hit pavement. One more block, and we came upon a large parking lot with two food trucks and five picnic tables of various sizes and shapes. There were about ten people milling around with drinks in their hands.

"Once a month, March through November, we have Food Truck Fridays. Anywhere from two to six trucks show up. Usually starts between three and four in the afternoon until seven-ish depending on the crowds, weather, and daylight. The trucks then head off somewhere else for the night. This started as a one-time thing for everyone that works in the business park but grew into one a month. Employees from Sherman's industrial loop also take part. Last year, it became a thing, and locals from Dome and Sherman started showing up. Plus, sometimes the nutters who follow food trucks. Occasionally, there's music."

"That's pretty cool. If this is our destination, I'll forgive you for my wet shoes. I see we got tacos and a beer truck so far."

"Grab that red square table next to the building, and I'll grab us some tacos if you're good with that?"

"Of course." I was still hungry but didn't think my stomach could handle spicy food. But it was a better option than alcohol.

I took a seat and watched as employees exited the vet clinic, Hedral Manufacturing, and other offices meandered over to the parking lot as a third truck pulled in. Several people were carrying camp chairs. The taco truck had turned up the music. I was beginning to actually enjoy this spontaneous outing.

"I don't mean to sound ungrateful, but those don't look like tacos," I said when Leo joined me at the table.

"Jaime couldn't get his credit card reader to work, and I have no cash. Beer, soft pretzels, and sausage bits are a fair substitute."

"Agreed." Despite the journey my stomach had been on today, the cold beer was the answer to a question I didn't know needed to be answered. "Cheers," I said.

Leo raised his cup to mine. "So what bothered you most? That Bo is supposedly back, or that Maz knew and said nothing?"

"I guess we'll not ignore the elephant in the room, and jump right in," I said.

"We don't have to talk about it."

"It's fine. I've calmed down. I guess it was the shock of it. Really, of it all and—"

"Steve, you were right. This was a good idea." A lady with spiky gray and purple hair stopped to talk to Leo.

"Thank you. I think it'll be a good turnout. Ellen, this is Sarah. Sarah, Ellen."

We did the hello exchange, and Ellen said, "I thought it might be tacky to have a festive afternoon when a girl is missing. Steve thought it might be a nice break from the gloomy world. I guess he wins. So, are you a new employee?"

"Friend," I said.

"I only said employee because I thought Steve implemented some weird uniform policy."

I looked at my light-blue flannel shirt and, for the first time, noticed Leo was wearing one almost identical.

He quickly answered, "I'm not organized enough for something like that. Just a happy coincidence."

"Cute," Ellen replied.

I missed the rest of what she was saying because I was suddenly picturing Leo and me as an old couple wearing matching knit sweaters, and it was kinda sexy. It was when she threw a twenty-dollar bill at him and swore off betting on basketball that I snapped back to the conversation.

"Nice to meet you, Sarah."

"Likewise."

And she was gone.

"Weird, you calling me Sarah. When did you drop Leo?"

"Probably when most of us did, when we leave the dome. We're a hundred yards from the edge of town, but it might as well be a hundred miles. You know, once you step outside Dome, no one understands or appreciates the internal workings of the snow globe where we grew up. I live not too far from here in Sherman. Nowadays, when some call me Leo, it just conjures up images from when I was young. At least you and I fared better than some. Can you imagine having to explain to your kids why your friends called you Jock or Crackers?"

"O-M-G, Butt Crack Craig—Crackers. Whatever happened to him?"

"He's a plumber," Leo said.

"No way?" I laughed.

He smiled. "Just kidding. Last I heard, he had some type of desk job."

I threw a piece of pretzel at him. "Not funny, Leonardo da Vinci. You got lucky you weren't named Da."

"No chance of that happening. Ski couldn't even pronounce Leonardo properly, much less the full name back in kindergarten, so he just called me Leo from the postcard I carried around for a week."

"Do you think Crackers is still eating pencil erasers? He was weird," I said.

"You're not supposed to say things like that these days."

I shrugged. "A person can be weird; you just can't bully him for it now a days. I remember when Bo learned her name. She thought we're making fun of her. I spent an entire morning explaining that it's a rite of passage. She demanded to know where her name came from. She didn't know what to say when I told her it was about the way she dressed. I literally had to spell it out for her . . . everything matching: the hair ties, earrings, bracelet, socks, and belt every single day. It was like she, Claire Cosworth, robbed a Claire's Boutique every week. She was mad and went to speak to Mrs. Quell, and I overheard her tell Bo, 'So? You got a problem with that, talk to John or Pitts.' "

"I loved when teachers could say things to kids and not worry about getting into trouble for not being politically correct. The good ol' days," Leo said. "These days, I rarely need to go to Dome. Have you seen all the development in Sherman Township and Maple Grove? Before today, I can't really tell you the last time I was on Main Street."

"I don't believe it. You don't even go to Hattie's?"

"Not for a few years, since there was that owner who changed everything. Try those sausages before they get cold," Leo said.

"They're delicious. I snuck in a few bites while you were talking with Ellen."

"Sneaking bites. What is that? Date eating?"

"This isn't a date. I don't worry about *date* eating. I eat what I want to eat."

"Let me guess, you got the whole women's lib movement from a few decades still going on?"

"No. There just have not been too many dates," I confessed.

"Oh, sorry. Sore subject?" Leo asked.

"It's just not a subject with much depth for me."

"Ditto," Leo replied. "First chance I get to take a lady out, and I bring her to a parking lot and start talking about our town's tragic history. So I'll leave it up to you if you want to talk about the elephant in the room or not. I seriously went to your place to check on how you were doing."

"I appreciate that. It's just strange to talk to someone about it. There were many times I was at a party. Someone would talk about something outrageous they had done, and I just wanted to shout, 'I HELPED SOMEONE DISAPPEAR!' You ever share with anyone? Wife, friend, priest?"

"No, no, and hell no," Leo said. "Shouldn't you shout, "I HELPED SOMEONE DISAPPEAR AND POSSIBLY RUINED A MAN'S CAREER?' "

"Fair point. Well, according to Maz, all is well with Olsen now."

"You and Maz really kept meeting up every year?" Leo asked.

I nodded. "It was kinda comforting. Well, at least for me. I was in the misery loves company mentality. Who knew he was keeping information from me? Did you ever see him? Living close to each other, ever run into him at a game or the hardware store?"

"Maybe two or three times since high school. You know these towns are small, yet combined with multiple communities and the city, you don't run into many people from back in the day. It could be I'm not good at recognizing folks these days. However, maybe I did some cyberstalking on Bo, you, Maz, and Olsen every few years just to see if anything was—"

"You don't have to finish that. I understand. I was too nervous what I would find on any one of us," I confessed. "At least for a while. I had to let it all go except saying no to the anniversary weekend."

"It surprised me to see the ring on his finger. Didn't know he got married," Leo said.

"Wouldn't it be funny if he found and married Bo?" I said.

We busted out laughing and talked for a few minutes about nothing in particular.

I showed him my empty beer cup. "Since this isn't a date, and I have no wallet on me, I don't mind asking you for another beer."

Leo went back to the beer truck, and I noticed the place had really filled up. People in khaki pants, a few in suits, but mostly, it was people in jeans hanging out. They had added more tables since we'd sat down. There was a line at the truck, and people were constantly engaging Leo in conversation.

A thud hit the table and broke up my people-watching.

"It didn't slide off or hit any food. I give myself an A," Dutch said.

"All the food is gone. Plus, the zipper is open. You could have lost half of your stuff," I said. "I give you a B-plus."

"What are you grading?" Leo asked, returning with two beers.

"Just an inside joke. Leo, this is Dutch and his friend."

Leo put down the beer and shook hands with Dutch, who introduced Quinn.

"Leo, give Quinn the twenty bucks you just got and let him find food for him and Dutch." I turned to Quinn. "Is that ok?"

Dutch answered for him. "Absolutely."

"Just keep an eye out for my mother. If she sees us apart, she'll have my head," Quinn said.

"It's ok. My dad knows Lou. The place is free of reporters," Dutch said.

Quinn took the twenty and disappeared into a food line.

"I hope I wasn't rude, but I wanted to introduce you to Leo. He's the other member of our . . . group. Please have a seat."

Dutch nodded and sat on the bench between us. His demeanor shifted, and he appeared intentionally quiet and reserved, like when we'd first met yesterday.

"This is it," I said. "This is the rest of us. I really don't know what Maz told you, but it was Leo, me, and Maz that day. There is one other, but he'll not be around."

"He mentioned both of you—well, he mentioned there were others but no names," Dutch said.

"This is probably not the time to discuss anything, but since we're all here, I figured introductions were warranted," I said.

"Sure." One-word answers from a teenage boy. Insert any boy's name here.

Dutch continued, "I came over here hoping you could help me on this assignment. Is this you?" He had his head in his backpack, going through folder after folder, and finally pulled out a photo.

It was an 8x11 photo of my English class sophomore year. The person with the camera had stood in the doorway and had gotten all the kids to turn around in their seats.

Mrs. Quell was top center of the photo. The writing was barely visible in the fading outside light, but I made out the words *Quell's First Class*.

"Holy shit," I said.

Leo got up, walked over, and sat next to me. "Where did you get this? Why are all the heads numbered?"

Dutch whispered her name, but the volume increased as he spoke. "Gigi and I are on the school newspaper. We were working on a story about Quell's retirement at the end of the year."

"She's still teaching?" I said.

"Yeah. Someone found this photo. Gigi had this idea to find everyone from the photo and get some type of quote or story about how Mrs. Quell inspired their life. Are you number eight?"

Before I could answer, Leo laughed. "What were you wearing?"

"Shut up. It was the eighties. Shoulder pads were high fashion." I elbowed him in the gut and felt his laugh ripple across me. My toes tingled.

"Why do some numbers next to the students have a line slashed through them?" Leo asked.

"From what I can tell, those are the people she could identify. If it's circled, she was able to make contact. In the notes, it looks like she has names for all but five. The kid in the top-right corner, his face is blurred. There are no notes on the other girl. She has some guesses as who the boys could be."

"Do you know how she was able to figure out everyone's name?"

"Yearbook, and then she made contact with a guy—one of the kids in the picture—who helped with a few names. I'm still sorting through her notes and figuring out some of her abbreviations. This morning, I saw your name. I was hoping you could help verify the names and give me a quote."

"I've been identified but not contacted." My hand holding the photo shook.

Leo placed his hand on my knee. His warmth ran through me. Then he did the gentlemanly thing and asked what I couldn't. "What does the box around the number mean?"

"I don't know. It's not in the notes. That's the one without a name or anything attached to it. We do our work on the computer. Mrs. Neimeyer, our newspaper advisor, can access our work at any time and give us feedback. Yesterday, Mrs. Neimeyer gave me access to Gigi's computer file and a folder with this photo and notes Gigi left in the workroom. She might have something in her locker or at home, but there's no way I'm going to talk to her parents."

"I understand. It's just that—"

Leo kicked me under the table.

Quinn walked up, balancing four red-and-white-checkered cardboard bowls with chicken fingers and fries. He handed two to Dutch but remained standing.

"Why don't I take a photo of the photo? Leo and I can confirm all the names for you. I actually might have some contact information on a few of them. You might be able to finish this project over the weekend. Stop over tomorrow, and I'll have the information for you."

"Thanks," Dutch said.

Quinn was done eating before I even knew he'd started. Dutch was a minute behind him.

The questions were burning inside me, and I fumbled with small talk. Leo got us through three minutes of conversation, talking about opening day for baseball, before the boys left to meet up with friends.

I exhaled the minute they left. "Holy shit, did we just connect the dots?"

My words hung in the air as we stared at the photograph on my phone and became as still as those in the old picture.

Despite the photo shrinking in size on my phone, there was one pair of eyes speaking to us—Bo's. The unidentified girl with the square around her was Bo.

NINETEEN

"Great. So we're done. Gigi figured out Bo had disappeared and copied it. She's escaping from something bad. The end," Leo said with the heart of no man.

"How can you say that?" I said.

"Look, we did what we did because we thought we were some self-righteous vigilante teenagers who knew best. And it may or may not have been the wisest thing we ever did, but Bo's situation was impossible and we helped her." Leo stood up but didn't go far.

"I get that. We orchestrated something that has been duplicated. But tell me why did Dutch call the police? Our plan worked because phones and cameras weren't everywhere back then. We could operate in stealth mode. We each had a role," I said.

"Exactly!"

A few people turned their heads, and he sat back down across from me. I felt his absence immediately.

"Gigi and Dutch had to adapt the plan as it worked for them," he said.

"What about her family? They are going crazy."

"That does not mean they're good people."

I just shook my head. "You're right."

We sat there silently, watching everyone slowly leaving the parking lot earlier than I would have expected, but the temperature was dropping. We got a good laugh at a young lady who made fun of her companion for getting salsa on his shirt when she dropped her full beer.

Our conversation comfortably meandered to ordinary life.

I found myself suddenly calm. We had solved nothing. Hell, we had only figured out one piece of the puzzle, but it had been a long time since I'd had a night out with a friend that didn't involve complaining about husbands, kids (her not me), the crappy spring weather (me not her), and the lack of good TV these days (her and me).

I surprised myself when I spoke out loud. "This almost turned into a very pleasant evening. Now what?"

"Now you clean up?" Ellen returned to the table. "Can I get the keys for the shed?"

"I left it unlocked when I pulled the tables out. If you get someone to move the tables in, you can go home. I'll clear the lot of trash and wait for the last truck to leave."

"Sounds like a good deal to me. I'll get the Hedral Manufacturing guys to do it. It looks like they're leaving. I better catch them." With a wave to me and Leo, Ellen was gone, but not before she said, "See you at the vigil."

"Shit," Leo mumbled. "I guess it won't be so depressing at the vigil since we know Gigi is ok."

"Or so we think. Tell me, what's going on? Are you the cleaning crew?"

"Ellen and I organize this whole Food Truck Friday thing. Well, it was my idea. She gets the different trucks to come and promotes it to the two industrial loops. I do setup and cleanup. Sorry, I didn't think about that when I went to check on you. Most everyone will be gone in a few minutes when the last truck pulls out. The weather is getting cold, so no one will stick around long, especially since it's still getting dark early. If you don't mind, I can walk you back then. I mean, not saying I need to walk you back, but I just thought since I picked you up, I should return you. Not return you but—"

"Stop, just stop talking. You're fine. However, I can see why your dating life is stagnant," I said.

"I've no response for that—you win."

"How about I help you clean up, and you walk me back halfway, just to the shortcut in the field since you said you live in the opposite direction."

"Hmm, paying attention to where I live. Planning on stalking me?" Leo was grinning.

"Maybe. Would that be a bad thing? I'm not sure I can find the path again. Oh—" I stopped short and looked around.

The parking lot was nearly empty. The beer truck was the only thing left besides three ladies sitting on camp chairs in the far corner of the lot laughing, not noticing the light was gone and evening was closing in on them.

"What's wrong?" Leo asked.

"Nothing. I just noticed how our conversation shifted from the reminiscent tragic event to giddy laughter. It almost felt like we were in high school again."

"Well, if we were in high school, I wouldn't have the courage to do this," Leo said. He stood up and walked around the table toward me.

I didn't know what he was planning, but my heart was racing and my palms were sweating. Great, another body part secreting fluids today.

A man walked up to the table. "Steve, here are the two last pours before we head out. We'll see you next month unless you come down to River Run Fest next weekend. We'll be there both days. Thanks again." The gentleman set down two beers, shook Leo's hand, gave me a wave, and then he hopped into the beer truck and drove away.

"I'm not sure if I can handle another beer." I wasn't necessarily tipsy, but my stomach had been throwing and going a little too much today.

"Good, but I want to go back to where we were before we got interrupted." He fiddled with his phone, music started playing, and he extended his hand to me. "Dance?"

My cheeks grew warm. With no more food trucks lighting up the parking lot and only the evening sky, I found myself thankful the darkness hid my blushing. It was cheesy yet romantic yet corny, yet something one hoped to experience one day.

I took his hand and followed him away from the table. One of his hands slid around my back, and he held the other one up.

We drifted with the music, and I was enjoying every moment. My hands stopped sweating, I didn't trip, and I didn't have food in my teeth, so I had to do what I do best—challenge the moment. Was I worthy of such a grand gesture?

"So this is a pretty good pickup line. Has it worked much in the past?"

"I'm just using you as a test subject. Hope to try it next month with Ellen," he said.

I couldn't turn my head to look at him because I liked the feeling of his breath across my cheek, and I could tell he was sporting a gruff and sexy smile.

"What do you think? Do I have a shot?" He zinged my snarky comment back to me and waited for my answer.

Our bodies were in sync with each step he led. He pulled away and twirled me. We stumbled on loose payment, but he pulled me back with ease. "You didn't answer. Do I have a shot?"

It was so comfortable being there with him, minus the corny move. It had been a while, a long while, since I was with a man. A really long time!

A car swung into the parking lot with fierce speed and lit us up like we were on a Broadway stage. Loud voices came from inside, and finally someone opened the window and gave a shout, "Hey man, do you know where Jaime's Taco truck is?"

"They left twenty minutes ago. Probably headed to the arts district downtown," Leo said.

We got a wave before they left, taking our whimsical moment with them. They were teenagers having fun on a Friday night. Images of Bo and Gigi flashed through my head. Then I realized whatever their predicament was had no bearing if I were to have sex tonight or not.

What affected my thoughts about sex tonight was Leo's sudden shift. He had jumped back three feet when the kids had driven up, but it might as well have been fifty.

"I got to pick up the trash before I walk you back." He grabbed his phone and three plastic cups off the ground.

I would not run after him or pout like I had just been stood up on a date. I took it as something to check off my bucket list that I hadn't known was on it—dance under the stars with a cute boy from high school.

We spent twenty minutes picking up. I grabbed two trash bags left behind from the beer truck guys and headed for the dumpster on the side of the building.

Leo picked up the third bag and took one from my hand. "We have to walk over to Hedral's building."

"Because logic tells you to use the dumpster that's farther away?" I said.

"This building here is empty, and no one picks up those dumpsters. We have to be careful not to leave anything behind. The leasing company doesn't know—or at least turns a blind eye—once a month when we use their lot. This monthly thing just sort of happened organically. We have no idea if we need a permit or license. Ellen and I have been going with it's better to ask for forgiveness than permission. So cleanup is key. I'm not even sure whose shed we're using. I assumed it belongs to this building. A couple of people have donated tables and chairs, and I paid five bucks for a padlock."

"So you work in the dark underworld. Clients pay you in cash and you avoid the IRS. Are you really Leo?"

"Who's Leo?" he smiled, and the charm was back on. "Come on, let's go."

We headed down the road to the shortcut through the green space in a relaxed silence. It was eight o'clock, and dusk had passed fast. The cool spring temperature had definitely run through me. Maybe the sudden loss of heat from Leo's body thirty minutes ago had made it worse. I wrapped my arms around myself as we walked.

The area was less than a quarter of a mile long, yet we found a second and far muddier trail. I stepped on a rock, slipped, and teetered for my balance in the mud field. I'd thought this night would have to end poorly because the morning started with me shitting my pants, and I hadn't been able to finish the dance. Why wouldn't I end up on my butt?

He threw his arm out and stopped me from going down. I finally had the dreadful luck skip me. He held my arm until I steadied myself. We stood nearly as close as when we were dancing, and I waited for him to lean in. I wanted the kiss but couldn't make the move myself.

Seconds ticked by like hours and nothing. He stepped back but held my hand until we were out of the boggy area. We spent five minutes shuffling our shoes through grass and along the curb, trying to erase the mud from our shoes.

We were two blocks from my parents' condo, and I needed to wrap up the evening before another non-kiss moment.

"I'm supposed to meet my brother for lunch tomorrow, but I'll be around otherwise. I hope to connect with Dutch about his assignment and maybe get some details out of him. He and his dad

—well, I think it's just them—are living across the street from my parents."

Leo was quiet, and I could tell what he was thinking.

I said, "I'm not sure if you're weirded out like I am about the photo Gigi had of Bo, the lack of notes, and the special mark around her name, but I have even more questions now."

"I've been thinking. Maz said Bo was back. Let's just speculate that somehow Gigi connected with Bo. Why would Bo share her secret? Obviously, all is well. Thirty years later, who cares what that bitch of a mother, Yvette, thinks. She left town too, who knows where she is now? If Gigi had to leave, all the better."

"What about Dutch calling the police? You think he's that good of an actor?" I asked.

"Maybe it's all part of the plan. With phones in everyone's hand these days, you need to work that into your plan," Leo said.

"You're thinking runaway and not kidnapped?" I pulled out the key to the condo as we walked up the driveway. "Because it's easier to believe?"

He waited before he answered. On the porch, he leaned against the side of the brick garage wall and pulled out his phone, shining his flashlight as I fiddled with the lock. The porch and the entire condo were dark.

I left the key in the door and turned to face him, waiting out his silence as he returned his phone to his back pocket. I truly believed he was thinking the answer through.

"Not because it's easier, at least not for Gigi. If she had to run, that means she was living in hell. Running is just one step. The next phase, whatever that is, won't be easy. If she was kidnapped, her hell is just beginning. I guess I'm saying she's a runaway because it's similar, although we don't have all the information like we did last time."

"Well, that brings us back to the beginning. Lots of questions and ever more confused," I replied.

Leo got a strange look on his face.

"What's wrong?"

"Actually, nothing. I just realized, if Bo is back, all is well. She got her happy ending," he said.

"We don't know that. We don't know what kind of mental state she's in or what she had to endure."

Leo shook his head and looked out into the dark street.

"What is it? What's bothering you?" I asked.

"I just realized, all day and evening, we've been flipping sides. One minute, you're fighting that we should do something. We must connect to the past and/or cover our tracks when I'm ready to walk away. Then we pivot, and I want to figure out this bizarre story, and you're ready to walk away—or in your words, you're 'done with it all.' "

"Humph, you're right. I've taken so many stances I don't know where I stand."

I shifted over to Leo's right side, and we both leaned against the brick wall and looked into the dark night.

I turned to him. "However, I know there are a lot of questions still out there. Bo is back. What does that mean? Is Gigi a runaway or kidnapped? What else does Maz know he hasn't shared with us? Same thing with Dutch."

After a minute of being lost in our own thoughts, Leo said, "It's been a hell of a day."

"Yeah, but a pretty good evening," I said.

"Only pretty good? It wasn't the Ritz but Food Truck Friday had some character to it."

Our shoulders were touching, and our hands dangled at our sides. I was acutely aware of how close we were.

"Food was good, but the company was questionable," I said.

"Questionable company? Should I be offended?"

"Not offended, but maybe the company should ask the question again?"

"Question?" Leo said.

Our hands touched, and neither one of us pulled away. Leo tangled our fingers together, pivoted from the wall, and turned to face me. Inches separated our bodies.

"Question? Let me think."

"You asked if you had a shot," I said.

"And . . ." He leaned in and waited for me.

I held our stillness as long as I could resist. Inches apart.

The tingling from my toes ran up through me like a volcano. He kissed my neck, and I was lost in the heat. I dropped his hand and grabbed his waist. His second and third kiss moved up my neck to my ear. His heat surrounded me.

I turned my face so our lips brushed each other's. We finally gave in.

The kisses were long, and his hands ran under my flannel, up around my waist, around my back before he dropped one hand between my legs.

It massaged my thigh as it climbed, and his thumb pressed into me.

I pulled back from the kiss, only to let out a breathless moan.

He dropped his head, and his kisses lingered down my neck to the center of my chest.

I wrapped my leg around him. His arms found their way back under my flannel and kisses continued back up to my neck. His hands were finding every inch of bare skin. Time was lost on us.

I couldn't believe, back at Food Truck Friday, I had hesitated when he'd asked if he had a shot.

He pulled away a few inches, and I followed for another kiss.

He paused. "This is nice, but . . ."

My heart was racing. "But what? Why is there always a *but*?"

"But could we go somewhere more comfortable?" he asked.

We giggled before we kissed again.

This time, it was me who pushed him back. Images popped into my head one right after another—my parents' condo porch, my parents' bed (eww), the double bed I'd slept in last night in my parents' condo—not ideal, but it works. Other images popped into my head as well—the diary still on the bed. Diary, Bo, Gigi, Diary, Bo, Gigi.

WORBy.

I could feel his chest rising and his breath on me. We were one body in the dark, but he seemed to know something had changed and retreated a foot.

His hands sliding out from under my flannel and catching my hands, he brought them up between us. "Well then, I should . . ."

"I wish we . . . I want to . . . it's just not . . . I can't explain it now." I gave him a long kiss but kept our hands balled between us.

"It's ok, you don't have to explain. It might be my first rejection, but I'll be ok." There was a forced laugh.

I pulled him in for another kiss before saying, "This isn't a rejection, only a deferment."

He stepped away, allowing room for me to move to the door.

After I pushed the door open, I turned and gave him another kiss and whispered in his ear, "Only a deferment."

He said nothing. He gave me a kiss on the cheek, turned, and left with sadness on his face. I watched him go into the darkness and almost lost sight of him three houses down when a car turned onto the street, lighting the way for him and for me to see he didn't even turn back to catch a glimpse of me.

I flicked on the light, put my back to the door when it closed, and slid down to the ground. It wasn't long before there was a knock at the door, and I was suddenly ready to have sex in my parents' bed, but that was a very wrong thought to have since it wasn't Leo returning.

TWENTY

"WORB," I said again to myself.

Through the window along the door, I spied Dutch standing there with his backpack. I needed to shift my sex thoughts away from Leo before I opened the door, so I quickly recited: sum of areas of the two squares on the legs—a^2 and b^2—equals the area of the square on the hypotenuse—the Pythagorean theorem. I did this anytime I was in public and didn't want to cry. I didn't even know if the theory was correct, but it diverted my focus so I ran with it.

"Don't tell me you're locked out of your house?" I said. "Come in."

"No, I got home five minutes ago, and I saw your light and thought you could verify the names on the photo."

"Now? I haven't had time to really look at it," I said.

"No problem." Dutch hesitated before he spoke again. "You said anytime I wanted to . . . talk."

"Of course, come in. I figured as much but didn't want to push. Unfortunately, I don't have any food or soda to offer you. My mother probably has an old jar of Tang."

"Tang? I don't know what that is."

"That's probably for the best. The jar might be as old as you are.

Have a seat at the table, and I'll get us some waters." I turned my back to him and continued talking. "Please gently place your bag on the floor."

He laughed, and I knew I was miles away from my evening with Leo.

"Does your dad know you're here?"

He nor his dad had ever mentioned his mother being around so I left her out. I thought about laying my phone on the table with a picture of my kids on the screen. I debated playing the role of a mother versus a peer.

Not knowing the situation with his mom, I thought, *Let's start as someone who has gone through the same thing. If he doesn't open up, then I'll pull out the bag of mom tricks.*

"He's having dinner with my aunt. He probably won't be back for another hour, and he thinks I'm with Quinn at a friend's house. Which was true, but I had Quinn drop me off. They started talking about Gigi. There were two girls there freaking out like they're going to be kidnapped. I just couldn't deal with people."

"I get that. If you don't mind, I have a few questions," I said.

"A few? I got hundreds. Really what happened, and why do you know so much? And the girl in the photo was that her? Is that Bo?" Dutch was almost out of air when he was done speaking.

"It's Bo. You probably guessed that with how Leo and I reacted. Before I tell you more, answer a few things for me. Why were you on the wooded path behind the baseball field? It isn't on your way to school from here."

"I was supposed to go a different route, but then someone said I had to go through the woods."

"Why, were roads blocked off for construction? Why did you have to go through the woods?"

He got up from the table and paced around the kitchen, finally sitting on the steps leading upstairs.

I wanted him to talk on his own, but I thought he might chicken out. "Whatever it is, you can tell me."

"So there's a group of us that go to the library before school starts, and we just hang out."

He watched my face light up, and I felt so sappy that it was still going on.

"We did that back in my day too."

"Did you guys have 4QBs?"

"Fourth Quarter Breakfast. Wow, It was one of my favorite days of the school year." No food or beverage was ever allowed in the library. No one even thought to have a water bottle back in the eighties. Once a year, around the beginning of the fourth quarter, the prelude to the end of the year, we would all bring in food and drinks. We operated on a system similar to Leo's theory of it's better to ask forgiveness than permission. We were always very careful to clean up and never overreached the generosity when the morning librarian looked the other way once a year."

Dutch said, "Someone had the idea we should have a real toast. Gigi wanted champagne. She knew someone that could get her a bottle. I knew we couldn't pop the cork in the library, so I volunteered to open it by the creek and pour it into my water bottle. The champagne bottle was supposed to be under that little bridge over the creek behind the hardware store. That morning I got a text saying it was in the woods."

"Who sent the text?" I asked.

"That's the thing I don't know. Only four of us knew about the champagne, and I have all their numbers in my phone. There was no caller ID. I tried calling it later, but no answer, no voice mail."

"Who were the other three friends?" I intentionally used *friends* instead of *kids*. Dutch needed to understand I wasn't casting parental judgment on him; I was a sounding board.

"Quinn, Saw, and Gigi."

"Under any scenario, do you think it could have been someone else, or would one of them block their number?"

"Quinn thought the champagne was stupid, and he was trying to get a flask of vodka from his house. He could have cared less about it. Saw is a junior, and he's too dumb to figure out how to block a call."

"That leaves Gigi," I said.

I hoped the booze was a onetime event. We had drunk alcohol in high school but that was weekends only. I couldn't get preachy if I wanted him to keep talking.

"Would Gigi know to block her text?"

"She wasn't nervous about it. She acted like it wasn't a big deal. The text just read *Let's walk the path.* Originally, that was going to be the spot. A couple of years ago, we dragged a bench into the woods. Before we started driving, we just would meet there before going to school or if we didn't want to go to the library."

The parent inside of me was screaming, and I couldn't let this one go. "Please tell me you don't vape or, god forbid, smoke."

I seemed to have caught him by surprise. "No, well, tried it. Hated it." He stood up from the base of the stairs and started pacing again. "As you said, no walks behind SMF Factory in the spring, but I figured someone had been at the bridge when she was supposed to leave the bottle."

"So it was logically the second option. Do you know when she was going to leave the bottle? The night prior or the morning?" I asked.

He stopped walking and seemed to think about the answer. "I just assumed it was in the morning, but I don't know. I got the text at six forty-five in the morning. I was halfway to the bridge and had to turn around."

"Where did you enter the woods, from the baseball field or from the tree section?"

He didn't answer. I kicked the kitchen chair back and waved

him in. Dutch sat, leaned forward, elbows on his knees and his hands holding his head.

I said, "Let me guess, you entered in from the baseball field but had to tell the police it was the tree section. They would have asked why you were going backwards away from school or the library, and you couldn't tell them about the champagne."

He nodded and leaned back.

I said, "Tell me what happened from the moment you got the text. Slowly. Not the version you told the police."

"I didn't drive that day."

"Do you always drive?"

"Just depends on what's going on. Living in London, I walked everywhere, and I got used to it. Coming back to Dome, if I don't have a ton of stuff after school, I walk.

"What would be the natural way for you to go the library or school?"

"Leaving out of here, I can either cut through the bird section and take the path behind the baseball field or cross through the lake section before crossing Simool Road to get to school. If I'm headed to the library, like I was that day, I always shoot two blocks through the lake section then cross over Simool. I turned right onto the second street in the flower section. There's a path between the second and third house that takes you to the bridge," Dutch said.

"Did you see or notice anything strange?" I asked.

His blank stare told me everything I needed to know.

I continued, "I know, lame question. I'm sure the police asked all the same stuff, but we already established you didn't tell them everything."

Dutch raised an eyebrow and remained still.

"Don't get defensive. We're trying to figure it out," I said.

"Sorry, it's just so many people asking me and when they're not asking they're talking about me or Gigi," Dutch said.

"I'm going to ask you something. Think long and hard before

you answer. Trust me, I'll understand, and the secret will stop with me if the answer is yes. Understand?"

Dutch nodded.

"Did you help Gigi runaway?"

He stood up and grabbed his backpack. "Why do you ask that? I'm not part of some vigilante underground support network or whatever you, Maz, and what's his name belong to."

He was out the front door before I could even stand up. I could not help but think he was right. What kind of group were we?

Are we some self-righteous do-gooders or self-serving keepers of our past?

TWENTY-ONE

I sat at the kitchen table, staring at my laptop and into the void of an empty corner. My thoughts bounced from from lack of job and income, Bo, Gigi, my kids, my ex, the last twenty-four hours, and finally lingered on Leo and our time on the porch.

The diary! Now was the time to read it again.

I ran upstairs, grabbed the cinched red bag from under the covers and went to my mother's chair, Waldorf, and turned on the reading light. The middle section piqued my interest.

I saw the bruise yesterday—on the top of her arm—is that your forearm? Today, she knew I saw it. I don't know why I'm mad.

I realized now what my sixteen-year-old self hadn't: I hadn't been mad. I'd been sad because I had known someone had hurt her, and I hadn't known what I could do to help.

The doorbell interrupted any further reading.

I didn't know who I hoped it was more: Dutch, so I could give him a hug or Leo since the diary was no longer in my bed. I slipped the diary back in the bag and slid it under the couch, feeling sixteen again and needing to hide my diary when no one else was even staying here.

Through the kitchen window, I spied Van holding the same bottle of Scotch from last night. This time the Post-it said *Cheers*.

I opened the door and pointed to the glasses, then went into the living room and turned on the television. He was wearing jeans that showed off his long legs and tight butt and a long-sleeve, form-fitting blue T-shirt, accenting his blue eyes and blond hair.

I took a seat on the couch, and he sat on the other end. Yesterday, when he'd sat on the love seat, we were an arm's length away and our feet could touch. Now on the same sofa, he was a little farther away, but it felt like he was invading my personal space. He poured each of us a large helping of the bronze liquid.

"What brings you here tonight?" I asked.

"No real reason. I saw your light on and wanted to make sure you were ok."

"Ok?"

"You said you were headed north for the weekend," Van said. His words were heavy, and I guessed this wasn't his first or second drink of the night.

"My friend had to bale because both her kids got sick. I might stick around until Sunday. Maybe get some food for my parents for when they return."

"So we can do this again tomorrow?" Van raised his glass to mine. "Cheers."

"Are you asking me out on a date without really asking me out?" I asked.

"Well, we don't have to go out," Van said. He laughed, seemingly as a cover in case I rejected his flirtation.

What was going on? First Leo and now Van. Maybe I shouldn't have stayed away for so long. My divorce proceedings started 384 days ago. Why was I just figuring out this was a honey hole of desirable men? Normally, I would have jumped at this fun banter, but after my brief session with Leo on the porch, it was making me feel a little slutty. I owed nothing to Leo, but I was not one to get it on with two men on the same night. Then again, it was just fun.

"Can I ask you a question?" I said.

"Sure." He swung his arm over the back of the couch. "What do you want to know?"

"What happened to Mrs. Van?"

"Ah, Charlotte." He took a long drink. "She stayed in London, along with our marriage. I thought our moving there was a chance to restart everything, our marriage, new job, and so on. She took it as an easier place to file for divorce."

"Sorry to hear that," I said.

"Not all bad came out of it. Dutch did great with both moves, and it made us closer. Just happy he's happy." Van said.

"Is he?" I asked.

"What does that mean?" Van's speech was slightly slurred, but his tone still sliced through the air.

"Sorry, I just meant to ask how is he doing since Gigi has been gone."

Van stood up and paced around the room, just like Dutch earlier in the kitchen. "I didn't mean to snap. Just, since Charlotte decided to separate herself from the family, I've been playing mom and dad. I'm not sure what I'm doing sometimes, and I get a little protective. He and Charlotte talk, but I swear from what I can hear, it sounds like Dutch is talking to his grandmother he hasn't seen in years. You know, basic updates, but no genuine connection. I can't wait to get back in the house and make a decent home for him before he leaves for college."

"House?"

"We kept our house in the constellation section when we went to London. We had renters who jumped out on us, and when a pipe burst, no one was around. Renovation is still going on, and I hope to move back in at the end of the month. The complete renovation won't be done, but it'll get us out of the rental. I feel like I'm living in a dental office waiting room."

I couldn't help but laugh. "I had the same thought when I was getting the house key."

We spent a few minutes laughing about the artwork and talked about their flat in London. He said he hadn't ever gotten used to the laundry being in the kitchen.

He sat back down on the couch again, but this time, he was on the middle cushion and much closer to me. I couldn't help but enjoy my time with him. He went to refill his glass, and I thought about that night in college.

We had gone to different universities but both found ourselves visiting high school friends at a college an hour from here. There was an amazing outdoor concert venue near campus and a favorite local Milwaukee band was playing. It was one of those weird nights when everything lined up right.

Three girlfriends and I met up with a group of guys tailgating before the concert. Parked next to our group were Van and his friends. We spent the preconcert time flirting, drinking rotgut hooch, and talked about meeting up afterwards. This was before cell phones ruled our lives. Plans were vague but promising.

After the concert, I rushed back to the car, hoping to see him, but it wasn't meant to be. My girlfriends and I found a house party and had way too much beer. Despite a great evening with my friends, I knew I had hit my limit. I was a little sad I didn't get to connect with Van after the concert. I left the party by myself, trying to find my way back to my girlfriend's dorm room. It was like a mirage when I saw Van walking with his friends a block away. It seemed like slow motion when I watched him separate himself from his friends without so much as a goodbye to them.

I'm not sure what we said, but we instantly took each other's hand. I was dizzy with excitement, and I wasn't sure who was leading our way. We walked into the dorm with a large group of people, and I laughed because we had walked past the desk security without issue and found ourselves in a dorm that neither one of us was staying in.

We ducked into the stairwell, went down a half a flight towards the basement, and sat on a step, laughing.

He raised his hand to my face and pulled me in for a kiss.

A minute later, I put my hand on his chest to hold him back. A nightmare rushed up to me. The beer, booze, beer, and more beer hit me with full force. Being under the age limit, I was still a novice drinker. I walked to the corner of the stairwell and dry heaved. I remember him saying, *Please don't, I can't handle the noise or smell, it'll make me*—he stood and went to the other corner ten feet away and dry heaved.

My stomach flipped again, and it was no dry heave. Sweat coursed from my hands, face and neck, and seconds later, a rocket of used beer sprayed the cinder-block walls. The smell must have hit Van, and he dry heaved again.

I didn't stick around to find out what happened. Mortified, I flung myself down the remaining few stairs and pulled open the basement door without looking back. I was like a mouse in a maze looking for another exit. I saw the laundry room twice or two different rooms once, lots of study rooms, one pathetic-looking gym, thankfully a bathroom, even though it had a urinal in it, for the second round of used beer being returned to the night. Somehow I made it to another stairwell and out of the dorm in time to find my friends walking back to the right dorm.

"Hey, are you ok?" Van asked, again sitting in the middle yet slightly closer than before, with a fresh glass of Scotch in his hand.

"Just lost in thought."

"Care to share those thoughts?" he asked.

"Kinda embarrassing, so no," I said.

"More embarrassing than talking about a failed marriage?"

"Nothing to be ashamed of for that. I'm also in that category."

"Then do tell; where did you escape to when I was in the kitchen?" He said it in a soft voice with a small smile, like he knew exactly what I had been thinking about. He put down his drink and turned his body towards me.

I got nervous. What was with me? Serious flirtation with two different men in one night. I had to break the mood, and I did a fake dry heave.

Van recoiled a foot and said. "Please stop."

We laughed, but it took him a bit for the color to come back to his face. I wondered if Charlotte had had to handle Dutch by herself anytime Dutch was sick.

"You still have a low tolerance for that," I said.

"Always have, always will," he said and put his hand on my leg. "But maybe I can switch the topic to something else?"

"And what would that be?"

"What we were doing right before you disappeared from my life?" Van said.

"You wanted me to stick around after the performance in the stairwell corner?" I said.

"Well, I don't know about that night in particular, but it would have been nice to have a night to finish that kiss."

I said nothing but held his gaze. His hand left my leg and touched my cheek. The soft touch transported me back to the stairwell. Van holding my face before kissing me. Now, years later, the same kiss with him holding my face. Time had stopped back then, and we were still on the stairs, but no beer had been returned yet. My inner nineteen-year-old was jumping for joy, and my fifty-plus-year-old self was, for the second time tonight, contemplating sex.

"Too bad it was just a kiss you wanted to finish," I said.

We remained inches apart with his fingers still resting on my cheek. Sitting so close and deep into the sofa, it was hard for me to move. My heel kicked the sofa, and I remembered my diary I had shoved underneath.

Images of Bo and Gigi popped into my head, and I was transported back to reality. I froze, and Van seemed to sense that something had shifted and he pulled back.

"Well, maybe tomorrow we can finish something else." He leaned in for another kiss that almost let me forget everything but the two of us.

I pulled back and said, "Tomorrow I promise no more dry heaving."

"With that, I best be going." Van was up and out of the living room and the condo faster than his son had left just an hour before.

I turned off the television, locked the door, and turned off all the lights. The darkness in the condo was a welcomed silent blanket covering me.

I sat at the kitchen table, reviewing the strange events of the day. Twenty minutes later, I wandered upstairs in the dark and cracked open the bedroom window. It was cold and damp, but the cold breeze kept me present.

I had no choice but to turn the light on in the bathroom. After I brushed my teeth, I went back to the bedroom and stripped off my jeans and wiggled out of my bra but kept the flannel shirt on. I pulled up the collar, and I smelled Leo. It was him that my mind returned to.

Outside, there was a faint noise, and I looked at the front door of the condo across the street. Dutch had a hoodie pulled up and seemed to be trying to leave the house as quietly as possible. Where was he going at this hour?

It wasn't late for a Friday evening, not even eleven o'clock. Why the need for secrecy? No reporters around. Was he meeting up with a girl his father didn't like? I couldn't see Van being very strict with dating protocols.

Was he going to meet Gigi?

Should I follow him?

What the hell was I going to do?

He headed on foot the same way Leo and I had come from. I fumbled for my phone, and I realized I didn't have Leo's number. I sent a text to Maz asking for it and got them on a group text.

Me: *Had a small chat with D tonight. He got angry when I asked if he helped Gigi. Now I watched him sneak out of the condo.*

Maz: *Could be going anywhere. He's a teenager*

Me: *Don't think he needs to sneak away to be with friends*

Me again: *He headed towards the business loop*

Maz: *11 am room five*

Nothing from Leo.

I sat on the lower bunk bed so I could watch Dutch's front door and pulled the flannel around me.

I tried staying awake to see if Dutch wandered back. Maybe homework had fallen out of his backpack, and he'd gone to look for it. I laughed out loud because of how ridiculous that sounded. A few minutes later, fatigue swept over me, and my head bobbed as I begun to nod off, and I finally flung myself onto my bed with thoughts of the porch and Leo. Occasionally, I could feel Van's fingers caressing my cheeks.

Hours later, I woke up to sunlight beating on my forehead and a heavy door slamming shut. I should not have been surprised. I only hoped they had aspirin.

TWENTY-TWO

It was seven fifteen Saturday morning, but I felt like it was two a.m. and I was standing at a rave. The previous night's sleep had brought Scotch-induced dreams about Bo thirty years ago. Yesterday, my stomach was throwing, my ass was going, my sex drive revved up to a hundred miles an hour for me to slam the brakes twice, and my head had beer, Scotch, and more dreams about missing girls. I needed to get away from here or to get some answers if I was ever going to sleep again. It had been a rough two nights.

Only one person would have had the nerve to show up this early. Three raps came from the front door before it opened.

"Two minutes," I yelled.

No time or need for a shower. I threw on a fresh pair of leggings, a sweatshirt from UW Madison, and a baseball hat that pressed too hard on my forehead. There was a faint bruise from the bathroom stall yesterday. I hoped it wasn't obvious to anyone else. I ran my fingers through my hair and did a twenty-second teeth brushing.

The kitchen curtains were now pulled back, and the front window opened.

My sister-in-law, Kay, stood there drinking coffee. "I hope I got your order correct—double blond shot Americano with nonfat milk steamed, light foam."

"Cinnamon?" I took the lid off the cup and inhaled.

"Extra cinnamon on top," Kay said. "Sorry I wasn't here earlier, but Hattie's wasn't open, so I had to go to the other place."

I loved my sister-in-law minus one detail. She thought I was a morning person like her. Sure, I had been a morning person by default previously. It happens when you have kids, but my twins were gone and so was my morning routine.

"Great coffee, but how do the pastries compare to Hattie's? Opening later on weekends now?" I asked.

"Well, you know the new Hattie does not bake anything except the special of the day or week. She orders all the pastries from the same local bakers as the other independent coffee shops."

That made me sad. I had never been part of the four a.m. baking crew, but it was sad to know that part of Hattie's was gone.

She must have seen my face. "Stop pouting and start eating. The croissants are amazing and still warm. I've no idea why Hattie's was closed. Just a handwritten note on the door. From the window, I could see some tables and chairs are pushed back, but it was dark inside. Almost like a blackout. I wasn't sure you were here. I thought maybe you went for a walk in the village." Again, she could read my blank expression. "I saw your car in front of Hattie's and hoped you would be back by now."

"Long story, but I left my car there yesterday," I said.

"Is it working, or do I have to get your brother to give it a jump start?" Kay asked.

"It's fine. You could say I went for a long walk and ended up here without the car. Just lost in thought."

"Well, I just wanted to say hi before I skip out of town. Can I give you a ride down there?"

"It looks like it's going to be nice today, and I could use another walk. It's not far. Thanks for the offer." I didn't know until I'd said it, but it sounded like a good idea—retracing Dutch's route from that morning. Not sure what I was going to find, but I had nothing else to do.

She gave me a hug goodbye. She's a serious hugger. Me, not so much. I leaned against the counter and just enjoyed the hot sugar disguised as coffee.

Two minutes after Kay's departure there was a knock at the door, no one was at the window.

I figured it couldn't be trouble at this hour, so I just yelled, "It's open."

Van stood there with two coffees in his hand, looking fresh in jogging pants that showed off his long lean legs again. There was no indication of any drinking last night. His hair was wet from a recent shower, and he had no bags under his eyes.

Damn, those Scandinavian genes make for a good-looking man.

"I know the food supply is low in the house, and I'm not sure what your coffee situation was, so I brought you one."

"Got that covered this morning, but I appreciate the thought. Actually, I may need a second cup."

He maneuvered gracefully with the two coffees, gently shutting the door with his body. He walked over and set the coffee on the counter behind me, like a pseudo hug. I drank my coffee so I wouldn't try to inhale his scent.

He lingered for an extra second.

If he grazes any part of my body, I will jump him on the floor of the kitchen.

It had been a while since I was with a man.

He interrupted my wicked thoughts with talk about milk and sugar. I didn't remember what I said to him, but I really snapped back to reality when he said, "I've been out all morning. Do you mind if I use your restroom?"

"Go ahead," I said.

He moved down the hall, and I couldn't help but wonder why he had been out all morning. Hadn't the morning just started?

There was another knock on the front door.

"It's open," I yelled again.

Leo opened the door looking tired with a shadow of a beard, holding two coffees and wearing a gray and red UW Madison sweatshirt. In Wisconsin, two people wearing Badger swag is no big deal, but after yesterday, with the blue flannel shirts, this was really playing into my vision of us as an old married couple wearing matching knit sweaters.

"I see I'm late with the coffee. Didn't figure you for a morning person."

"I'm not. Thanks for the coffee. You can put it on the table by my laptop," I said.

"Here, take your newspaper." He swiveled sideways so I could pull the paper out from under his arm.

"Could you not have packed something else? How about a Northwestern sweatshirt? Isn't that where your son goes?"

This all felt rather intimate: the matching clothes, him remembering where both my kids went to school, and bringing morning coffee.

Leo continued, "Support the boys in your family. What's wrong with you?"

I couldn't help but laugh.

Van said, "I don't think there's anything wrong with her."

I silently said WORB, and my leg twitched. I so so so needed to call my best friend. How could I excuse myself to call her and tell her the two men I'd kissed the night prior were both standing in my kitchen before eight a.m.

At least let me put her on speakerphone? This is too good not to share.

I'd heard a saying from somewhere—*everyone needs a friend*

who they probably shouldn't be allowed to sit next to at a serious function.

Well, that's how it was between us. She would so have enjoyed this moment and understand how epic it was for me. I so wanted to zap out and get her on the phone, but I didn't think it was possible because she was traveling in Alaska, and with the time difference— *oh hell, this is worth waking up for. Crap, my phone is upstairs.*

I had to focus on the present so I made introductions. "Leo, remember Van? He was in my year. Van, Leo was a year ahead of us."

They exchanged handshakes. Leo remained near the table, and Van stood near me, leaning on the counter. There was plenty of space in the kitchen. I couldn't decide if it was a romantic move, suggesting possession or just a lack of perception of personal space.

Leo got a funny look on his face. His eyes darted past Van and me. He spied the Scotch bottle and two empty glasses sitting on the counter.

With Van standing so close, Leo might think Van spent the night or showed up after he left.

Where was my friend when I needed her the most? I needed an inappropriate joke (told by me, not her) or the nearly-saying-the-right-thing to say to finagle out of this moment (that's her role, not mine). Seconds ticked away, and I needed to do something.

A car door slammed, and the front door wasn't even open yet when Stew's voice echoed through the kitchen. "Yo, let's go . . . Oh, hi everyone."

"Gentlemen, you might remember my brother, Stew. He was two years ahead of me."

Van already had his hand stretched out.

"This is Van, and this is Leo," I said.

"Leo, it's been a few years. How are you doing? I was sorry to hear about Gina. How is she doing?" Stew said.

"Thanks for asking. She's pretty much the same," Leo said.

Gina? His daughter's name is Jenna. Just Jenna, no nickname, because they don't live in Dome. No ring on the finger. All conversations about spouses were past tense. I don't remember a sister, maybe a cousin or mother?

"Didn't expect a crowd here this morning. So I'm assuming you're all talking about the news?"

The three of us looked blankly at Stew.

He seemed to need a second to realize we were not up to date. He finally continued. "They found that girl. The one who was missing."

"Are you serious? Is she alive?" The only motion in the kitchen was my lips moving.

Leo maintained his composure and focused on Stew.

"Is she speaking?" Van asked.

"It's not good, well, not bad. She's alive, but in terrible shape. Some early morning jogger found her in the woods. That's all the press is saying. No statement from the police or the family except confirming the identity."

"The woods? Where she was last seen?" I asked. There was no relief floating through my body.

"Did I say woods? I meant the parkway. I think somewhere between the golf course and the picnic area where they have Fall Fest."

"Wow, incredible. Maybe a long road to recovery, but she's alive," I said. "What about the family? Is anyone saying what happened to her?"

Stew shook his head. "No statement."

"What about the family? What did they say?" I said.

"What do you mean?" Stew asked.

"There's a difference between not making a statement because they're with their daughter and just having no comment," I said.

"Not sure what you mean. The story online just shows the same photo of the girl as before and only repeated where the jogger found her."

We chatted like strangers at a coffee shop watching the news unfold, united only by the community where they lived.

I was watching Leo's reaction while avoiding eye contact. I didn't want Van or Stew to pick up on any connection Leo and I had to the story.

Leo broke up our huddle in the kitchen. "Well, I see you're all set here with coffee, so I'll head out. I got somewhere to be. Stew, good seeing you. Don't be a stranger. Come over to the shop sometime. Van, Lou, take care." And he was out the door.

Van asked Stew about his truck, trying to make small talk with my brother, but Stew wasn't in the mood, so Van also excused himself and left thirty seconds after Leo.

"What is going on here? I get a text from Kay about you needing help with your car, and I find two guys at the condo? What are you doing? Having some sort of weird overnight boy-toy party while Mom and Dad are gone?"

"Gross! Shut up! Van lives across the street and gave me the key to the condo. Leo—forget it. I don't need to explain anything to you."

"Do you need help with your car or not?" Stew went to the fridge.

"There's no food in the house. Mum cleaned out everything before the trip."

"What's in the pot?" he asked.

"The only food I have, so leave it alone."

"If it's stew, I'm taking it."

"There's probably more downstairs, so leave this for me. Who is Gina? You asked Leo about Gina."

"His wife. I'm going to see what's in the freezer downstairs. Kay didn't leave much food behind." Stew ran down to the basement.

I shouted after him, "I know that isn't true. It's probably all healthy stuff you wish to avoid."

Wife? Leo has a wife. Gigi found alive, and Leo has a wife.

It was eight a.m., and this was too much for me.

Wife?!?

Stew came up carrying a potpie when his phone dinged with an incoming message. He looked at it and said, "Well, I gotta go."

"What's up?"

"Kay got a flat tire. She's on the side of the highway, one mile up from the Sonraw Road on-ramp. Roadside assistance said it might be an hour. I'm going to see if she wants to take the truck so she can stay on time."

"Well, there you go. Kay *almost* had it right. She needs car help, not me." I slid over and stood in front of the stove, blocking Stew's view of the pot. If he knew I had wasted half of it, I'd never hear the end of it. I contemplated finishing it for breakfast, but it had sat out all night. If it wasn't for my weak stomach yesterday, I might have risked it.

He had one foot out the door when he turned back. "I didn't forget about lunch. I'll text you where to meet. Afterwards, you can head back to Chicago."

I ran upstairs for my phone. It was too early to call my kids, but I left messages about Gigi being found. They had been following the story, having been to Dome countless times. They had even walked that same path.

Since the guys had left the house and that drama was over, I conceded it was also too early to call my friend in Alaska. She would get the story when she got home and would give me pointers for next time I was in an awkward situation with two men.

I sat on the edge of the bed with coffee and phone in hand.

What did it mean that Gigi was found alive, but was she awake or unconscious. Did she have any memory of what happened? Did this end our ties to Gigi? Should we have not said so much to Dutch?

Dutch!

I wondered if he had heard the news and what time he had gotten back last night. He was probably still sleeping, but surely, Van would wake him with that type of news. I looked out the window, and like the previous days, the window blinds were closed at Van's house. The place looked lifeless. No car in the doorway, garage door shut, not even a plant on the porch.

Standing at the window, I tried digging for peace and happiness for Gigi, but everything kept going back to Bo. I had a feeling the story wasn't finished.

I grabbed my tennis shoes. I was going to walk off this anxiety. Who would have guessed what I was about to walk into.

TWENTY-THREE

I took off the sweatshirt because I didn't want to associate it with Leo. I threw on a long-sleeve black T-shirt and tied a black North Face pullover around my waist. The pullover had belonged to my ex. He had three of them, so I hadn't felt bad about making sure it wasn't around when he moved out. I thought the sunny weather may not hold, and I liked being prepared—well, at least for weather, because who knew what the rest of the day would bring.

In the kitchen, my head pivoted like I was watching a tennis match. Two coffee cups were screaming for my attention. It was like choosing Leo or Van. Leo had a wife. Van was overly comfortable in my personal space, yet had no wife.

My shoes squeaked on the floor. One of the men had dragged in red mud. I got some rags and cleaned up the floor and then did the most ridiculous thing I could. I took my first cup of coffee and rinsed out the paper cup and poured half of Leo's coffee and half of Van's coffee in my cup. Satisfied with my answer, I grabbed my wallet and keys and went for a walk, retracing Dutch's route.

Mixing coffees hadn't been my best decision, but I kept drinking. Few cars were on the road, so it was easy to spot Van driving past. Dutch was in the passenger seat, and I caught him looking at me. I tilted my head to the right. He knew I was retracing his route. It wasn't just a head nod; it was an understanding of wanting answers.

Fifteen minutes and three neighborhoods later, I found the small path between the second and third house leading to the creek.

For many years, this area between the shops and the houses in the flower section had been ignored, except for the neighborhood kids who played in the creek looking for frogs. Eventually, the ladies in the Garden Club had gotten their hands on the space. They had cleared away the years of dead leaves and broken branches, held a fundraiser, and planted five hundred tulips. Their biggest accomplishment was getting the Men's Club to build a four-foot bridge. A swing set was added, but I wasn't sure when.

I stood on the bridge, pretending to enjoy the view. Several rows of trees lined both sides of the creek. The small green space between the creek and back alley was maintained by the Garden Club. During winter and spring months, someone in a house could see through to the alley and the back of the shops. The houses closest to the bridge only had a thin row of trees.

Dutch had said he'd gotten the message before he got to the bridge. If someone had been watching for him, it could be from any one of these houses or even the one on the other side of the street. Maybe in the alley they could see him once he stepped foot on the path.

Still retracing Dutch's route, I retreated out of the flower section and walked one block. Across the street from left to right was the small SMF factory, the narrow section of woods, with a path leading to the sidewalk from the woods beyond centerfield, the baseball field, and overflow parking. Way off to the right was the main parking lot and finally the high school. Something inside me wasn't letting me go to the path. I was going to have Maz walk it with me.

Cars were turning into the high school lot, and I figured there must be a game or some type of practice. It had only been two years since my kids were out of high school, and I could not remember what sport kids played in springtime; however, I could recall every minute of one particular morning thirty-four years ago.

I walked down Main Street several blocks to check out if Hattie's had opened up. Before I got there, I stopped at the hardware store to duplicate my parents' house key.

"We don't need that in here," the old lady behind the counter squawked, referring to my coffee cup.

"I can throw it away, ma'am. I won't bring it inside."

"Not you, hon, that fellow behind you. Yes, you." She pointed. "Clean those boots, come back then."

I turned around to see the young man quickly retreating.

The four foot tall centenarian with gray tight curled hair shuffled around the counter and kept talking to me. "Ah, those young fellows with no common courtesy. The whippersnappers working on the new store signs have been dragging in mud, and that garden crew brings the red stuff. That's the worst. They track it in here, and it's impossible to get off the floor."

"Eunice, leave this lady be. She didn't come here for your lecture," said an older gentleman, walking up to us.

The lady tapped my arm as a gesture of goodbye and shuffled away.

"I'm Henry. What can I do for you?"

"I need a copy made of a house key," I said.

"That I can do. Follow me this way and just ignore Eunice. She thinks my hardware store should be spotless, like her kitchen sink. Give me that key of yours. How many copies?"

"Just one key, sir. Can I ask you something? The red dirt Eunice mentioned, what is it? Is it red clay like you find in the South?"

"Oh, she likes to chat. Sorry if she was bothering you. If she wasn't so good with the books, I would make her stay home," Henry said.

"She's no bother, but about the red clay?"

"Ah, it's not clay. The landscaping company that handles the park started using red mulch. Then they sprayed with something for bugs, and when the sprinklers go off, there's some runoff from the mulch mixing with the bug spray, and it gets in the dirt onto their boots. The company is a mess. I heard the village is ready to dump them anyway and hire their own crew. Probably cheaper for them too."

"How much for the key?"

"A dollar eighty-three with tax. I can ring you up here if you got cash, otherwise Eunice will have to do it."

By luck, I had two dollars with me and told him to keep the change. Henry put the cash in his apron pocket. If I had to guess, Eunice would not see it in the accounting books.

Eunice was helping the same young gentleman she'd kicked out three minutes ago pick out a tarp. "Goodbye, dear. Thanks for coming in. Please stop by again," she said as I walked to the door.

I nodded to her, then walked three doors down to Hattie's. Several people were retreating to their cars after seeing the Closed sign. Just as Kay had said, some tables were pushed back and the entire dining room and counter area was in a blackout. I could not even see a red light on any of the coffee machines. However, there was a small light coming from under the kitchen door, but no other signs of life. In all my years, I had never experienced complete rejection at Hattie's. This was my happy place, and it was telling me to go away. I felt like crying for myself, for Gigi, and Bo.

"It's closed, but I would love to get a comment from you," someone said behind me.

I turned around. It was the same reporter from yesterday. Every muscle in my body froze. The cameraman was three feet behind the reporter. He had to adjust his stance, which allowed me to shift away from the lens.

"No comment." I held my hand up to block my face.

"We're collecting well wishes and reflections now that Elle has been found."

"Who?" I asked, still holding my hand up.

"The missing girl. I thought you were local."

"Guess you were wrong." Denying my ties to Dome sliced through me.

The cameraman grumbled. "Find someone else quick. One more and we can go."

I clicked the key fob, and the lights on my Land Rover lit up the reporter and cameraman.

When she stepped towards the news van, she looked over in the passenger window and saw the folder I'd received during the group interview process with my name scrawled across the top. "You work for the church? I tried to do a story about them and got shot down on every angle. I would love to talk about them and their expansion into the Midwest."

"If I didn't give you a comment about a missing girl, do you think I'm going to talk to you about that?"

The reporter stepped back and looked at the folder again. "Ms. Loudowski, if you will not talk to me, can you give me a contact name? If the church has nothing to hide, someone should be willing to talk."

"Should there be something newsworthy besides the mission to support the communities they are in and the gossip they spread, I will contact you immediately," I said.

She clearly did not understand my sarcasm because she handed me her business card. "Yes, please get in touch with me anytime." The reporter left after she got a quote from another lady trying to get into Hattie's.

When the news van pulled away, I spied there was no ticket on my car for parking overnight. I'd thought for sure the Illinois plates would have attracted a ticket, but maybe the Packer frame around my license plate had spared me. Before I reached the driver's-side door, I got a message. It was the group chat between me, Maz, Leo.

Maz: *We need to meet now*

Me: *Library isn't open*

Maz: *Hattie's*

Me: *It's closed. I'm standing in front of it*

Maz: *Stay there*

Leo: *No thanks*

Maz: *It's important*

Leo: *Not anymore*

Maz: *There's more*

What did Leo mean, no thanks? I wonder if he couldn't get away from his wife.

I sat on the bench outside Hattie's and wished I could have enjoyed the epic people-watching. Hattie's being closed on a Saturday was like someone shutting down the water pipes to their house—it just didn't happen. A girl going missing and being found in the same week as Hattie's being closed was a cosmic event so big people might not have believed it to be true. Not saying moon landing conspiracy big but close to it. Nothing like this happened under the dome.

TWENTY-FOUR

Four minutes later, I was surprised when Leo pulled up. He hopped out of the truck and shut the door. I wasn't sure if he saw me because a group of teenagers were standing in front of me with their heads in their phones looking for another place to meet a friend. He could have been ignoring me, or maybe he'd had something on his mind, like his wife. He retreated two steps and reopened the truck door, took off his sweatshirt, tossed it inside, then grabbed his sunglasses and shut the door.

I scared the kids when I howled, "Oh, hell no!"

They retreated quickly to their car.

"Put your sweatshirt back on," I said.

He was wearing a black T-shirt as mundane as the one I was wearing. I couldn't read his expression, and he didn't banter back.

"Surprised you decided to show," I said.

"Couldn't put this one off till later," Leo said.

"What does that mean?" I asked.

We were standing two feet apart, but it felt like an ocean. Leo didn't answer me and just said, "Maz called."

"What, your wife answered? Sent you on your way?" I said.

No answer. He looked like his mind had been teleported to another planet.

Our phones beeped. It was Maz telling us to come around to the back side of Hattie's.

"Hmm, back door? So our mystery continues. I wonder if Maz has another job and a key to the place."

I didn't know why I was trying so hard to maintain conversation. He was the one with the wife.

"Whatever," Leo said and walked ahead without me.

I was relieved when I noticed his T-shirt at least had a logo on the back. I stayed a foot behind him. We passed a couple of shops, and I looked into the hardware store and saw Eunice sweeping the floor.

We rounded the corners of the last shop and walked along in silence circling around the dumpsters. Leo avoided walking on the green space next to the creek and clung to the back side of the long building. I expected to see Maz on the bridge, but he was a no-show. I started to make my way over to it.

Without looking back, Leo said, "This way."

Maz ran up behind us, wearing the same clothes as yesterday. He pulled out a different key ring and unlocked the back door of Hattie's. Leo was unfazed and followed behind Maz. He caught my eye when he held open the door for me.

I said, "Must have been a hell of a call. You don't seem surprised we're in here."

Leo replied, "You might want some of that Scotch of yours for what you're about to hear."

Damn, one shot and it was a takedown shot. Did he have a right to be jealous of Van?

One soft overhead light illuminated the kitchen area. For the most part, it was exactly as I remembered. The stainless-steel tables, industrial ovens that still intimidated me, the walk-in cooler, and the bulletin board with the safety rules pinned to it. If I hadn't been bothered by Leo's last comment, I would have loved strolling through memory lane.

Maz grabbed the the chair from the tiny office and one from the front of the store and tossed them into the prep area. We declined Maz's offer for coffee. He disappeared again into the front of the shop.

Leo moved a chair to back door and sat down. "Just making sure you don't do a runner like last time."

Maz returned with bottled water for each of us. I took the second chair when Maz started pacing around the metal prep tables.

He stopped in the middle of the room with his back to us. "I'm sorry."

I waited for more from Maz, but that was it.

I finally looked at Leo.

He said, "I only got a twenty-second highlight on the phone. Give him a minute."

Maz turned towards Leo and me, focusing on a spot in the corner between us. "Eighteen months ago, I met up with Bo. We chatted. It's amazing how we connected. I never expected anything . . ."

My heart rate was steady, nerves were calm, no sweating palms. Maybe it was Leo's warning that made me settle in and accept whatever Maz was going to tell us.

I said, "Whatever it is, please just tell us."

"We are married, and we have a house not far from here." Maz paused to seemingly get a reaction from me, and without it, he continued. "I actually found her years ago."

"WORBy," I muttered. I was still calm, but my breathing was heavy. "Maz, just lay it all out for us."

And so Maz spilled it all. "About eight or nine years ago, I found her living in a small town in Oregon working in a bakery. After Bo left Dome that day, she did as she said and went to live at the commune in Colorado. She stayed there for a while before doing some traveling and landing in Oregon."

"How?" I wasn't even sure I said the word out loud for fear of breaking Maz's confessional.

"For the most part, she used her name. She figured no one would be looking for her. The only person to miss her would be her mom, and she figured once she escaped that hell, her mother wouldn't have courage to come after her. I've been calling it a commune, but I really don't know much about it except what she tells me. When I went searching for her, I started there. I called and convinced some lady on the phone to pass on my information to her.

"I just wanted to know if she had a good life. Bo and I started with simple emails. She begged me not to ever tell anyone we connected. I thought about what she was asking. Lou, I know we met every year, and I tried to justify not telling you and I don't know if I'll ever have an answer for you. We did what we did so she could have a good life. It wasn't about us."

In the same whispered tone, I asked, "What about Olsen?"

"Like I said the other day. It's true he's living in Idaho, teaching and helping troubled youth. He had it rough for a few years, but he finally got his drinking under control. This is where . . . I feel bad . . . I should have . . . I should have told you."

Leo and I made eye contact, and he shrugged. We were lost in Maz's story together.

"Bo went to see Olsen. She went to thank him and ask for forgiveness for us using him." Tears welled up in Maz's eyes. "He said we probably saved his life. He had such deep regret for not being able to properly help her and never hated us for using him. At some point, after losing a job because of his drinking—these are his words—'I used my guilt, admiration of Bo's bravery, and your actions to help stay clean.' "

"You talked to him?" Leo asked.

"I haven't. When Bo went to meet him, he had letters written to each of us. Should anything happen to him he wanted us to know how much we impacted his life in such a positive way. He honored the pact we made on that first anniversary to never speak of it and would never seek us out."

"You have our letters?" I asked. My voice was barely a whisper. I thought any sound would shatter the confessional.

"That's the thing." Maz walked to the other side of the kitchen. "The letters are gone. I never even read the letter addressed to me. Bo thought we should read them together. I only know what she has passed on to me."

"What? Was she planning some great reunion?" This time, bitterness seeped out of my voice. I stood, holding onto the metal prep table, and continued. "Does she think we've moved past it all these years? Good for her for having a happy ending. Did you ever explain our angst about her and Olsen? Could we not have been granted some peace? She was in our lives for three months, and we were in her shadow for decades!"

Neither one of them interrupted. The hum of the refrigerators rattled the silence, and my hands shook the table. "Where is she? Why are you telling us this? Why are we in this damn kitchen?"

"She's gone. I can't find her," Maz said.

I put my hands on my hips. "What do you mean? Gone?"

Maz said nothing. He stood with his back to the wall, and his eyes scanned the room looking for the words and the courage to explain it all.

How dare he bring me to Hattie's the place of my first job, the place of our anniversary peace gatherings, a place of home for me, and shatter it with a sucker punch.

TWENTY-FIVE

Maz laid it all out for Leo and me. "When we were kids, she left Dome to find her own shelter. A place with peace and safety. As I said before, she lived at the commune and then traveled the world and then wanted a quiet life, but she wasn't settled. When I finally went to see her a year and a half ago after years of emailing, we connected in a way I never expected. We fell in love and got married three months later. It was her idea to come back here. She told me she wanted to prove to the three of us that she earned the life and opportunity we gave her."

"You got married? Ah, yes, the wedding ring," I said. It was a subtle but direct hit, and I forced myself not to look at Leo. "Why keep it from us?"

"She was getting ready to reach out to you. Tell you everything, but something happened. A few weeks ago, I thought it was nerves, but then it seems like something spooked her. One night, I caught her sneaking out of the house at midnight for a few hours. She thought I was sleeping. I didn't confront her outright but tried to get her to open up. All she kept saying was she needed to take care of something. Bo said she would tell me when she could. She had been getting these real bad headaches. She has some medicine that works half the time, but otherwise, she sleeps them off. I begged her to go to another doctor and . . . sorry, I'm rambling . . . Bo said she had things she needed to do. She started acting more erratic these last few days—"

"Could she have helped Gigi? Copying what we did. Sort of like paying it forward to someone else in need." I was sorry I had interrupted him, but my mind was going a hundred miles an hour. "What do we know about her family?"

"Bo and I know them. Gigi's father, James, is a CPA and does the books for Hattie's. I always thought he was a good guy. The stepmother, Patty is a little uptight. My interactions have been limited, and what do you really know about someone?"

We let that thought hang in the air.

Maz continued, "She didn't come home last night and isn't answering calls."

"You go to the police?" I said.

"It hasn't been twenty-four hours. They won't do anything," Maz said.

"Yeah, but with one girl missing, they might."

"But if she's involved in helping Gigi, I don't want to interfere."

"What about work? You said she has a business," I said.

Maz said nothing.

Leo got up from the chair and stood behind me like a support pole.

"What are you not telling me?" I said.

Leo said, "C'mon, Lou. You can figure this one out." He put his hand on my shoulder, and I wasn't sure if it was for support or to keep me from running.

My gaze spun around the kitchen. I looked from wall to wall, around the prep tables to the storage racks.

My mind zoomed back to yesterday. The lady with the dark hair helping customers who retreated when I stepped up to order. The hair was dyed black, not brown like in high school, but the bracelets. Too many bracelets. I was stunned I hadn't recognized her.

On every vacation, the question *What if I ran into her* would creep into my head. Each new city was another opportunity to have that chance encounter. I had forever tattooed her image to memory. Then I realized it was a memory, but she continued to grow old like me.

Now I was standing in her kitchen. The girl can disappear and reappear without a fuss, yet I'm the one shaking.

TWENTY-SIX

"You ok?" Leo asked.

"I . . . I . . . I guess so. It's just the surprise of Maz knowing," I said.

"She was going to tell you," Maz said. "I didn't mean to . . . I was . . ."

I held up my hand. "Stop. I'll deal with you knowing later. There's a lot to process." Leo's hand was on my back, and I wanted to lean into him. Just like our anniversary afternoons, Leo's half hug felt like a warm blanket during a snowstorm. I was mad at myself for wanting a full embrace from him.

There was solace for the first time in decades standing with this weird tribe. We had shared a secret, and things had grown out of that—some good and some bad. It was just nice to verbalize all my thoughts and feelings. I realized some knew more than I did, and I needed to know how much more. I had to figure out a way to get the truth out of everyone. I knew Bo hadn't told Maz everything regardless of their newfound connection.

When I stepped away from Leo, a look of panic came over his face.

I shook my head. "I'm not running, but I think I know what we need."

I went to the office, and the boys looked at each other. The office held the desk and one side chair. The office was so small, the door hadn't been able to close with the desk chair, so it had been removed before I started working there. I sat on the desk and hauled myself up. The ceiling in the dry storage area and the office had a low drop ceiling with white tile boards. I pushed up the tile in the corner, and my hand struck a paper bag.

Maz finally got the courage to speak to me again. "What are you doing?"

"Praying it's something better than apple Schnapps. Go find three glasses," I said.

Leo walked over, and I handed him the paper bag. He held my hand as I jumped down. Maz pulled three coffee mugs from the rack behind him, and they looked at me like I'd just performed some magic trick.

"Not sure when it started, but I know when I worked here under Ms. Hattie Number Three, this was the tradition. Working the Friday afternoon closing shift sucked. Hattie Number Three would provide the extra-long cleaning detail list and then leave for the evening. I never knew who brought the bottle or who replaced it when empty. When Hattie Number Three left for the evening, we would do a shot and then do the cleaning. Once a week, we did one shot. We felt like such rebels."

Leo removed the bag and revealed a cheap tequila. "You were always the rebel. Your life in the underworld started early."

I knew he meant those words as humor, but it was also a reminder of some of our decisions we had made thirty-four years ago.

"You know it's nine in the morning?" Leo said.

"You know it's nine a.m., and Bo is back. Oh wait, she left

again. Pour us each a shot. This is it. We'll figure it out. Bo, Gigi, and . . . everything."

Maz was reluctant, but after twenty seconds, he raised his mug to Leo and then to me.

I said, "It ends now."

We put the empty mugs aside, and Maz went to the storefront and grabbed a chair for himself. We sat in the center of the kitchen between two stainless-steel prep tables under the single yellow light.

My phone beeped with a message from Stew asking if everything was all right, and for some reason, it felt good to ignore him. He could be an annoying doting older brother, or Kay might have told to him to check on me again since I hadn't been as fresh and clean as she was at seven in the morning.

"What do we know about Gigi? Maz, are you ok if we start with her as it might bring us to Bo?"

"Anything that can help find Bo is fine with me," Maz said.

"I've been doing some digging," Leo said.

This was news to me. I thought he would have said something during Food Truck Friday. Not during the porch scene, that would have been weird.

"After you sent the text about Dutch leaving last night, I got online. The papers ran the same photos and background stuff about Gigi. High school senior, cheerleader, and member of the glee club. Wants to be a reporter. Personal information has to come from the family. I tried tracking her through social media, but I'm not very good at it. From what I can tell, she posted almost every day. She had a sizable gap a month ago, and then it started picking up again."

"Maz, you said you knew her through the library. Do you know if she was a regular here?" I asked.

"Most of the high school kids are here at some point. When Bo took over Hattie's, James, Gigi's dad, was doing the books for the previous owner, Glenna. Bo was impressed with the detailed accounts of the business, but Glenna insisted that was all James. I thought she should find someone else. The store's business wasn't great, and I thought a fresh perspective might be good, but Bo insisted. I think they meet a couple of times a month. He has an office with a couple of accountants over in Sherman Township. He's a typical accountant, kinda boring. I brought champagne when Bo signed the papers for the bakery, and he said he and his wife don't drink. He would not even do a sip for a toast. Bo thought that made for a good accountant—someone always in their right mind even if they killed the mood at the signing party.

"As for Gigi, I got to know her and Dutch when they did a report for the school newspaper. They were in the basement, sorting through the old village newspapers. They were doing some retrospective piece. She was one of the semi-regular morning patrons of the library. So was Dutch," Maz said.

"Did you know they still do 4QB?" I said.

For a brief second, we all flashed a smile.

Leo rubbed his face. He was an early riser, getting me coffee this morning, but I could see he had spent no time shaving. "Forever trapped inside a dome, of course, traditions continue. Your bottle still being stashed above the desk, 4QBs, and now let's add missing girls."

Maz and I looked at each other, and we didn't know how to react. There was more anger than humor in Leo's voice and then a lot more silence.

Leo finally spoke again. "Sorry, this is all too much. Not enough sleep and definitely not enough food."

Maz stood up and walked into the front of the store. I thought our tribe was lost, but I was pleasantly surprised when Maz returned with a tray full of pastries, napkins, and plastic forks. "These are yesterday's but still should be pretty good."

Leo tried using a fork to split open a scone, and it shattered.

Maz said, "Bo has been experimenting with biodegradable flatware."

"Well, that is a new tradition," I said.

The boys gave me a pity laugh, and I explained my conversation with Dutch last night. His work on the Quell retirement story, the account of the morning Gigi disappeared, the champagne, him storming out when I asked if he helped her runaway, and him sneaking out later.

"Did you tell him too much?" Leo said.

I nearly choked on the lemon apple strudel, but Leo corrected himself.

"Didn't mean you. I meant *us*. Did we get him involved in Bo's disappearance when we didn't have to?"

"Too late now," I said. "Plus, with Gigi being found, he could probably couldn't care less about some old folks."

"Tell us again when you last had contact with Bo," Leo said.

"Yesterday. After you guys left the library, I came here. We talked for only a second because the place was busy. She seemed irritated, but it could have been anything. I went back to the library tunnels to get some work done. Moving the last of the boxes out of there. When I was wrapping up at five, she texted that she would see me at home later that night. All that isn't unusual. When she wasn't home by six, I called and got no answer and no text update. I tried one or two more times. At seven, I walked here and Rosie was locking up. She told me Bo left around five thirty to run some errands and told her to lock up. When I tried calling, it went straight to voice mail like the phone is off."

"She goes missing, and less than twelve hours later, Gigi is found unconscious in the parkway," I said. "Does she keep any type of diary or something?"

"Not that I know of. After she left the house that night when she thought I was sleeping, I scoured the house looking for something, anything. The only thing personal she brought with her from

Oregon was a box of a few mementos from her travels. You can see in here that the office is wide-open, so I don't think she would hide anything here."

"What about her car?" Leo asked.

"It's at the house. We thought about selling it since we're two blocks from here. She hardly drives," Maz said.

"Would she go for a walk? Have you walked the trail?" I asked.

Maz shook his head. "Nothing. I can't find her." Tears came to his eyes again.

My phone beeped. Maz excused himself to use the bathroom, and I was shocked to see the message.

Five Now?

Followed by a second text.

PLEASE.

What could Dutch want?

TWENTY-SEVEN

"Dutch wants to meet."

"We shared too much with him," Leo said.

I shook my head. "It seems like he's asking for help."

"You think he knows something about Bo?"

"Who?" Maz asked when he returned to the kitchen.

"Dutch is asking to meet in room five," I said.

"Great. Let's go." Maz was almost to the door before I could form a thought.

I needed a moment to think this out. "Easy. I don't want you jumping on the kid."

Maz was frantic. "You said you saw him leave during the night, and Bo is missing. I want to talk to him. Tell him to come here."

There was no way I was going to let him attack Dutch before we know what was going on. We had built a relationship with this kid, but Maz might destroy it in seconds.

"Absolutely not. Not until you calm down."

"Don't tell me what to do!" His anger surprised Leo and me. He grabbed his phone. "I'll tell him."

"Lou already told him we'll be there at ten." I'll give Leo credit for not spoiling my lie.

My text read: *Does the bridge work in five? Hang back until you see me alone.*

"I'm going now." Maz walked back and tossed the remaining food and dirty mugs on the tray and threw all of it into the deep wash sink.

I grabbed the bottle of tequila. Leo picked up the brown paper bag that had fallen on the floor. When I tried grabbing the bag, he held it back, trying to catch my eye. I snatched the bag and returned it to the proper spot, and again Leo was there, helping me off the desk.

Maz was a nervous ball of energy. He held the back door open for Leo and struggled to lock it.

I nudged him out of the way and secured the door. "Before I give you the keys, promise me you will not attack the kid. You've got to settle down. If we get nothing out of him, go to the police and at least try to report her missing." I gave him the keys. "We have some time before he meets us. I'm going for a walk to clear my head."

"Good idea, I'll join you," Leo said.

Maz turned and scurried along the back side of the building and was out of sight before I turned to Leo. "You don't need to walk with me."

"Oh, I'm not walking with you. I'm going with you to meet Dutch."

"What do you mean?"

There was no response from Leo.

"Ok, you got me. I'll not let Maz jump all over that kid without warning him."

"What's the plan?" Leo asked.

"I told him to meet me at the bridge and that I would be alone."

"Then you're going to bring him here."

"Nothing gets past you."

"Maz might be losing his mind, and maybe it's the nine a.m.

tequila shot keeping me focused, but I know there should be a loud click when you lock a metal door."

I shook my head. "Never fear the morning shot. It isn't always bad."

"True, but it's never good," Leo said.

"Ah, you're wise. Now get out of here. Go settle Maz down. Try to get more information. He's holding back from us, or Bo held back information from him."

"What makes you say that?"

Oops. I was praying Bo had withheld information from Maz. Leo and Maz and I had carried out our plan flawlessly. The last time I had seen Bo things had taken a dark turn. "Ah, let's just call it women's intuition."

"I'm not leaving you with that kid."

"What can he do to me?" I said.

"Look at what we did thirty-four years ago?"

"Wow. Point, set, match. You won that round, but remember, it was three of us."

"You don't know he's alone," Leo said.

"Ok, here's the plan. Go back inside and sit in the dining room near the kitchen door. Make sure no one sees you from the front. The last thing we need is someone pounding on the door."

"Ok, but if you go somewhere else, let me know you're ok, but if you take off, I'm calling the police, saying I saw you being dragged away, and both you and the kid will be in trouble."

I started to object but didn't want to waste my energy. "WORB," I mumbled and rolled my eyes.

After Leo retreated inside, I looked down and saw a piece of fresh paper under a rock. It was an invoice for baked goods and scribbled on the back was *Waited as long as I could. Second trip can be done with extra charge. Contact Irene at the shop, Zack.*

I realized the operation of Hattie's was still in play overnight.

The delivery hadn't been called off, but employees had not shown up at the backdoor. Was Bo able to contact them?

Was her disappearance premeditated? I couldn't think about that now and walked over to the bridge. No one was out this early. The sun was shining, but it was still spring and the cold had not completely slipped away yet.

A minute later, Dutch showed up out of breath.

Whatever happened, the mother gene in me always prevailed. My first reaction was to hug him after I saw his damaged forehead. I'd missed that last night in my dark kitchen, or it maybe happened after he left.

TWENTY-EIGHT

I reached for his eye, but Dutch retreated three feet.

"Sorry, I won't touch it. What happened?"

"Can we go to the library? I don't want to stand out here," Dutch said.

"Of course, but first come with me. At ten, we'll meet Maz." I led him to the back door of Hattie's.

"I don't want to see anyone," Dutch said softly. This kid needed a hug badly, but I refrained.

"It's closed. We have the space for ourselves. I'll explain it in a minute, but you will have to tell me what's going on."

The kitchen remained as we had left it, with the single light on in the center. However, the desk and second office chair were sitting outside the small office. The third chair was nowhere to be found, but I spied the swinging door to the front of the store cracked open.

Leo must be right on the other side, listening.

I grabbed Leo's unopened bottle of water and handed it to Dutch and told him to sit.

He stumbled for the second time in two minutes, but he sat. His shoulders sloped, and the energy seemed to drain from his body. He sat back on the chair but quickly shifted to the edge of the seat.

I asked, "Now tell me what is going on."

"This is between us. You said, well, all of your group said I should trust you."

"Yes. Remember, we told you stuff as well. We trust you." I felt bad for not bringing in Leo at this point, but I didn't want to break the moment. "What happened to you?"

"My dad and I went to the hospital. I was so relieved when he said they found her, but I didn't think we should be there. But my dad said her parents wanted to see me. That's where we were going when I saw you walking."

I just nodded, wanting him to tell his story.

"We got to the waiting room, and her stepmother attacked me. She went ballistic. She grab me, demanded I tell her about the drugs, and her ring gave me this bruise."

I pulled his hand away from his head. "Don't touch it. It hurts."

"I guess when that jogger found her, Gigi was repeating 'Help, Dutch, help, Dutch.' She was in and out of consciousness. There was some other stuff, but that jogger couldn't understand what she was saying. Her mom thinks I did something to her. She thinks Gigi was naming me as the attacker. She was furious the police didn't take me into custody. She wanted to deal with me directly."

"That's awful. I'm going to ask some questions, but don't feel pressured. Do you know if Gigi will make a recovery?"

"I guess so, but she is—was—I don't really know. I think she was unconscious."

"Where is your dad?" My question seemed to surprise him.

"I don't know." There was a long pause before he spoke again, "After I got away from Gigi's stepmom, he started yelling at them. Security pushed us out of the hospital. He dropped me off at home and said he was going to take care of things and to stay home. I waited until he pulled out of the driveway before I went over to your place. I heard a car and thought he was coming back, so I ran to the back side of the condo and knocked on the patio door. What's her name—the old lady next door saw me—so I sat on the porch like I was supposed to be there and texted you. When I got your message, I ran here."

I wasn't sure if his story fit the timeframe. He might have been lying, but I let it go.

"What happened since you left my place last night?" I needed to know how far the lying would go.

His face lit up. "Oh, I found this in the file Gigi had for the report we were doing on Quell."

"Mrs. Quell," I corrected. "Sorry, it drives me nuts when my kids don't know how to address an adult."

Dutch ignored me and dug into his backpack. He was holding it in front of him like he was scared someone might steal it. He pulled out several sheets of paper on top of an empty folder. He stood up, spread them out on the prep table, and kicked the table.

"You're stumbling around. Are you ok? Do you want some food?" I asked.

"It's kinda stupid," Dutch said. "I have my dad's shoes on. They're a size bigger."

I couldn't help but laugh. It was endearing, watching him act like a teenager and blush at his own actions. I confessed, "I've actually gone to work with two different shoes. One black, one brown. I get it."

We shared a laugh.

"Does this mean anything to you? I think Gigi found something and was working on a second story," Dutch said.

I stood next to him and put my hand on his back to shift him over a foot, but he jumped three feet.

"Didn't mean to startle you. Just trying to get a good look."

"I thought maybe they were phone numbers for people she was trying to contact for a quote, but I'm short a number."

Sweat poured out of me. My stomach rolled, and I was fearful of another water balloon bursting through my underwear. I grabbed the metal table for support and kept my head down. Dutch couldn't see my face now.

"What else do you have?" I asked.

He moved the papers around and pointed to Mrs. Quell's class picture. "Here, I'm not sure of this either . . . is this Hattie?"

"You got it."

"But Hattie is Claire Cosworth, Bo, and according to you, she disappeared. What is this, some type of prank?" His voice was getting stronger. "You guys tell me she disappeared when you were in school, and now I'm standing in her kitchen. Is this a hoax?"

"Gigi's stepmom attacking you proves otherwise. We're still trying to figure out how the two incidents are related," I said.

Dutch was silent. His hair fell forward, and he swept it back as he looked at the papers and photograph spread out on the table. Watching his profile immediately took me back to standing next to his father and me watching television and betting on which house people would buy. My train of thought shifted to watching television and us kissing. My mind lingered a little too long.

When I came back to reality, Dutch had gone very still, but I didn't know why. I followed his eyes behind me and noticed the swinging kitchen door had shifted closed.

"Is someone there?" Dutch asked.

"It's ok." I walked over to the door and held it open for Leo to come in.

With a swift motion, Dutch scooped up the papers and his backpack. He flung it on himself like a baby carrier, holding it in front of him, and bolted out the door.

Leo started for the back door.

I said, "Let him go."

TWENTY-NINE

I flung myself onto the desk chair and put my head on my hands. I finally turned to Leo. "How much did you hear?"

"Some. Obviously, I couldn't see whatever he was showing you. Sorry about the door. I saw it slipping and didn't know what to do."

I waved him over to the chair next to me. "Gigi figured out Claire is Bo is Hattie."

"I don't trust that kid. He knows more than what he's telling us. Why is he so willing to talk to us if he is only a witness?" Leo said.

"Would *you* trust us?" I said.

"Fair point. Last night—"

Thank god, I was still leaning forward and could sink my head into my hands again because when he said the words *last night* my mind flashed from me kissing Van to me and Leo on the porch.

"—ran, and I couldn't see anyone roaming around the industrial park. Maybe someone picked Dutch up down the road so Van wouldn't catch him leaving. Hell, maybe Bo and the three of them are working together."

"He's hurt."

"Gigi's stepmom attacked him," Leo said.

"No . . . it's more . . ." Exhausted and hunched forward, I could see mud on the floor. Something made me pick it up and give it a closer look before I walked over to the garbage can. "Why are you so against the kid?"

Our phones beeped. It was Maz looking for us.

I groaned. "Shit. How am I going to tell him I chased Dutch away?"

"I'll do it. Why don't you go home and watch for Dutch to return?" Leo said.

"Who knows, maybe he'll go to the library. Maz said he knew Dutch and Gigi from their school assignment. Maybe Dutch will trust him," I said.

"What about Maz? He kept all that from us. Who's to say Maz isn't helping Bo? All these years I was more worried about Olsen than Bo. What we did was really shitty, but what Maz did is worse."

"What do you mean?" I asked.

"Really? I had a lot of time to think about this. Let's start at the beginning. I mean thirty-four years ago, not a few days ago. You come to the library one morning, and you're all freaked out because Bo isn't there. Not everyone showed up every morning. We had the same people but not every morning, but you're still upset. Plus Bo, was new at the mornings at the library."

I said, "Yes, because days before, I confronted Bo about her bruises. I remember thinking it was so odd when she said she would help me with my science grade if I kept my mouth shut. I was trying to be an afterschool-TV-special superhero, and she was acting like it was no big deal. It was confusing. I was ready to get her help and yank her away from home. I nearly told my mother about it. Simultaneously, I was angry at her for ruining our English class reading assignment and worried like a parent for her. This was her first school in years. Her mother was moving her all around, pulling her from schools after just a few months. She even made Bo homeschool herself, and that wasn't like homeschooling, as we know it today."

"Maz and I had to talk you off the ledge. You were ready to call in the army. You hinted that something bad might have happened but wouldn't tell us. We didn't fully know until we overheard her talking to you the next afternoon."

"Somehow I felt guilty knowing her secret. I saw her in school, and she avoided me. I couldn't understand it."

"We knew little about that stuff or what to do. Maybe you had watched a TV show where someone reports trouble at home, and they sent the kid to an aunt's house to live happily ever after. We weren't prepared for this type of stuff back then," Leo said.

"You got that right," I said.

"Actually, we had proof before we knew that we knew it."

"You lost me on that one."

"Maz and I had study hall first period. It was so stupid having it first thing. Either you were rushing to finish what you blew off the night before, or you were completely bored. So Maz and I helped in the front office. It's amazing the shit we found out. The three secretaries loved us. We practically had free rein of the files, and we were looking at stuff students should not be seeing. Probably much like those files in the tunnels Maz talked about. We even got Mrs. Schneider to amend Bozz's absent days to a respectable number. He just had to clear her car of snow anytime it snowed during the school day. The first day back after Christmas break, this girl comes into the office to complete her registration.

"Mrs. Schneider hands her a schedule and says something about gym class and giving her a pass today because she probably doesn't have a swimsuit with her. The girl freaks out and says something about needing to miss all of swimming. Mrs. Schneider says, 'Oh, girl, I can only give you a pass for a few days, and by then, you should be done. Nothing to be ashamed of, hon, we all get our periods.' Maz and I were mortified hearing Mrs. Schneider talk about that stuff. After you told us what you saw and because she always wore sweatpants and long sleeves to gym class every day, and never shorts, we put it together."

"You knew what she wore to gym class? You were not even in her grade."

"Don't make me sound like a pervert. We were in high school, and a new girl started. You bet every guy was checking her out."

"Fair enough. What I never understood—because we promised never to talk about it, even when we were together—is how she got you guys to help?"

"Do you remember when one of the library bathrooms was shut down?"

"Not sure if I want to hear this, but at this point, nothing can surprise me," I said.

"Bernie was in there as usual, so I tried buying some weed. Anyway, when we were in the stall, some kid walked in and made some joke about the cops being outside the library. Bernie panics and starts flushing everything down the toilet. He's freaking out because he's losing all his inventory, and somehow, in the process, several plastic bags and a brown bag got dropped into the toilet bowl and clogged up everything. Water overflowed and he runs out. I knew if I went out with them I would be seen with him, so I went the other way."

"To the rear of the library that leads to the basement that leads to the tunnels," I said.

"My dad, working as the maintenance guy at the middle school, paid off. Sometimes my brother and I would go with him on weekends and run around the old steam tunnels. I always thought it was kinda cool, Dome having secret tunnels under the village. Bo was in the library that afternoon and saw me go and not come back. She took my math book I had left behind. The next day, she would only give me my book back if I explained about the tunnels. She was really focused on where they went and if the other doors were locked or had alarms on them."

"I can't believe I never thought to ask before."

"You probably did, but we promised never to speak of it even when we're together," Leo said.

"So she had dirt on you. Do you think she set us up? Stage that eavesdropping conversation?"

Leo looked like I had dumped a bucket of water on him. "I never thought of that angle. You think she made up the whole bad family life?"

"Just something else to consider at this point. Any idea how she got Maz?"

"I'd figured it was the same way as you. Blackmail and pity. Are you going to tell me your story?" Leo asked.

"Just pity."

Our phones beeped again.

"Tell him we're on our way," I said.

We shut the back door behind us tight. It wasn't locked, but I wasn't concerned about that at this point. We walked side by side along the back side of the buildings, and the small creek was flowing to our left.

Leo asked again for my story.

"You might not like it," I said.

"Try me."

"I did it because I thought it was the best thing for her. She told me she had a place to go, and I figured it had to be better than home with her mother."

"Calling BS on your story."

"What?"

"There's no way you felt guilty or not at peace, as you put it, if you did the right thing without being blackmailed," Leo said.

"I don't think there was much blackmail in your story. Who cares if you ran from a bad drug deal. You did it for the same reason —we wanted to be superheroes."

We were at the end of the building and made the turn towards the storefronts. The guys working on the signage for the stores were moving all around us, so we walked to the corner of the parking lot and had a view of the library. We watched a news van drive down the street and a few more cars pull in front of Hattie's and immediately leave.

"Asking again, why all the guilt years later?" Leo asked.

"We screwed with Olsen. We stole his car keys and car!"

"Borrowed!" Leo corrected me.

"Seriously, you're still saying borrowed! We took his keys. Convinced him you would have your uncle, the cop, look for his car. I still don't know how it ended up at the mall."

"Maybe instead of catching the bus in Madison or Iowa, she felt bad and just hopped the city bus. It doesn't matter. I freaked out when I saw it there the next day. At least we were able to get it back to Olsen faster than expected, and we didn't have to do anything with the fake bottle of liquor. I was so nervous when we gave him his keys back and told him we spotted his car at the mall."

"He was so confused about his keys. The next day, he pulled the three of us into the corner of the library and asked what we did."

"I was so proud how we kept it together. What did we say, something like, 'You helped save a girl's life.' We said someone had to get away, and this was her only chance. He was so mad. He thought we set him up to lose his job."

Leo said, "It took him two months to figure out it was Bo. No one else missed her. He had gone to the high school and pulled some report and figured it out. Any other person would have turned us in. We picked the right guy. He was a mess."

"With his record, he had to avoid any involvement in a scandal even if he was innocent."

"Keep your voice down."

"Whatever." I dug my toe into a tiny pothole and kicked out some pebbles and muttered, "WORBy."

"What the hell is that? Woobe? You've been sputtering that nonstop."

"I've been doing that since that week. WORB—Woods, Olsen, Rook chess piece key chain, Bottle. It started as my to-do list that morning but morphed into my go-to expression. Some people swear, some sigh or breathe heavy, and I just unknowingly mumble WORB. My kids think I'm asking Woody from *Toy Story* for help."

"What about the *y*?"

"There's no *y*, just a long *b*. There's no logic," I lied. "It isn't even a word, and you're correcting my spelling."

Sometimes, in real angst, I added the *Y*. Yvette had not been not part of the plan. She had been the reason for all of it, but she had never been part of it. Then she became as real as my nightmares.

THIRTY

I stepped towards the library.

"Wait," Leo said.

There was no reason for his hand to linger on my arm when he held me back, but neither one of us could pull away. We stood a foot a part, but it was almost more intimate in daylight as opposed to being on top of each other on a dark porch. Both of us were suddenly aware of how close we were, and it made for an awkward silence.

"So, where does that leave us—ah, I mean what now?" Leo said.

I steadied my breathing and pulled myself mentally away from him. "You need a ten-second recap? We made Bo disappear and decades later—"

Our phones beeped again.

"We better get there before Maz has a meltdown," I said.

We crossed Main Street, and Leo said, "Aren't you going to continue the recap? It seems I'm slow, and I'm lost on how to feel and do."

I elbowed him in the ribs, and we laughed.

It took everything in me not to reach out and touch him again, so I had to cut off our connection. "Are you dependent on your wife telling you what to do?"

He walked ahead and opened the first library door for me. No comment. No explanation. No excuse.

I held the second door for him, and we walked single file down the hall to room five. It was vacant.

Suddenly, instead of an empty study room, it became a confessional.

"I need to explain something," Leo said.

"No explanation needed." The words were like ice coming out of me.

Leo shifted his tone from apologetic to sounding like my ex, Joe, before our divorce was finalized. "If I recall, this morning you—"

He never got to finish because Maz came back in.

"You guys are finally here. Where's Dutch?"

"I don't think he'll show, but let's give him time. It's still early," Leo said, giving me a pass for freaking out Dutch and making him run.

We each stood in a corner, not unlike boxers in a boxing ring except we were supposed to be on the same team.

"I hate to assume, but I'm guessing you haven't heard from Bo," I said.

Maz shook his head.

I continued, "You looked like hell before, but now you're a mess. What happened since we saw you twenty minutes ago?"

"I walked the tunnels. In case she was hiding down there," Maz said.

"You think she's trying to repeat her disappearance or hide?" My heart was breaking for him, but I had to press on. "Any proof she was there at some point?"

"Not that I can tell," Maz said.

"Do you know how and when she told the employees not to

come today?" I asked. "When we were there, not one employee showed up. Customers were at the front door, but no one was coming to the back door. She must have put some thought into leaving."

"You're saying she's gone? Disappearing again, like it was planned?" Maz said.

"I'm not saying she took off for good, but something spooked her and made her prepare to not show up today. Where have you looked?"

"Last night, I came to Hattie's at eight, and it was all locked up," Maz said.

"When you were at Hattie's, was the sign on the front door saying they're closed?" I asked.

"I went through the back door. It was locked, and just the one light was on."

"What about the tables in front? Was everything in order? I noticed a few of them pushed out of the usual layout."

"Don't really know. Sometimes, when they mop the floor, they don't move the tables back until the morning. I left there and walked back home until I got your message about Dutch sneaking out. I drove around until midnight, went back home, and dosed on and off for a while.

"This morning after the news broke about Gigi, I went to the parkway. The police had the area blocked off. I was scared they would find Bo, but in a worse state than Gigi. I walked around the parkway for a bit, but couldn't get anywhere because of the police."

"Is that why you have red mud on your shoes?" I asked.

"Probably," Maz said.

"You need to go to the police," Leo said. "Forget the twenty-four-hour rule. At least report it, even if they won't or can't do anything."

"I can't," Maz said.

"Why not? She could be in danger," Leo said.

"I promised. Bo made me promise. A week ago, she sat me down and said I should not go to the police if anything happens to her. I didn't understand, and all she kept saying is that she would explain everything as soon as she could. For days, I thought she might run. I thought we were a happy couple, but given her past, I thought maybe staying in one place is just not something she's comfortable with." Maz kicked the wall behind him. "Maybe she was planning something, and that's why I can't call the police; she made me promise."

"That changes things," I said and received strange looks from the men. "If she had a contingency plan in place, like you not calling the police, this is an orchestrated event. I'm sure it'll all work out."

"Just because I'm not going to call the police doesn't mean she isn't in danger," Maz snapped.

"Ok, you have a point." I couldn't help thinking again we might be pawns in her game.

Leo's phone beeped, and without explanation and only a half-ass apology, he said something had come up, and he had to go. He went to Maz and gave him that half handshake, half hug routine guys do. I got a head nod, and before he was out the door, he reminded us to keep him informed.

Ignoring my feelings of abandonment from Leo, and with my skepticism about Bo behind me, I went to Maz and put my hand on his shoulder. "It's good of you to keep a promise. She was in danger once, and we helped her. Bo knows you'll keep her safe. Go home and wait for her."

"I have to wait for Dutch," Maz said.

"He's probably not coming. He was doubtful in a text message. I lied. I'll stay here. You need to eat, shower, and wait. If you stay here, the parents at toddler time will think you're a nutjob and call the police. I'll wait for Dutch, and if he shows, I'll text you. If you want to help Bo, you need to keep it together."

"Maybe you're right."

"We'll find her. Now go."

He left, and I took a seat. Maz had left wondering where Bo is. I was left knowing Bo had died thirty-four years ago, and I had to find the new Hattie.

I hoped our secret would not be revealed.

THIRTY-ONE

I sat in room five, and the silence voided any rational thoughts running through my head.

I had to figure out where Bo had gone. Bo had become Yvette for decades, and now she was back but what did that mean for her? For me? How far would she go to carry out her plan? Helping her once was . . . I didn't have a word for it, never had and never would. Maybe it was justifiable, but to repeat it would be unthinkable. More importantly, I had to figure out who she was protecting or who she was going after.

WORB!

Gigi had figured out Hattie was Bo. Was Gigi blackmailing her? Did Bo feel threatened? Why would it matter if Gigi figured it out? Did Bo negotiate Gigi's release for herself? Maybe Gigi escaped on her own.

I was forgetting about Dutch. He lied about going out last night and his timeline this morning. He was more beat up than he was letting on. Had Gigi attacked him before she escaped?

He must be the key to all of this.

I texted him an apology. It was weak but honest, and I offered the library as a place to meet. I told him the guys were gone.

He replied: *Bench*

Me: *Walking from the library*

Never had I thought I'd be on this route again under these circumstances.

The sun was bright, but the temperature was in the high sixties. I unwrapped the North Face fleece from my waist and put it on. I wished I had something warm to drink. More traffic was on Main Street, and cars were still headed to the high school. Some kids were playing kickball on the baseball field. It was tempting just to sit and watch them having fun, and let everything dissolve away.

From the sidewalk, I followed the worn path to centerfield and cut into the woods. It wasn't as muddy as expected, but I had to watch my step.

Dutch was on the bench playing with his phone.

I texted him one more time. *It's just me. Sorry about last time.*

Dutch looked up from his phone and gave me a nod as I sat on the bench, his backpack between us.

"I just want you to know there was no weird motive, with Leo being on the other side of the door. We just thought you would be more comfortable talking to me," I said.

"It's ok." Dutch was barely audible.

I waited out his silence.

He finally said, "So Hattie is Bo, who is Claire. This girl who you helped disappear."

"She was in an abusive situation at home. We helped her run away," I said.

"If it was for the best, why are you guys worried she'll come after you?" Dutch asked, pouring a metaphorical bucket of ice water on me. He must have seen my reaction, and he continued, "Isn't that why you guys are freaking out?"

"Honestly, not really sure at this point. So much information has come out, I don't know how to feel. Did you know Maz was married to Hattie?"

"You're kidding?" There was a slight laugh from Dutch.

"It's true. I don't know what hit me harder: that Bo was back, that Maz had been communicating with her for years, or that they were married. It's a toss-up for me—pick one out of the hat—surprise, betrayal, or nausea from riding the crazy train."

The sky was blue, but the thin row of trees set between the baseball field and the SMF factory cast shadows all around us.

Dutch stood up and put his foot on the bench and stretched. He resembled his father so much, it was a little unnerving.

"Not to sound too motherly, but I have to say how you're handling everything is remarkable," I said.

"Really? I've been freaked out. All the attention when Gigi disappeared was uncomfortable, and then Maz—"

"Maz and I cornered you. Again, sorry, we were trying to help you, Gigi, and maybe protect ourselves. Well, I was protecting me."

Dutch just nodded his acceptance and said, "Why is it not better now that Gigi is found? Last night was different when she was missing. Why were you still being so secretive at Hattie's kitchen?"

"I don't mean to sound defensive, but you asked to see me this morning," I said.

"I just thought I had a great story about a former student coming back to Dome, kinda undercover, as Hattie. I think Gigi had figured it out too, and I could finish her story. It would help my grade."

"Bullshit." I think I startled him with my candid response because he didn't move. "You could have asked your dad if Bo and Hattie were the same person. You know he's a Dome alum, and I'm sure he has been to Hattie's."

"That would be great if we were talking," Dutch said.

This was the opposite of what Van had told me. I tried keeping a poker face, hoping to keep him sharing, but he stopped, so I said, "Not always easy talking to the people closest to you." No response, so I switched directions. "Tell me how well you know Gigi. Same group of friends at school?"

"I guess so. It was weird coming back after London. It seems like this place is frozen in time. I missed a few parties and some inside jokes had to be explained, but everyone was right where they'd been when I left. About four months ago, I was leaving a party early because I was over everyone, and Gigi asked for a ride home. Instead of going home, we got to talking, and everything was great. We drove around for about a half hour, and at one point, we sat in my car in the parking lot of the diner before I dropped her off. I swear, just talking, nothing else! I gave her my number.

"She never texted that weekend, and that following week, she was all weird at school and was mad at me when I didn't start acting like her boyfriend. Later, Quinn told me she was telling people I thought everyone was such a loser and I think I'm hot shit for living in Europe. I confronted her later in the library and asked what her problem was. She said something about *Me Too*. I nearly flipped out. She must have seen my panic was real, and she asked why I had sent all those texts to her.

"I said I never sent her anything because she had never given me her number. Right then, I asked for her number, and I sent her a text. She realized she had my phone number wrong by one digit. Some creep was pretending to be me, and he was kinda harassing her."

"How do you mean?" I asked.

"I don't know. I think she was embarrassed and wouldn't show me. After that, we were fine. I was still mad at her, but we started having fun with this Quell project. She tried making up for her trash-talking by setting me up with her friend, and I gave her a solid no thank you. I didn't want to mix with her anymore like that. A couple of weeks later, I heard she was seeing someone. I asked her one day when we were digging through the old village newspapers, but she wouldn't tell me about him."

"So, that morning, you were on friendly terms with Gigi?" I asked.

"Yeah, we were both semi-regulars for the morning shift at the library."

"Let me get this straight. You got the text about the champagne being in the woods. You walked over here, picked up the champagne, and when you were walking back, you saw her get into a car and that she had dropped her backpack, correct?"

"Yup, I thought it was odd, but she can be dingy, so I grabbed her bag and went to the library. I figured I would give it to her there. We had plenty of time that morning since it was 4QB. We are all early risers being part of the morning crew, but on that day, most everyone was there around seven. I figured she would show up at some point. I went to one of the study rooms, popped the champagne, and poured it in my water bottle. Everyone threw food on the table, and we had fun. Poppy, Quinn's girlfriend, texted Gigi but got no response. Quinn, Poppy, Julz, Saw, and I passed the champagne between us, and we thought it was strange Gigi never showed."

"Then what?" I asked.

Dutch stood up and casually paced around the small open space. "Quinn drove us to school."

I mentally pinned this conversation to circle back at some point because I wanted him to keep talking. The drinking and driving lecture was for another time. It had probably only been six sips of champagne, but it still wasn't cool.

"Did you look in Gigi's backpack?" I asked.

"In the car I did. I thought about putting the champagne bottle in there before I turned in the backpack. But I changed my mind when I remembered she had apologized for the rumors. I think she actually felt bad she'd started them, so I left the bottle in the car. She was going to put it in the old steam tunnel and retrieve and dump it later. There are these tunnels that run under the buildings."

"I know about the tunnels."

"Ok. Like I was saying, I opened her backpack to put the bottle in it when I saw my name on the folder she kept our project in, so I pulled that out. I didn't really look at the rest of the bag. I sent her a text—by this time I had her number—saying I was leaving the backpack at the main office.

"I thought nothing of it until fifth period, when I got called to Principal Hayes's office. The police were there, asking what I had seen. Everything I told them was true, beginning with me walking through the woods on the way to the library and that I had seen her in the overflow parking lot. The village snowplows were parked there, so I only had a partial view. At first, I didn't even know if it was her, but I saw her pink and purple backpack on the ground. Two other people confirmed they saw her walking near the plows as they drove past. A teacher drove past as well and confirmed seeing her walking with the backpack. Because of the plows and because I was looking at my phone, I didn't see what type of car."

"Do you have any idea why the police were called so fast?" I said.

"Poppy, Quinn's girlfriend, told me later that Gigi had been skipping first period two days a week, and the school called her stepmom and I guess she got into trouble. Her parents put one of those tracking apps on her phone. Her phone got turned off near the time I saw her. When her stepmom called the school to verify if she was there, the secretary said something about me dropping off her bag, and I guess that's when they called the police. I don't think the police took it too seriously at first because of her skipping school for weeks."

"What did you think? Could you see her running away?" I asked.

"Not really," Dutch said.

We listened as the wind twirled in the trees and watched a rabbit nibble on a small patch of grass. I thought Dutch was going to run or collapse like a sobbing baby. He balanced on his heels before he spun around and dropped on the bench.

"What else is there? You can tell me," I said.

He reached into his pocket and pulled out a sheet of paper. He held it out to let me read it.

I hadn't been ready for this one.

THIRTY-TWO

T,
You are better
Sorry
—H

"What does this mean? *T*? *H*?" I asked.

"Theo and Hannah. Our actual names. That night that we drove around, we talked about leaving Dome and what it was like once you lifted the lid and left this biodome and got to leave Gigi and Dutch behind. As far as the note, we always joked who was the better writer on the school newspaper, so I am assuming it was about that."

"But you are not a hundred percent sure?"

"I don't know anymore. Why would she write it down and leave for me to find in her backpack. Anyone could have picked it up and taken it to school I keep going over every conversation we had. Does that relate in any way to when Bo left? Was there a note? Can we talk to her?"

Just when Dutch should have been relieved because they'd found Gigi, I had to tell him Bo was missing.

Occasionally, a ray of sunlight streamed through the trees, giving us brief moments of sunshine. The sunlight was like the thoughts in my head weaving in and out. All of it slowly coming together.

Why wasn't Dutch more relaxed? If he had done nothing wrong, he should have been fine that Gigi was back. She had been saying his name, but maybe that went back to when she was first pulled into the car and was asking for his help.

I had to choose my words carefully. I wished I'd paid more attention to those articles about reading people's reactions and how to look for small clues to see if they're hiding something.

"Bo is missing. She has not been seen since early evening yesterday."

The blank look on his face was pretty telling. This revelation was a surprise unless he was a talented actor.

"What do the police say, or do you think she just left again?" Dutch asked.

"It's hard to say, and unfortunately, it hasn't been twenty-four hours and she's an adult, so Maz can't report it yet."

"I just want it to be done. When I heard Gigi was found, I was so happy and then her parents attacked me, and it just keeps going. Why me?"

There was no whining in his voice, and I wasn't sure he was aware he had spoken the last part out loud.

I picked up a twig and started fidgeting with it. It crumbled in my hands. I wiped the dirt away and soaked in the sunshine.

I needed to carefully steer the conversation in one direction but in a very roundabout way.

"After this is all over and you go to college, you can get as far away from here as possible. Will it be back to London, or are you going to settle here, figuring the worst thing that could happen already has occurred, and you can live out a peaceful life in Dome?"

The change in topic rattled him, and he took his time answering,

"I'm going to Madison for college, but afterwards, I'm not sure. Downtown would be cool or maybe somewhere warm. I don't have a desire to stay in the Dome. It's not bad. I just want something different."

"My son talks about living in the house he grew up in—I still live there—and making it cool. I don't know his definition of cool, but I currently like it. What about you? You have any say in the renovations?"

"Not really."

"At least when you're back in the house, you won't have to walk this path again. The bird section is just on the other side of the library."

"Actually, the house is in the constellation section, but just barely," Dutch replied without answering my unasked question, so I had to press on. "What do you mean? This is Dome; all houses are in a section."

"I just mean the property line is questionable, and most of the yard ends up being in the city of Nallwhit. Come fall time, the leaves are a pain to rake up. I'll not be taking over that house."

"Wait a minute. Help with my old-lady memory. Is the house you're renovating the same house where your dad lived back when he was in high school?"

Dutch nodded. "There will only be two generations of Van Dijk's owning that house and not a third unless some random cousin pops up at this point."

We lapsed into silence again and went back to rabbit watching.

"Is there anything I should be doing? Even though GiGi is safe, I still feel like I should have some answers or being doing something. It's like it's not over," Dutch said.

"I wish I had the right answer for you. Part of that is because Maz, Leo, and I telling you about Bo leaving all those years ago was like us anchoring you to another problem that was not yours. It probably was not fair to you, but our intentions were always meant to be helpful. As for right now, if you did nothing wrong, you have nothing to worry about."

Dutch jumped up. "*If* I did nothing wrong? I didn't do anything!"

"Sit down." I pointed to the bench, but he stayed standing. "I'm just saying you didn't do anything wrong so you have nothing to worry about. Gigi, god willing, will make a complete recovery and can recount what happened to her. You will be fine."

"What if she doesn't or lies?"

"Don't start on the what-ifs. That will drive you crazy," I said.

He looked at his phone and said, "I gotta go."

"So fast?"

"Quinn had swim practice, and I've been waiting for him."

He put his foot on the bench and flexed it. The white rubber base of the shoe had turned red.

My head swirled with all the pieces lining up. He stood up and flipped back his hair. My head swirled another way, and my stomach flopped.

He grabbed his backpack again, throwing it on in front of him.

"Wait!" I said a little too loudly. "Just give me an answer, and I'll let you go. Do you have a girlfriend or a curfew?"

"Why do you ask?"

"Just struggling with my kids when they come home. They're just a few years older than you. Taking an informal survey if I hover too much."

"I don't have a girlfriend and not really a curfew."

"What do you mean, no real curfew?"

"My father never really cares about what time I get home as long as it's before midnight or he knows where I am or who I'm with."

"Do you have a tracking app on your phone?" I asked.

"We put it on our phones while we were in London. My mother

isn't the best with directions, and she was worried I would get lost in the city. Not sure it's working since the last phone update."

"Which app? My kids and I have one, more for safety than parental hawking."

Dutch swiped a few buttons on his phone and showed me the app. "Take a look. It's pretty easy to use."

"I'll hold your phone while you tie your shoes."

He handed the phone to me and bent down to tie his shoe.

"See, too much mothering—but I can't let you walk away with your shoes being untied. Maybe I shouldn't upgrade our tracking app."

He gave me a courteous laugh and didn't notice me fiddling with his phone while he fixed his shoes. I wanted to ask more about his mom, but I didn't know how to steer that conversation without looking like I was stalking his dad.

Dutch took his phone back, and I tried to reassure him everything would be fine, Gigi would heal, she would clear up any confusion about calling his name, and we'd find Bo.

I wanted to hug him as if that would make my words true and my lies less damning.

THIRTY-THREE

Dutch left me on the bench. I followed a minute later, standing in the full sun on the edge of the woods, looking at centerfield, and watching him cut through the grass to the high school parking lot, when I started to shake.

Without realizing it, I was back to where I had been thirty-four years ago. Literally standing in the same spot, asking myself what I would do to protect Bo, and now asking what I'd do to protect myself.

I picked up a stick and broke it into a hundred pieces, channeling my nerves out of my body. The shaking stopped, but my heart was bouncing out of control so I closed my eyes, inhaled the fresh air, and let the sun's rays ground me mentally and physically.

My thoughts returned to Bo. She must have planned something, otherwise why would she make Maz promise not to go to the police? Right now, I didn't have enough to tell them anything but my suspicions. I couldn't count on Maz to make a rational decision, and Leo apparently had something else to do, so it was up to me to find Bo.

I didn't know what scared me more . . . finding Bo or finding out what she was willing to say.

WORBY?

THIRTY-FOUR

I walked back to my car in front of Hattie's and saw someone pick up a flyer about the vigil from the sidewalk and toss it in the garbage. Word spread fast when someone like Gigi was lost and found. Of course, people were upset Hattie's was closed, but was anyone concerned about Hattie? Once again, Bo was gone and no one in Dome noticed. I hadn't even really seen her when I'd come in a few days ago. I'd only seen Hattie as a boss and owner, more like a character in a play versus a real-life person.

Across the street, a woman took two little kids into the library for weekend story time. I wondered if they would check out books, and if they had ever left a mitten behind so they could search lost and found. Imagine the joy they would get from playing hide-and-seek in the tunnels.

I dug in my pocket for my car keys and came up empty. I'd had them when I left the house. I would have heard them drop on the sidewalk or Hattie's kitchen tile floor. That left the library or woods, so I retraced my steps to the library. Walking in this time with a simple mission of looking for keys should have been easy. Past the reception desk and computers, I found a group of blue chairs and plopped myself down.

Two toddlers ran past, and their mothers just watched them go. One elderly gentleman was reading the newspaper and there was more, but everyone and everything just blurred away.

My mind went to that morning thirty-four years ago, and I saw everything clearly.

I had been so careful that morning. Preplanning was key, and I'd actually planned my morning conversation with my folks. Not too much talking, not too little, just the usual chatter. It had turned out better than expected. My dad had left early, and my mother had been preoccupied giving me instructions for starting that evening's dinner to notice anything.

Stew was getting out of the shower when I left. He only ever showed up for a morning library session if he desperately needed help on homework, and that was rare. His 4.0 GPA was as annoying as his farts in a car. I'd known I wouldn't have to worry about him getting up early. He was more than pleased when I went to the library early, and we didn't have to fight about sharing the car.

In my hand was a Hot Pocket for breakfast as I casually left the house, using my nerves to count and pace my steps, mentally walking through my part in our plan.

After eating the Hot Pocket, two blocks from my house, I began mumbling the words that would become my mantra in life when sometimes just a simple *oh shit* would do.

Each step I took, I said a word. I had to control body and speed. Nothing could be out of the ordinary.

Woods. Step. *Olsen.* Step. *Rook.* Step. *Bo.* Step.

And repeat.

Woods. Step. *Olsen.* Step. *Rook.* Step. *Bo. Step.*
WORB.

Slow and steady was the way I had to go. I had learned that line from a Donald Duck book—slow and steady, steady and slow, that is the way to go. If I hadn't ran on this walk before, I couldn't run that day.

The weather was doing its job, and the rain was starting. My hood was up, and my jeans were cinched at the bottom and rolled like '80s fashion demanded. I would have preferred my black shoes, but they didn't match the plan. My walk took me to the woods behind the SMF factory, where I dropped my pink backpack and picked up Bo's identical one. There wasn't much variation in our book bags back then. Most everyone had same type of backpack. Everything I owned was a deep-dark color tone. I thought the pink backpack was funny against my normal style and that it made some type of statement. I didn't know what kind of statement I was trying to make that year, but a bright-pink backpack was going to be it for me. Bo had come to school that January with the exact bag I was now carrying out of the woods.

My shoes were muddy from the path, and I walked on the grass behind the baseball field. The Hot Pocket was long gone, and my stomach turned a bit. I could hear my mother's voice about eating right, especially on a school day, but I had to push her voice away so I repeated my list. This time, I added a check after the first step.

Woods ✓

Olsen

Rook

Bottle

At any point, any one of us could have backed out, but I knew the second I stepped out of the woods, there was no stopping me. From the woods to Edward Olsen. Maz was waiting for me across the street from the baseball diamond. He saw me approaching once I rounded left field but would not look at me directly. I feared he might be the weak link in our plan, but he showed up on time maybe because he still believed in what we were doing, or he was scared we would kick his ass if he backed out now.

We barely exchanged hellos. Maz was bouncing back and forth on his feet. I asked if he had what he was supposed to bring, and he nodded. We took a few steps, playfully sparring with each other. A simple jab and a light shove. We had to really slow our walk down because timing was critical. Maz walked backwards and tugged on my backpack, and we held this stance for two minutes.

Finally, his eyes went wide. His face shimmered with sweat. I tugged hard on the bag. He pulled harder, and he/we flung my bag into the street. I went to retrieve it, forcing the oncoming car to swerve.

The brown four-door sedan pulled over.

Holy shit, it worked!

Mr. Edward Olsen pulled over in front of us, but Mrs. Canslow, the art teacher, stopped behind us. I pretended to trip when I went to pick up my bag.

The rain was coming down at a pretty good rate at this point. I kicked Maz as I fell, and that must have finally triggered something inside him.

He yelled to Mrs. Canslow, "We're fine. Don't get out; you'll get wet."

I jumped up, gave a wave in her direction and a half embrace to Maz as if this was all fun and not something serious. Supervision from teachers in the '80s, it seemed, was based on the weather because Mrs. Canslow stayed in her car. I'll give credit to Olsen for stopping to help some kids, but then again, it involuntarily enlisted him into our plan.

Mrs. Canslow watched as Olsen picked up my bag, and he waved her off. We told him we were on the way to the library, and he offered us a ride. Middle school teachers, police officers, and village merchants parked in the village overflow lot next to the police station and between the middle school and library.

We let Olsen get inside the building before we ran after him and found him walking from the office. I said my book must have fallen out in his car. He turned to walk out with us, but Maz made a point of the rain and how clumsy I was. He suggested I go out alone, and Olsen tossed me his key. The key ring with the rook chess piece on it. I told Maz he was a wimp and left them standing there. Maz walked with Olsen to his classroom, making sure he didn't see me go left past the cafeteria towards the gym, into the maintenance room, and finally down to the steam tunnels.

Each step was working as planned. I wasn't nervous; it was like this was my eighty-seventh performance in a play, and I was operating like a well-rehearsed actor. At the same time, I felt like I was watching my own performance from the ceiling stage lights.

My biggest concern was navigating my way through the tunnels. There had been no way to rehearse the route, but I followed Leo's detailed instructions. The steam tunnels had been shut down for a few years after a more efficient heating and cooling system was installed. Each tunnel held a single overhead light bulb and was mercifully clear of any rodents. Leo had emphasized not touching the walls or pipes because we could leave a trace that we were there. He'd really highlighted the fact that ceiling height varied, and we needed to be careful.

There was something poetic about seeing Bo then. I realized we were probably at midpoint, which meant we were closest to the police station. A wrong turn, and we could be in the tunnel that led to the firing range.

We met each other's eyes but didn't speak. We exchanged key rings. I took the key Leo had given her for the tunnel door, and I gave her Olsen's key ring. She slipped it into her pocket.

I gave her my jacket and her backpack, and I walked away.

Bo put her hand on my arm but said nothing. She took off towards the middle school.

Leo had warned us it would be hot, but I hadn't realized just how hot he meant. It was suffocating, and I wanted out but didn't want to rush it.

Woods ✓

Step

Olsen ✓

Step

Rook ✓

Step

Bottle

Step

I climbed the short stairs to the library basement door, reviewed the plan, and pushed open the door to the storage room in the basement.

Everything was still clicking into place. However, sweat poured from me, and I panicked because I looked like a mess. After I exited the basement storage area, I was supposed to be circulating with the crowd and be seen, but I had to stop in the bathroom.

Inside the restroom was MayMay. She gave me one long stare before she said, "So the rain got you too?"

"Absolutely dreadful," I replied, using paper towels to wipe the rain/sweat from my face, and left the bathroom.

The open table section was full of regulars. My book bag and my second jacket hung on the back of a chair.

To my left, the first table held an orange and yellow rain jacket, yellow hat and orange umbrella, everything very matching but the seat was empty. There was one notebook on the table.

Leo was at the third table with a notebook and textbook out as if he was actually doing homework. His body was rigid, but his head pivoted from the notebook to the textbook to me several times before his shoulders dropped. His wide eyes pressed so many questions my way, and all I could do was give him a simple nod.

We were running short on time, so I made my way to the common area and chatted with as many folks as I could. When some got up to head to the high school, I gathered my jacket and book bag and walked out with them, even telling MayMay I would see her in five minutes after our second rain shower of the day. Everyone went running for their cars, and I retreated two steps back into the library.

Maybe it was ignorance, but not having a cell phone tracing our movements and security cameras tracking us really made things easier.

Leo was waiting for me. I slipped him the tunnel key and grabbed the notebook and put on Bo's raincoat, hat, and pulled up the hood while Leo stood guard. I kept my head down as we trotted past the reception desk.

Mrs. Layne, the morning librarian, walked up and left us with this treasured nugget: "Bo, be sure to share your umbrella with that nice young man who is too proud to carry his own."

Under his breath, Leo said, "Holy shit, that just happened."

Everything was working, except Maz had never showed up.

We stood between the entryway doors, waiting for Leo to find his car keys, but his hands were shaking.

The hot-air blowers in the double entryway were suffocating me like the steam tunnel. I jumped outside, not so much for fresh cold air but the space. The open space and away from our plan. In that moment, I grasped the reality of the role I was playing.

I stood there in the rain until Leo pulled me by the elbow to his car and opened the passenger door for me. We didn't speak during the five-block drive to the high school parking lot.

Leo stopped short, nearly bumping into the car in front of us at the one stop sign on the short drive to school, and took the turn too short and rode the curb. I kept my head down and slid out without as so much as a goodbye as soon as he put the car into park. There was no need to count my steps or slow my pace in the rain.

Woods ✓

Olsen ✓

Rook ✓

Bottle

I had the school day as a safe zone before the last—well, the *next* step. At the time, I thought it was the last step.

Thunder cracked in the distance, and kids were running from the parking lot. Even the Corner kids had to halt their smoking habit that morning. Snow and ice they would be there smoking, but rain and thunder had them going without their last smoke before class.

I went straight for the locker room near the gym and pool area. No one would be there yet, and if someone was early for first-period gym class, there were enough rows to slink into and remove Bo's hat and jacket. I tossed them in a bag and into a locker. I would later retrieve the rain gear. There was no fear of anyone stealing it. Someone might steal a coat from your book locker or something from a car, but no one went snooping through the gym lockers for dirty gym clothes. And, most definitely, no one would want a neon-yellow and orange raincoat.

Nerves were setting in on me. First-period French, I answered two questions immediately, knowing I would be ignored for the rest of the class, and I sank into a fog.

It was like the intermission of the play. I went over all the steps in my head, making sure I missed nothing. The second act was coming up, and I had to get through the day. In the hallway next to my second class, Maz was at his locker. He told me Lowman had offered him a ride, and it hadn't made sense to continue walking in the rain, so he'd just gone with him instead of coming into the library.

He also said the handoff had been almost flawless. Bo, never having attended that middle school, had taken a few wrong turns navigating the hallway. Maz had hovered in the classroom doorway and acted like she had given him Olsen's car keys. Maz tossed Olsen a key ring back—but Olsen had two key rings. Each one had a small wooden chess piece with a hole drilled through it. His house or apartment key was on a ring with a knight, and the car key had a rook on the ring. Last year, some kids in shop class had made the key rings for him.

Olsen caught the key ring Maz had tossed him and put it into his canvas bag with two of his chessboards.

The rest of the day sailed by smoothly. The rain let up, and I had Jam drive me to the library before her shift at Hattie's. I wasn't a member of the chess club but would hang around when friends were playing.

That morning when I was putting on Bo's raincoat, Leo had slipped a pint of vodka in my backpack. I made my way over to where three chess games were going on and Olsen was mentoring students. I let my backpack fall open and some stuff spill out, and while I was on the ground, I dropped the bottle into Olsen's canvas bag.

Leo suggested leaving the bottle as a backup plan, and I thought it was a pretty good idea. He even got bonus points for saying it should only be water in the bottle in case one of us got caught with it.

I thought, of everything we did that day, Leo had the hardest part. He was more or less admitting to Olsen that something was going on. Olsen usually left the chess club shortly before five, and that day was no exception. Leo was following closely behind him. Maz and I had the job of cutting off anyone if they tried talking to Leo or Olsen on the way to the parking lot.

Maz and I hung back near the library and watched the exchange between them. Leo later told us that Olsen had walked towards where he parked his car and looked around for it. Leo said he hadn't waited long before he offered Olsen a ride. Olsen said he didn't think it was right for him to have a student drive him home, so Leo countered with "How else will you get home at this point." We knew he couldn't file a police report.

Olsen had let it slip once that he had no car insurance. He tried playing it off as being a teacher who makes no money. He was caught between being a teacher and trying to fit in.

After a day of talking to seventh and eighth graders, sometimes he said too much to us high school students. He had not been in Dome long, and some of us had never had him as a teacher. We only knew him as the cool young guy in the library that made chess fun.

Remember when I said we didn't give teachers nicknames, and the closest one ever got was Olsen—just vodka, just mouthwash, or just too much.

Leo had his uncle the sheriff pull up his rap sheet. He told Leo, under the strictest confidence, that Olsen had several driving-under-the-influence charges on his record. I thought his uncle was trying to scare Leo straight, but he had just handed Leo some hard facts about a teacher. Sometimes even responsible adults could tell kids too much.

It didn't take much for Olsen to accept the ride. Leo offered for his uncle to run the car plates to see if something turned up. Olsen really pushed back on not accepting the ride to school the next day, but Leo said it wasn't a problem and, hopefully overnight, his uncle might be able to locate the stolen car.

Leo said Olsen lived six miles from Dome in a depressing-looking apartment building that had more vacant parking space and for rent signs than it probably had renters.

The next morning, Leo picked up Olsen and said no report yet, but maybe later that day. Olsen told him a friend was going to take him home that afternoon. Leo said Olsen looked like he'd barely slept, barely spoke on the way to school, and insisted he be dropped off on the far side of the overflow parking lot.

When Maz and I watched them drive away from behind the bushes, he started talking a mile a minute, asking questions without waiting for any answers, probably because he knew I didn't have any.

Did we do this? Did it work? Is Olsen going to kill us? Are we getting kicked out of school? Where do you think she is?

That last question bitch-slapped me across my face. I bent over forward, placed my hands on my knees trying to catch my breath, not out of relief or terror for Bo.

Every step this morning was about what I'd had to do. I mentally checked off Woods, Olsen, Rook, Bottle.

Even when I'd seen Bo in the tunnel, it hadn't been about her. She didn't even get a ✔ by her name. Never once had I thought about her.

I left Maz standing there and walked away with tears streaming down my cheeks.

Just like now, I hadn't been thinking about Bo or Gigi. Always thinking about myself and especially about how the next twenty-four hours would impact the rest of my life, and would Bo tell everyone our secret?

THIRTY-FIVE

"Do you think she's ok?"

Two girls were laughing, and I realized they were talking about me.

Back to reality, I thought.

I wasn't sure how long I'd been sitting in the chair in the open study area of the library. I got up and walked to room five. My heart flopped when no one was in the room nor were my keys.

We had told Dutch someone would always be there for him, and I had sorta hoped someone would be in room five for me. The emptiness cut deeper when I compared this moment to a recurring nightmare I had twice a year about being the only one working on a high school group project assignment. I would scream at people in my dream to get them to hear me, but my voice couldn't leave my body.

I left the library without asking anyone about my keys and figured they were in the woods.

Stew texted that I should meet him at the diner in fifteen minutes. I was about to tell him to come pick me up when Leo's truck pulled up in front of me.

He rolled down his window. "Get in."

"Déjà vu," I said. "Not today. I don't need rescuing."

"No rescue, but an explanation."

I was curious what crap he would come up with but not enough not to ask him to explain, so I told him to save it for another time and kept walking. He followed in his truck and yelled to just give him one shot. I stopped walking mainly because it would be a double win for me: I could laugh at his explanation about having a wife, and I could get a ride to the diner.

Leo unlocked the door, and I hoisted myself up.

He said, "Push my stuff to the side or toss it in back."

I tossed a hat and notebook onto the back seat.

"Can you move—" Leo said.

"I need a ride to the diner."

He just nodded.

I had to give Leo credit. He knew when to shut up. A similar skill Joe—my ex—had, and that gave me goosebumps.

Leo saved his explanation for a later time. Halfway to the restaurant, I received an email from my desperately needed but slightly ethically questionable job prospect, the megachurch, stating my future employment required further background information. I couldn't imagine what they needed to explore. Had that reporter immediately called the church office and used my name already on a Saturday afternoon?

I was looking at a future of no's. No income, no sex with married men, no answers about Bo and Gigi. I just wished my day had stopped there. I couldn't think about the lack of income. I just had to freeze that out of my head.

The restaurant parking lot was half-full, and Stew's truck was nowhere to be found, so I had time to ditch Leo without having to explain him to Stew. We had to wait for two cars to leave before he could maneuver his truck into the right size parking spot.

"Thanks for the ride. I'll give you and Maz any information I find out," I said.

"I'm coming in there with you."

"There was no invite. I just needed a ride."

"It's a restaurant. I'm going to eat too. I thought you might be good company even if you won't let me explain," Leo said.

I hopped out as he was adjusting the position of the truck for the third time.

He yelled, "Most people wait until it's in park to leave a vehicle."

He was still maneuvering his truck when I pulled open the first door. The flyer for the candlelight vigil was still up. Someone had scrawled *Bitch be found, save your candles* across it. Shock ran through me. I yanked it down and tore it in half. Kids could be cruel when they thought they were being funny.

My rage against teenagers sent me clambering into the dining room. My head spun back to see if I'd damaged anything when I'd flung the second door into the bulletin board. Unfortunately, I kept walking as I looked back and stepped into Monica carrying a full tray of dirty dishes.

Simultaneously, cold and warm liquid cascaded over the half collar of my North Face pullover and streamed like a babbling river into the crevasse between my boobs and pooled at the elastic band. I dry heaved when the smell of half-eaten scrambled eggs and breakfast potatoes clung to my fleece.

Instinctively, I jumped back but slipped a little. My leg kicked out at the same time as an empty orange juice glass was dropping. My foot connected with the glass when I jumped. The glass went flying over a customer's head into the large coffee urn behind the counter. The clink of glass against the metal sent the customers into a large round of applause.

Warm syrup pooled on the top of my hand as it ran down my sleeve. Monica brushed off some gravy and a chunk of biscuit from my fleece with a rag. I ran my hand across my neck and could feel some unidentified chunkage, which rolled under my fingernails. I dry heaved again, and Monica pushed me towards the bathroom.

In the bathroom, I threw off my fleece and top. I was pumping soap into my hands when Monica walked in with a shirt and an empty garbage bag. She left without saying anything.

My face had been spared of food and beverage debris, but my neck and chest hadn't fared so well. I could have done without the brown paper towel exfoliated skin treatment I gave my neck and chest. Across my chest, I was leaving a collage of paper towel lint when removing the congealed substance.

It was a mix of tears and laughter when I pulled out two hash browns from my sports bra. No spot cleaning could resuscitate my bra, so I swapped it for the shirt Monica had brought in, and I threw my clothes into the garbage bag. My leggings were clear except for a small spot of juice near my ankle.

I gathered my garbage bag and went into a stall. Two girls came in to use the mirror, and I couldn't help but eavesdrop.

"I told you she was faking it," said Girl Number One.

"How can you say that? She's in the hospital, nearly dead," Girl Number Two said.

"Not the kidnapping or whatever you call it. The boyfriend. If he was so amazing, why didn't he come forward to grieve or support her family?" Girl Number One said.

"Maybe he's the guilty one," replied Girl Number Two.

"Doubt it. Although you could never trust her judgment. Remember when she suggested you wear that green dress for the homecoming dance? That wasn't good. Besides, if he was the man she said he was, he would have come forward. So I call BS on this so-called boyfriend or whatever she called him, what was it—oh yeah, her 'man-friend,' just because he wasn't in high school."

"I bet he was hot. She would never go for an ugly dude. Oh, maybe that was it. He wasn't good-looking, and she had to keep him hidden." Girl Number two laughed.

"Damn, I owe her some cash, but thank god, she's back before finals. I need her *vitamins* and—"

The bathroom door opened and shut again without me hearing the rest of their debate on Gigi's character and what she was able to contribute to their final exams and why the funny emphasis on vitamins.

Sitting on the toilet listening to the girls, I had time to read the long sleeve T-shirt I was wearing. I would have to spend the afternoon promoting the diner. After I washed my hands for the fourth time, I returned to the dining room for a second round of applause.

Leo was sitting at a table in the middle of the room and didn't turn or applaud with the other diners. Still feeling defeated and trudging into a melancholy mood, I lost my gusto to avoid him. I should not have been surprised when I got closer and saw the back of his shirt, and again, I recognized the smudge logo.

I plopped down opposite him.

With a straight face, he said, "Nice outfit. Imitation is the sincerest form of flattery, thank you. Your black T-shirt wasn't close enough to mine so you got a matching diner shirt. That's flattering. It's a fine-looking shirt."

"Not really. At least this shirt you can read. You buy yours off the discount rack?"

"Remember, I own the print sign and shirt press company. We have the account for the diner, and I was trying out a new press and I screwed it up. The shirt is still good, even if the logo is blurred."

"Define good," I said.

Monica put a coffee mug in front of me.

"Thanks, but I had enough coffee for the day."

"It's not coffee. It's chicken soup broth, and here's some warm bread. Eat and drink. It'll do you some good, and it'll help wipe away the last five minutes," Monica said. Then she weirdly continued to push her agenda. "If I can make a suggestion, dip the bread in the broth. Believe it or not, it's better than butter."

I did as I was told. It was as comforting as fire in the fireplace on a winter night with a bowl of buttered popcorn and my favorite show. If it had been served with a pour of whiskey, I would have added to my daydream a well-built man sitting between me and the fireplace. Instead, I was staring at Leo with our fourth matching outfit in under twenty-four hours.

Leo went back to letting the silence hang over us. That was better than the hug I had been looking for back in room five.

I contemplated my morning, going over everything I'd learned and thought I knew. Gigi had been lost and was now found, and Bo was lost. Something had happened to Gigi, and Bo was trying to help her.

Without asking or taking my order a few minutes later, Monica delivered a grilled cheese sandwich with a side of mac and cheese for me and chili for Leo. I asked for the check, which she produced on the spot.

"What about the shirt? How much do I owe for it?" I asked.

Leo said, "I'll throw an extra shirt on the order coming this week."

That seemed to satisfy Monica, and she waited for Stew to take the seat next to me. Without looking at the menu, he ordered chili and a Coke. In the last fifteen minutes, I had forgotten about Stew coming for lunch.

"You couldn't wait for me to order? I'm five minutes early."

"You look like a mess." I couldn't help myself.

"I just got done with a run. Since you don't recognize it, let me explain what exercise looks like," Stew said.

"Fine, you win whatever point you were trying to make. I don't have the energy for you this afternoon."

"Rough morning?" he asked.

Thankfully, I didn't have to answer because Monica dropped off the soda, and the men chatted about college basketball. I excused myself to use the restroom because three people at this table suddenly felt overwhelming.

I tossed a little water on my face and came out and stood at the large window opposite the bathrooms. I got lost thinking back to when this had all started.

Bo had really been a stranger to us back then. She had started school in January and had been gone by April. It was one afternoon in early February I suspected something about Bo's shitty home life. After avoiding me for several days, she finally told her secret or her lie. We were working on our world literature assignment in the back of the old library. She reached for a book on the top shelf of the stacks, and I saw a bruise on her side.

She was reluctant to say anything at first, but then it finally poured out of her. The abuse, the constant moving, only taking clothes with them because that's what fit in the car, the loneliness, trying to be perfect, thinking that would make it all stop. The whole time she spoke, there were no tears, no anger, just a steady narration as if she was reading from a book.

I wasn't sure how, but we ended up sitting on the floor. I felt like I was holding the rows of books on my shoulders. The weight of her words pushed me into the carpet, and I was worried it could vacuum me up. When she stopped talking, I didn't know what to do. I knew it was serious, and that would stop gossipy little me from telling anyone.

Some stories are shared, but some are just too big to comprehend.

When I said nothing, she finally said, "That's why I don't tell many people because they have nothing to say, and somehow it becomes their problem." She stood up, looked down at me, and said, "I could get into trouble if someone finds out."

"Why would you get in trouble?" I asked.

"Forget about it. You don't understand. Just be quiet," Bo said.

A book dropped in the next row over, and Bo's stoic face dropped.

She rushed to the end. "Keep your mouths shut," she said to whoever was on the other side and walked away without looking back.

Maz and Leo came around the corner and sat down with me. I had known Maz since fourth grade. Leo, being a year ahead of us, I only knew from our morning time at the library. Leo asked if I was ok, and I laughed at the irony of me receiving sympathy from just hearing Bo's miserable story, but then again, she wasn't around to accept it and she hadn't appeared to be looking for any.

The next two days, I couldn't find her at the end of the long lunch tables sitting by herself, and I didn't know where she was. I shared two classes with her, and she suddenly became the last person in the room when the bell rang and the first one out. I was more shaken the next two days than during any part of the next three decades because I couldn't shake that wretched feeling from hearing about Bo's home life.

Wednesday after the last bell rang, Maz and Leo pulled Bo into an empty classroom and closed the door, and I quickly followed them. She walked to the far wall, putting distance between herself and them. They stayed in the middle of the room, and I remained near the door. I didn't know what they were going to do or say.

Leo and Maz said they hadn't really meant to eavesdrop on our conversation. Maz suggested she go talk to Mrs. Kaplin, one of the school counselors.

Bo laughed at them. "No thanks. Not in the mood to move again. I was hoping to make it to the end of the school year. You can't help. Don't worry, I can take care of myself. Just keep quiet."

I couldn't believe her courage. I was withering away in the doorway corner because I couldn't handle any part of this conversation, and here Bo was rejecting help.

The boys kept talking, but she shut them down. "Fine, if you want to help, then find a way for me to get to Colorado and away from hell." She stared at them and finally over at me. "There's a retreat co-op center where I can live. I just have to get there." We were all quiet, and she finally said, "That's what I thought. All talk. Don't bother me anymore."

After she left, the three of us sat down in Ms. Ganel's classroom, and we started thinking about how we could get her out of Dome.

Monica snapped me back to present day. "Hon, are you all right? I'm not talking about our dance by the front door. You seem to be lost in space."

I had no desire to share my thoughts with Monica. However, it was touching to know a stranger can spot someone in trouble and would reach out to them.

It suddenly hit me. I had to find Bo now. I couldn't believe I was saying this after all these years. Had she played us? Had it been our plan or hers? I wondered if the boys had done anything outside of the original plan.

THIRTY-SIX

"You ok? You were gone awhile," Stew said.

"I just returned a phone call, and I got another one to make. Just came back for some water." There was no way I was going to get Stew off my back. He would insist on looking for my car keys with me, and I would have to endure listening to him mock me for consistently losing or forgetting my keys, so I came up with Plan B.

I left the boys to make the phone call, but actually I swiped Stew's car keys and left out the side door. It took me longer than I would have liked. I had forgotten he had Kay's car because of the flat tire this morning. Three blocks later, I pulled over and shot Stew a text.

Thanks for the car.

Will return it in a few hours. If you don't complain, I'll get it washed.

Leo can give you a ride home.

Don't bother replying

I drove through the parkway looking for any signs of where they'd found Gigi this morning. Even growing up in Dome, I was always confused by the streets in the parkway. I never knew if the good sliding hill was the second turn or if that was the botanical garden center. My thoughts weaved through my head like the streets crisscrossing in the parkway.

A car beeped behind me. I realized I was barely going ten miles an hour, so I pulled into a picnic area parking lot.

It was the same now as it had been when I'd grown up here; we never had to break the safety capsule of Dome because all the answers were here.

Ten minutes after leaving the diner, I finally pieced it all together.

THIRTY-SEVEN

Two policemen were standing in front of their squad cars one block into the constellation section. I parked two blocks over, and when I got out, Leo pulled in behind me.

"I dropped off your brother and saw you coming out of the parkway. He wasn't as mad as I would have been. What's with the two of you? I would have been pissed, someone stranding me like that."

"Sometimes when we're together, we act like we're still teenagers who don't like one another, and other times, it's just fun to annoy him."

"I get it. Do you mind if I join you?" Leo asked.

"You might as well. This involves you. Plus, aren't you going to follow me regardless of what I say?"

"Probably, but can you give me a minute? I need a sweatshirt."

"You can put the gray one back on. As you can see, I've moved on." My arms crossed, I was suddenly very conscious I was braless again and could have used a sweatshirt.

"That would be nice, but someone pushed it onto the floor and got mud on it." He went to the back seat and fiddled with some boxes. He reappeared, tossing me a nice light-blue sweatshirt. "Turn it inside out so you don't look like a River Bend high school senior." His sweatshirt made him the River Bend varsity basketball coach. "I really don't make a habit of pilfering my clients' merchandise, but when I do, I replace everything, so feel free to keep it."

"Thanks, I guess."

That was our fifth matching outfit.

"I take it you have a plan, or there's some reason we're here?" Leo asked.

I just nodded.

We strolled through the neighborhood like a couple enjoying the weekend. We were not the only curious people on the street. A golden retriever found me very interesting and wouldn't let me pass without giving it some belly scratches.

The owner introduced himself and the dog, but I could only remember the dog's name.

DD's owner said, "The police are doing a door-to-door canvass of the area because of the girl that was found. I think they got most of the houses on the west side and are working their way over here."

We thanked him, said goodbye to DD, and continued our walk to the rear of the neighborhood. The cool weather kept the front doors shut, but most people had the blinds up or curtains pulled back to let the sun in.

The house I was looking for was at the end of a dead-end street that backed up to the parkway. It was easy to see the appeal of the house, for the beauty of the modern square structure contrasting to the rustic backdrop was eye-catching. The house was distinctly different from the ranch-style and colonial-style homes of the '60s and '70s when most of the houses in Dome had been built.

Bare trees were tipped with green buds, but plenty of dead leaves from the previous fall covered the lawn. I could understand Dutch's aversion to raking leaves. Backing up to the parkway, during the fall, it must have been a continuous stream of never-ending foliage.

"At some point, could you fill me in on what we're doing here? Wait, I remember this house. Back in high school or maybe my freshman year of college, some girl a year older had a wild party here the Friday after Thanksgiving. Not sure if I can remember who it was."

"Probably Mimi. She was the middle kid. I think Lemi the other girl was much older. Van was the youngest of the three kids in the family."

Leo said nothing.

I continued. "Van owns it now—"

"Want me to turn around?" Leo asked.

I ignored him. "They're renovating it, so no one is living here."

Shades were drawn on the large front windows and gave no insight if anyone was inside. Coming all this way, I wasn't about to turn around so I walked around the property. This tall modern straight-framed house differed from most every house in Dome but blended in, between the tall pine, birch and aspen trees that followed into the oak and maple trees of the parkway.

The driveway on the right side of the house led to the detached garage. There was a ladder lying on top of a tarp securing some construction materials in front of the garage door.

The neighboring house on the right was set at an angle to maximize privacy for both homes. The driveways ran parallel, only a few feet apart. The neighbor's front door was hidden from Dutch's driveway by a large garage and shrubbery. There was only one small window on the left side of the house. The closest house on the left was actually on the other side of the cul-de-sac. A large green space between the houses led to the parkway. It was understandable why this was such a desirable neighborhood.

The garage door had five large rectangle windows on the left side that mirrored the modern look of the house. No lights were on, but patio furniture was set up inside. It wasn't piled up in the corner and covered for the winter. The two chairs and couch were set up, facing each other for easy conversation. I could imagine this would be a great place for kids to hang out. The front door and rear doors didn't have any doorbell cameras that I could see.

The rear of the house had large sliding doors on the right that stepped out onto a deck that held no grill or empty flowerpots. Leaves and a garden hose were the only occupants of the deck, contrasting with the cozy space inside the garage. I wanted to check the lock on the rear door, but common sense told me to run. Leo walked along quietly.

Next to the sliding door was a large glass door, and I spied a beautiful modern kitchen, black cabinetry mixed with blond wood floors. Piled on the counter were spare floor planks, tarps, and a toolbox.

Straight ahead led to the living room, and to the right, in front of the sliding doors, sat a large table. No view of the living room from the kitchen prep area, and I suspected the only view of the backyard was through the sliding doors on my right. One would have to be at the kitchen table to enjoy the view of the parkway. I thought that was the only miss of an otherwise amazing home.

I raised my hand to knock when a figure approached from the living room.

It was only a hunch that had led me and Leo here. Now, everything came to mind: *run, call the police—still don't know what I would tell them—cry for joy, cry for sadness, laugh, hug, or just wait it out.*

I'd waited this long, and I figured that was all I could do: wait and follow her lead.

"Lou, come in." She pulled the door open, and I entered the house, but after that, I didn't know what to do, so I stepped to the side.

She touched my arm like she had in the tunnel. Leo took a step back on the deck, and it seemed to take him a second to connect the dots. I was still calculating what to do.

"I'm not surprised you found me."

Erasing decades, I could finally see Bo. Before me stood the lady with the black bob and all the bracelets from Hattie's. Her eyes had deep lines like most women our age. Her pale complexion was flawless; however, sweat was traced around her forehead. Her movements and words were deliberate, but her voice shook just a tad.

There was no doubt, after all these years, it was her.

"Really, I have been looking for thirty-four years. I figured it was finally time," I said.

Her voice raised with a smile. "Leo, good to see you."

Leo stepped inside and gave Bo a hug, which they held for a while. Leo's face and posture switched from rigid disbelief to genuine warmth. After they separated, he stepped back, ran his hands through his hair, and rubbed his chin. He held her shoulders, and they hugged again.

I was watching a beautiful reunion. Suddenly, I was sad, but I should have felt what Leo was feeling. I was jealous of his relief and bitter with my anger.

They let go, and Bo simply said, "Shut the door and come to the front room."

Leo did as he was told and looked at me with wide eyes.

I whispered, "It was only a guess she was here."

The family room had two midcentury-modern chairs with metal frames and a brown leather sling seat that actually looked comfortable. A folding table with a television sat on it with miles of cords and cables. I'd thought things were supposed to have fewer cords these days. Maybe when the renovation was complete, the electronics would get an upgrade.

Most of the blond flooring was covered with strips of protective brown paper covered in dusty and muddy foot tracks. There was an open modern staircase near the front door leading upstairs. The black floating steps were wrapped in an industrial plastic wrap. Paint cans and brushes lay near the front door.

She stood against the far left outside wall and gestured to the two chairs for us. I couldn't breach the space in the family room or break the decades of questions.

She became all business. "I prefer you don't stand where people can see you from the rear door."

"That's all you have to say?" I asked and sat in the chair against the kitchen wall Leo was leaning against.

There was no reply. It was as if I was talking to an empty house.

I had to make her acknowledge the present, so I said, "Would you at least text Maz and let him know you're ok?"

"I can't do that. Not until I finish this. I want to do this for all of you," Bo said.

"All of who? What are you talking about?" I asked. "You know you can't stay here. The police will be back."

"I figured as much, but I have to wait. I'll just tell the police I came over to borrow a cup of sugar, and the back door was open." Bo laughed. "He can't tell them otherwise. He has to come back and clean up his mess."

She turned her attention to Leo. "It's wonderful to see you. Of course, I never thought it would be like this. I had it playing out so differently. I actually hoped to see you at the cafe and surprise you."

"I'll be your first customer on Monday," Leo said with a smile. "Maybe I'll buy two weekly specials to make up for my absence from Hattie's."

Their reunion was a bitter aftertaste for me. "If you're here, it'll be bad for everyone. Please let Maz know you're ok, and let's leave."

I didn't tell her I had texted Maz when she and Leo were greeting each other. *She's fine, give me time*, it said.

My phone was silenced to all incoming messages. I had to know what she'd do and admit.

"This isn't about you," I said.

"Sure it is. She asked for advice or was it blackmail or me wanting to pay it forward?" Bo said playfully.

"People ask me for advice all the time, but it doesn't lead me to sitting at a possible crime scene. If you think something happened here it is not good for you to be here."

"Good for you for always doing the right thing. I am not worried about the police. I want him to understand what it means to hurt a teenage girl." There was no anger in her voice. It was almost robotic. Everything about her suddenly had a mechanical edge. She was here in front of us, but it could have been a mannequin. I questioned my reasoning for bringing Leo with me.

This could get messy.

I figured I had to give up something in order for her to really start talking, so I said, "Gigi figured out who you were."

Bo continued to stare at some imaginary target beneath the floating staircase, so I kept talking and confirmed my suspicions.

"She forced you to help her?"

"That's not bad. Actually pretty close, but disappointed in your choice of words. You see, I needed to pay it forward." She paced along the left side wall. Her hands seemed to have a slight tremor, but when she walked, she crossed her arms against her chest.

When she spoke this time, her voice softened, and there was a slight smile. "She pieced it together. Her father was the accountant for the previous owner, and I wanted to keep him as my accountant. I had to submit all my personal information. I was so nervous. Without realizing it, buying Hattie's was the culmination of everything I went through. The first month I owned Hattie's, on the way to the shop, I had tears of joy trickling down my face.

"Then one day, this girl comes in and doesn't have enough money on her. The girl at the register was going to deny her order.

I recognized her as one of the regulars though and, of course, as James's daughter. I told her she could pay for it tomorrow. She comes in the next day, and the same thing happens. She orders and has no cash or card. This time, I pulled her casually aside and said it wasn't acceptable. Then she says to put the charges on her account. And If I have trouble with one account number, use the other number. She handed me two nine-digit numbers and thought she had some blackmail story on me. She thinks I'm stealing from my mother. Her father had complained about the extra work some client is making him do, and later, Gigi saw his notes in his home office. She said there was no way a hippie from Oregon could have all that money to buy Hattie's without stealing it. She and that punk thought they could pull one over on me, but I have always prepared for this moment. I cut her off and knew to end it once and for all. I had to befriend her and use her father to tie up the legal loose ends.

"It turns out, the same time I was buying Hattie's, she started on a newspaper project. Maz became friends with the kids. He gave them too much freedom in the library basement. He and Martha were not so diligent with all those old school files they had pulled up from the tunnels and were supposed to be destroying. She connected the dots. I wasn't Yvette." She paused. "Let me back up a bit. This is all thanks to you."

"Me?" Ice went down my back. Where was she going with this? "You mean us. You, me, and Maz, Leo—and I guess—Olsen."

It had been such a mistake bringing Leo here if Bo was going to confess everything.

"This isn't the time to be modest. I owe everything to you. The true leap to freedom."

I dared not flinch or look at Leo.

She had a wistful voice as she told me the story. "I remember my eighth birthday. We were living outside Fort Worth. A month after my birthday, which wasn't celebrated or even mentioned, my mother allowed me to have one friend come over to the house to play. I had told my school friend, Shelly Hireck, it was my birthday.

"Shelly's mom came to the door with Shelly and gave me a present. Standing next to my mom, I could see her physically shift into a different person. My mom invited Mrs. Hireck into the house and became the perfect host. My mother had Shelly and me bake a cake and make frosting from scratch using an old cookbook that had been left in our rental house. We made our own party hats with cardboard boxes. During Shelly's visit, my mother acted as if this had been the plan the whole time.

"Throughout the three hours, Shelly's mom could not stop saying, 'Oh, Yvette, this is so much fun. Yvette, I would be a wreck with my kitchen covered in flour. I wish I could relax like you, Yvette.' As much fun as we were having, I knew it would end before Shelly and her mom pulled out of the driveway. All I could think was I want Yvette, this fun mom, to be my real mom.

"I was right. The second our front door closed, the fun-loving Yvette personality disappeared, and the mother I knew was back. I spent the next three hours cleaning the kitchen and made fourteen attempts to write the perfect thank-you card for the doll I never got to play with.

"When we all came up with the plan to leave, I spent the week thinking I wasn't running away but *to* something. I was looking for an Yvette, for a family."

I was sitting there, hearing Bo's words bounce off the walls and fall into the empty space. I wasn't sure if she was speaking to us, making a confession, or letting the quiet thoughts in the back of her mind and heart finally have a voice.

When we came to know Bo, she'd had sixteen years of living with an abusive mother. She had never met her father and wasn't allowed to ask questions about him. These days Yvette would be labeled with some behavior disorder and prescribed medicine, and better options would have been available for Bo.

Those neglected now did not have it any easier, but there might have been other avenues for us to make sure Bo got the help she needed. Maybe something had been available back then, but we were too naïve to know, and liked the idea of playing rescue and superheroes.

She had gone looking for happiness. But I'd spent the next few decades looking for my moral compass.

Bo went on. "I made my way to the ranch in Colorado."

"The commune you talked about?" Leo asked.

"It was far from a commune, or at least what I pictured. It was a working ranch, and I had to pay an entrance fee, but I also earned a decent wage. We had to attend either anger management classes, AA, or highly spiritual and sometimes drug-inducing meditative sessions. The counselors and owner asked very few questions about where we came from or why we were there.

"However, they were trying to operate within the law. Everyone had to be over eighteen and complete payroll records and file taxes. I accumulated a decent-size savings while I was there. I never touched it after I left the ranch. Over the years, I invested the money and watched it grow. When I came back here, I realized it was kismet that I was buying a life here in Dome with Yvette's' money. Thanks to you back then, I had Yvette's Social Security number. No one at the ranch questioned it."

I said, "You keep saying thanks to me but you—"

She shook her head. "I dreamt about leaving it all behind, waiting until I was eighteen but then . . ." Bo couldn't or wouldn't continue.

I looked at my phone and saw I had several messages.

Maz: *Call me.*

Maz: *Let me talk to her*

Maz: *On the news, Gigi's family is going after Dutch*

I stood up and paced while searching online for more news stories. Sure enough, Gigi's stepmom had contacted a reporter and demanded Dutch and his family come forward with everything they know. She didn't name Dutch directly. She must have been coached by a lawyer since he wasn't eighteen, but she referred to the young gentleman who spoke before but must be hiding information. Gigi is still unconscious.

I must have mumbled *WORB*.

Bo asked, "What's going on?" After I told her, without hesitation, she said, "Let him deal with it. He messed things up for Gigi."

"How can you say that?" I asked.

Bo ignored the question. She spoke softly, but again without hesitation. "After that first day with Gigi trying to weasel free food from me, we got to talking. Almost every day we would talk, and I enjoyed our chats. She came to me a few times about situations with her friends. I don't think she got along well with her stepmom.

"Eventually, she confided in me she was seeing someone. That caught me off guard because I never saw her with a boy. She said he was different, older, and then something shifted. She stopped coming in as frequently, and I heard her friends say she was spending less time with them. When I did see her, she acted nervous and almost like we were never friends. I thought it was drugs, and I slipped different leaflets and telephone numbers into her book bag. Then I thought maybe the new boyfriend was knocking her around. It was hard not knowing the situation, but it became my mission to help her."

"To pay it forward," I said.

Bo nodded and continued. "As I said, she didn't like her stepmom, Patty. I, however, found both Patty and James to be very kind and honest people. I know better than most that people can put out two different personas into the world. I didn't know if I could completely trust Gigi, so I knew I had to go to James before she did. I figured he would take pity on me if I was honest."

"You mean if you were the victim?" I said without thinking.

"I was the victim." Her voice sliced through me, and she returned to the other chair.

"I didn't mean to imply you weren't. Just trying to follow your thinking that James might get into trouble if he set up a fraudulent account and loan using Yvette's information. If you go to him as the abused child, he would help you clear up everything legally for you while protecting himself."

"You're good. It would have been nice to have you with me after I left here, but it was comforting to know I could always trust you to keep my life a secret. Like I said, I used Yvette's Social Security number on all the bank loan forms but wanted to clear my name. Once and for all, I wanted to be done with Yvette. I went to James and told the story I had been cultivating for years. I told him my mother took me to a commune to be raised by a group of women. That the place operated like it was the '60s and '70s. There were lots of hallucinogenic drugs and stuff beyond my comprehension. I said I wasn't sure, but I think my mother overdosed or was involved in some weird cultlike stuff that went horribly wrong. I said my mother had gone to the afternoon chapel, and I never saw her again. She and several women died, and the place quickly shut down. One of the other mothers took me with her to a new ranch in New Mexico, and I lived there until I was eighteen."

"That is quite a story."

"I had prepared for years because I knew at some point I would want Yvette officially gone from my life. I read about a ranch where something like that had actually happened. It was perfect; the place had shoddy bookkeeping, most participants used fake names, or were baptized and given alternative names. Witnesses were unreliable and hard to find. It was perfect for what I needed. Every once in a while, you can see some investigative report on TV about messed-up cultlike retreats, and that one always gets a mention. I just felt bad lying to James. He offered to help me get Yvette declared legally dead and to make sure Hattie's Cafe and I personally were in the clear and, of course, himself too."

"You had plenty of time to work out the details," I said.

"For years and years, really, until Maz and I connected, I'd had no one but me and lots of time to come up with a story. As I was saying, Gigi had confided in me but would never tell me what she was involved in. After a while, I wasn't sure I believed we were actually friends. I had become a good judge of character and spent years observing people. I was trying to figure out if she had been playing me all along or maybe she was upset because her little blackmail thing backfired on me. Then a few weeks ago, I heard some of the other high school girls talking smack about her. She was skipping school and wouldn't tell them much else but alluded to a boy and all the money he had or they had. There was a lot I could not hear, but I knew she was in some kind of trouble." Bo's voice was becoming slower. There were longer pauses between sentences, and she slurred ever so slightly.

Sitting there, I wondered if we were being played like James. Bo was the victim, getting herself worked up now. Were we to feel sorry for her sitting in the house we were not supposed to be in?

Bo continued, "I finally suggested she tried to secretly record the person if they were harassing her. Maybe he had naked pictures of her, or it was drugs and she helped sell them. I really wasn't sure and was just trying to help her."

"What brought you to this house? How did you know to come here?" I asked.

"Last week, something shifted with Gigi. Suddenly, she said everything was fine, and that I didn't need to worry. She had figured everything out, but I didn't really believe her. I had been watching her and her friends and noticed when her behavior shifted and saw money. Lots of money. When she went missing, I watched his behavior and knew he was involved. It just took me until last night to piece it together from some things I heard from two of my employees."

"What did you expect to accomplish coming here by yourself? You could have been in danger. Why do this?" I asked.

"You're asking me why? You of all people asking me why. I can't believe it." She slowly paced around the room. "For years, I had this recurring dream that my mother was in the next room, ready to come after me. I would lie in terror and slowly watch a light appear under the door. It was a soft glow that got brighter and brighter. It would start as a nightmare, yet as the light got brighter, the more peaceful I felt. Sometimes in the dream, the door would be open, and you were standing there telling me I could go in peace now. I understood the euphoria that Gigi was living with this last week. Raw emotion of finally getting out from under whatever was weighing her down. What she couldn't know was that would not just end. It wasn't until the final time I saw you that I knew that— while our plan was good and would help me escape—I would never fully let myself be out of my mother's control. Only when you said to go be her, did I feel free."

"That isn't exactly what I meant."

She was saying too much. Was she making sense?

"How were you able to follow her movements after you left? When did she stop reporting taxes? Was James able to track all that information?" Leo was asking practical questions, and I didn't know how to stop either of them.

She walked to the corner, keeping her back to us. I could see she raised her hand to her face, but not much else. Was she crying?

"Are you ok?" I asked.

She not so much as ignored me but it was like she didn't hear me, and I went to stand beside her. Her face was rigid and sweaty. Leo stayed glued to the wall and waited for me or Bo to say something.

I assumed a migraine had hit her, and I knew from experience a cool dark room and sleep were what she needed. I thought she might have medicine at home or in her purse, but neither seemed accessible at the moment.

"Sorry, I get these headaches. They come and go in a flash." She dug into her jean pocket and pulled out some loose pills and walked to the kitchen. "I just need some water."

I dropped myself back into the chair next to Leo.

"I think I'm missing something," he said.

"Clearly she is too," I said.

"I got so many questions," Leo said.

"You and me both."

I didn't know how far Bo was going to go with her thoughts and how much of the past she was willing to talk about now. I had to divert her and Leo from talking about what we had done. "Dutch played us from the beginning and—"

The sound of running water came from the kitchen, then the kitchen door opened, and it sounded like floorboards dropped from the counter.

"What are you doing here?" Dutch yelled.

"How could you? She's just—" Bo said.

I jumped up from the chair at the same time Leo pushed off the wall, and we hit heads. I ended up back in the chair. He pulled me up, and we lunged around the kitchen wall.

Bo was raising a hammer to Dutch.

"What the hell?" Dutch screamed. He ran into Leo and me as we lunged into the kitchen.

Bo tripped on the fallen floorboards, and the hammer went flying towards Leo. Dutch swiped the flying hammer away from him. Dutch had been spared, but he sent the hammer's claw into Leo's right temple. Leo flung his head sideways, slamming it into the cabinet.

Without hesitation, he ran to Bo and held her back. Her words were harsh, but her voice was softening, and her advance on Dutch weakened. Leo raised his hand to his face. When he moved is hand, his face was covered with blood. He held his stance to block Bo from coming forward.

"What are you doing in my house? Who are you people?" Dutch yelled.

Bo's energy amped up again, and she lunged for him again.

Leo blocked her way.

"It's not him! It's not him. You got it wrong!" I yelled.

He trapped her in the corner, and the dripping blood landed on both of them.

I kept my hand on Dutch. He was shaking.

Bo slunk to the floor, pulled up her knees, and buried her head.

Leo was muttering under his breath and continued to wipe his face. When he turned around, I don't know what was more startling —the deep cut above his eye from the hammer claw and smacking his head into the corner of the cabinet or the blood coming from his nose.

We looked around and only saw a painter's drop cloths and several old rags. He went to grab one.

"No, leave the rags. Who knows what infection you could get. Take off your sweatshirt," I said.

Leo did as he was told. I grabbed it and tried to pull off the sleeve to no luck, so I asked Dutch for help. He was as helpful as the wall he was pressed into.

"Kid, are you all right?" Leo asked.

Dutch slowly came towards me, and I tossed him the sweatshirt. He tried, but nothing would tear off. I was getting blood on my sweatshirt, so I took it off and held it to Leo's forehead and nose. His face was clammy, and his eyes were dilated. I held the sweatshirt while he moved to the sink to wash his hands without soap.

Dutch rooted around the toolbox, found a five-inch knife, and started making cuts. He came up with seven long strips. Leo leaned against the counter and tilted his head back.

"How did you get here?" I asked Dutch.

"I thought you would be here," he said.

"I didn't even know I was going to be here."

"All those strange questions you were asking me, and you left the tracking app open on my phone," Dutch said. "You were looking for where we had been."

I didn't know how that had gotten him here, but it was time some of this was finished. "What I meant was, how did you get here? Is Quinn outside?"

"He dropped me off," Dutch said.

I turned to Leo. "Gimme your truck keys."

"What are you doing?" There was no argument in his voice but general wonderment at what was going on around him.

I didn't wait for him and dug into his front pocket, retrieved the keys, and handed them to Dutch. "Run over to Orion Street, and you'll see Leo's black pickup truck. Bring it here so we can get him to the hospital."

Dutch looked from me to Leo to Bo. "But—"

I finally pulled out my mom voice. "Go, *now*."

I wished I could have harnessed that mom-voice power into more things because it got Dutch moving with no more hesitation.

Leo was moaning, and I helped replace my bloodied sweatshirt for one of the fresh strips Dutch had cut up. As he tilted his head back, I put his hand on my shoulder for stability.

I kept my hand on his for a nanosecond longer than needed, and Leo slipped his hand over mine. It made me want to lean forward and kiss his injury.

The words *Leo's wife* popped into my head, and I wanted to split open his wound.

I pulled away and saw Bo was still on the floor in the fetal position without even a whimper.

"Let's get you some fresh air while we wait for Dutch." We left Bo curled up in the corner, and I guided Leo outside and had him sit on the one step to the deck and leaned him against the wall.

"What is going on?" Leo asked softly.

"You were hit in the head, and we're taking you to the hospital."

"No shit. I was hit in the head, but I'm not a dumbass." I couldn't help but laugh, and Leo spoke again. "What have you figured out that you're not sharing?"

Silence and time were on my side, or so I thought.

Leo asked again, "Lou, what's up? I can sit here all day and maybe bleed out, and you will have to answer a whole lotta questions from other people besides me."

"Stop being so dramatic. You're not going to bleed out. Maybe have your head cave in from all your dumbassery."

"Excuse me, is that even a word? Now stop stalling and tell me what you know. *Everything.*"

"Gigi was here in the house. I think she ran away and was hiding here upstairs. You heard what Bo was saying. Gigi was in trouble, and Bo told her to get the person to admit what they had done and record it. Gigi had drawn someone here, and it probably backfired. Then she refused to leave or someone refused to let her go."

"Since you just gave Dutch the keys to my truck, I'm assuming you think it was Van." Leo shifted his head towards me.

"Keep your head back. The bleeding has slowed; however, the wound is still open, so keep the fabric on it."

Avoiding eye contact felt right. I had nothing to hide. I'd just made out with Van, a guy who may or may not have slept with a teenage girl, but probably was. That was his problem, not mine.

Although you can judge a person by their friends, I thought.

Right now, the last two friends I'd made were an adulterer and a pedophile, or maybe since Gigi was eighteen, just a skeevy old man.

"Are you telling me we're done? We found Bo, and Gigi is recovering," Leo said.

"You got it," I said and stood up when I heard Dutch pull into the driveway. "Let me help you up."

"I call BS," Leo said, refusing my hand. "You're holding out. I'm not going anywhere until you tell me."

"You can't see how bad your forehead is right now. You need to go."

Leo pulled himself up and used the wall for support but short-stepped the porch stairs and stumbled into me for support.

"Easy there. You need to get to the hospital," I said and turned him around without much resistance.

Dutch got out and tried handing me the keys. "You have to take him. The emergency room on 35th is the closest," I said.

"I'm not leaving her in my house," Dutch said.

"Understandable, but you saw her reaction the first time. She had it all wrong. Let me get her out of the house, and I'll come get you," I pleaded, but he wasn't moving. "I won't be long. Just be in the waiting room. I'll tell you everything."

He would find out sooner or later, and I thought for some reason it would be best coming from me.

Dutch dropped his head and stared at his shoes. "Was she here?"

I didn't say anything, and I was holding Leo by the elbow like a child who might wander off.

Dutch spoke again. "Was . . . what's inside? Who else?"

In no more than a whisper, I replied, "I'm not sure but most likely she was. We didn't go upstairs or in the basement, but if I had to guess, I think Gigi has been here."

I reached out for his shoulder, but he turned his back to us. I let him have his space and walked Leo around to the passenger door. It took Leo two attempts before he could hoist himself up.

I was about to text Maz to come get Bo when Dutch hopped into the driver's seat.

I said, "Are you good to drive? You don't have to . . ."

Dutch turned the key and put the truck in reverse.

I can't stop mothering. "Keep the windows open and keep him talking. Don't let him fall asleep. I'll be there as soon as I can."

Dutch wouldn't look at either one of us.

Leo grabbed my shirt and pulled me close. He whispered. "You still have more to tell me."

I pulled back, shut the door, and watched them drive away. Now I had to figure out how far Bo was willing to go or if she could let it be.

THIRTY-EIGHT

After a few minutes of me squatting next to her, Bo declined my offer to get her water and acknowledged her migraine with a slight nod. She accepted my hand as I led her towards the back door. I had looked around the living room, bathroom, and kitchen and didn't find a purse. Her phone was in her pocket. I had no interest in going upstairs or to the basement. I had nothing to hide from the police, but I didn't want to spend more time in this house.

Bo accepted my sunglasses and easily walked alongside me with my hand on her elbow. We made it to Stew's car, and I debated taking her to her house or mine. I knew a migraine could suddenly stop someone dead in their tracks. Whatever she wanted to tell me would have to wait.

There was no sense in making Maz more worried than he was, so I texted him for the address.

He responded immediately and called, but I ignored the call. I texted that I would see him in three minutes.

Bo kept her head down, avoiding sunlight. She stumbled a bit getting into my car, then slumped down into the front seat. The ride to her house was uneventful.

Maz flew out of the house as I pulled into the driveway. He ran to the car to help Bo out. He threw his arms around her and guided her to the front door without badgering her on what she had been doing. His affection for her was genuine.

I got out, and he didn't yell at me or ask me a hundred questions about where I'd found her and why I'd kept him away. I was sure those questions would come but not until Bo was put to bed.

Their house was behind Hattie's, the same street I'd walked down earlier. I got back in the car without saying anything. Out the rear window, I could see the path to the bridge where Dutch and I had stood a few hours ago. I backed out of the driveway and just started driving. I drove out of Dome and sat in a parking lot of some store so I could gather my thoughts.

Bo was out of commission, but I didn't know for how long.

Maybe if I finish paying it forward for Bo, she'll stop talking.

Unfortunately, I didn't have a way of contacting him, and how was I going to get him to confess? He had to know Gigi would recover.

It suddenly hit me; what had Gigi's end game been? Blackmail for money? Blackmail because he ended the secret relationship? Would she risk exposing herself? Would she want that to be public information? So what if he confesses? Yes, he could be in legal trouble, but would that be embarrassing for her? Maybe she was a victim of rape but that did not match what Bo said about her behavior and how her friends talked about her in the bathroom at the diner.

I drove out of the parking lot hoping, as the odometer rolled up, I could pull the pieces of the puzzle together and somehow that worked.

I slammed on the brakes in the middle of Simool Road. A car honked and swerved around me. I found myself lucky there had been only one car behind me. I hit the pedal hard, and a quarter mile up the road, I did a semi illegal U-turn. It was only partially illegal, because I didn't get caught.

It was time for Dutch to tell me everything Gigi's friends had failed to.

THIRTY-NINE

I called Dutch for an update on Leo and told him I was coming to pick him up. He said the nurse had just taken Leo back, but he had to wait because he still had Leo's keys. I told him to take Leo's truck to the village overflow parking lot and meet me there. Even if Leo didn't have a concussion, there was no way the hospital would let him drive himself home. His wife or kid would have to get him, and I would deliver the truck later.

Twenty minutes later, Dutch showed up in Leo's truck.

I sent Stew a message:

Car behind library.

Keys under floor mat.

Did not read any of your texts

Thanks for the car.

Talk soon I promise

"It's my brother's car, and he lives a couple of blocks in the tree section," I said.

"I can follow you there," Dutch said.

"Appreciate the offer, but I like to make him walk. Now, where can I drop you off?" I asked.

Dutch cinched his forehead and dropped his eyes. "I thought you were going to answer some questions."

"I didn't know if Leo filled you in, or if you were over us," I said.

"Leo didn't say a lot. I had to fill out the hospital form because his vision was a little blurry. I even asked if I should call someone for him, but he said no."

"Text him you're with me, and I'll get him when he's ready." I really meant when *I* was ready since he was a putz and wouldn't call his wife when he was in the hospital.

"Let's make this a ride-and-talk session. Let me get in, and you can drive us to the baseball field."

"The high school field, by the woods?" Dutch asked.

"My car keys are missing. I think I dropped them when we were there earlier."

Dutch pulled out of the lot and kept his eyes straight ahead.

I asked, "Earlier, why did you ask if Gigi was at your house?"

He didn't respond, so I unloaded a few of my own.

"Last night, after we saw you and Quinn at Food Truck Friday, you said you went to a friend's house, but did you go hang out in your garage? It's a pretty safe spot to drink with no parents around."

Dutch swept a hand over his ear and brushed back his hair. After three blocks, he finally said, "Yeah. We had been there before. A couple of friends like to smoke so I won't let them in the house. Out of the garage windows, I looked up at the house and saw something in the window. I assumed it was my dad, so I had everyone leave."

"Wouldn't you have seen each other's cars?" I asked.

"He has been parking on the street. The construction guys can be messy. They left a few nails on the driveway, and he got a flat tire once so he parks on the street when checking on the house. We come in through the woods. The garage has a back door."

"That's pretty smart; hide the cars so parents and cops can't follow you or the weed."

"Did your kids ever get away with anything? You seem to have figured out a lot," Dutch said.

"I know the ways of Dome. My kids got into plenty of mischief, some I knew about and probably lots that I didn't. After you left there, you came to my place. Why at that hour?"

"I did have all those questions about the girl in the photo, but really, I didn't want to be home when my dad got home."

"You thought it was him at the house?"

"He has done this before. Cheat on my mom. My parents don't think I know, but it was part of why we moved to London temporarily—a fresh start. At least over there, the nighttime yelling stopped for a while. How do I tell her not to come back for him?" Dutch said. He pulled into the parking lot and turned off the truck.

"How about her coming back for *you*?"

He didn't flinch when I put my hand on his shoulder and continued to look ahead. After some silence, he opened the truck door but stayed seated. "I'd rather have them fighting than pretending everything is fine. I hate it when people are fake."

He hopped out before I had time to process what he'd said.

I took the giant step out of the truck, and my boobs bounced under the diner T-shirt like branches on a tree when the wind kicked up. Dutch started walking but waited while I rooted around the box in the back for a new sweatshirt. He declined the sweatshirt I offered as payment for driving Leo to the hospital.

We walked the long way to the path leading into the woods to retrace my steps. Neither one of us said anything. I was processing Van's lie about work ending his marriage, but who would confess if he was cheating on his wife when he was flirting with someone?

"Do you think my dad kept Gigi at the house?" Dutch asked.

"I don't know your dad well enough. It's just a guessing game at this point. You know your dad better than any of us. We don't know for sure if he was involved."

"Why that house?" There was real anger in his voice. "Don't you guys have the answers?"

I was so taken aback by Dutch's direct question, I stumbled when we stepped off the sidewalk and onto the dirt path. My hand flew up and hit him in the back. He caught me before I fell, but not before I saw him flinch.

"Are you ok?" he asked.

"I'm good. How about you?"

"Fine, but I'm not the one who almost fell."

With everything going on, this was one of the most terrifying questions I had to ask him, but it could not go unasked. "Are you ok? Has . . . does . . . did you . . . had someone?" Oh shit, I just had to say the words. "Did someone hurt you?"

Dutch's eyes went big, and he took a step away from me. "Why would you ask that?"

Damn, I didn't know what to say or if I should approach this head-on, but I knew this should not be ignored. "Twice today, I touched your back, and you jumped like a toad on fire."

"Toad on fire?" Dutch laughed.

"I don't know where that came from, and don't change the subject."

Dutch pulled up his shirt and turned for me to see his back. His left shoulder was bruised, and there were several scratches. I gasped in horror. He put his shirt back on, turned to face me, and dug his right shoe into the ground. His face was flushed. "Last night when we went through the woods, I tried hurdling a fallen tree, and I didn't do so well."

"That's a relief," I said.

"Relief?"

"Yes! It's child's play and not someone hurting you."

"My dad may be a jerk to my mom, but he isn't a scumbag. Well, at least I don't think so."

"See you do know your dad. Don't jump to any crazy

conclusions. Look what happened to Leo when Bo jumped to a conclusion," I said. "This is a strange question."

"This is all strange," Dutch said.

"Fair point. Did you wear the same shoes you wore in the woods to my house last night?"

"Those are in the garage. I washed my pants twice, and there's red dirt that I can't get out."

"So there's no chance of you or your dad bringing red mud into the kitchen."

Dutch said, "Remember I was wearing his shoes because mine were so messy. He would spend the time to get a pair from upstairs rather than wear my shoes, clean or dirty.

We walked in silence looking at the ground for my keys.

Dutch finally said, "Don't do that. What's worse than my parents fighting are the quiet times when everyone is in the same room, but no one is talking."

"I didn't mean to shut you out. Just trying to process everything. The red dirt is found in the parkway because of some landscaping fiasco. The parkway where Gigi was found near your house. I'm not sure if it's connected, but someone brought mud into my kitchen and into Hattie's. That person had to be in the parkway."

"You think there's some connection," Dutch asked.

"I did at one point, but I'm not sure it's relevant. The only person who's been in both is Leo."

"You think Leo did something to Gigi or Bo? Is that why she attacked him?"

"She was attacking you, but Leo stepped forward. Bo thinks you were blackmailing Gigi or something. I can't read Bo's mind, but she had you or your dad pegged as the bad guy."

We walked into the woods, walked around the bench area, and sat down without finding the keys.

"Here's what we know. Gigi went missing on Tuesday; Bo went missing Friday night. They found Gigi in the parkway near your house. We found Bo waiting for your dad in your house, and she claims she was trying to pay it forward with Gigi because she was in some kind of trouble."

"Pay it forward?" Dutch asked.

"Remember when we first met in room five?" I said. "Thirty-four years ago, Maz, Leo and I helped Bo escape her abusive mother, and now she wanted to help someone in need. Last night, it wasn't you sneaking out of the house. It was your dad?"

"I'm confused."

"Last night, your dad came over for thirty minutes. After he left, I went upstairs to go to bed and saw someone leaving your house. Does that tracking app keep records of where you've been?"

Dutch pulled out his phone, and we looked at his father's history.

"The accuracy isn't always exact and can be off by several hundred feet. So Dad showing up at your parents' condo may not register on the app," he said.

Van's history showed the condo, work, grocery store, his aunt's house, a couple of office buildings downtown, once to the house on Wednesday, and one other location.

Dutch said, "The renovation has stopped until a city inspector can approve the electrical work. All the work was stalled until the inspection happened, so not much reason to be there."

"Would it be possible for someone to be upstairs and not be found?" I asked.

"Maybe. All the electrical work was done in the basement. The main level got new floors and kitchen cabinets, and the upstairs got new floors. The bathrooms were updated two years ago. I guess someone could be upstairs, and no one would know unless they went looking. Do you know the other hits on his location?"

"The downtown locations look like office buildings, but I don't know the other spot. He was there each day this week," I said.

"If it's near his office, it's probably the coffee place," Dutch said. "So my dad hasn't been going to the house. It wasn't him there last night, and it was someone else's shadow I saw in the window. It was Gigi, wasn't it?"

"Probably. It could have been Bo, but I doubt it. I wonder where she was last night if she wasn't at your house."

"You said you saw my dad leave the condo last night, but it shows he was there all night." Dutch's words were slow and deliberate. "He wanted to appear to be home all night."

Yikes. My ego took a hit. Was I supposed to be an alibi? For the second time, my high school crush had ended in embarrassment, but at least this one didn't involve projectile puking and a hangover.

The wind picked up again. I wrapped my arms around myself for warmth. Dutch got up in silence, and I thought he was done with me since I couldn't give him the answers. I was gladly mistaken.

He walked to the edge of the clearing that led to the path and retrieved my car key.

We cut across the green space between the football field and baseball diamond. There was no need to go the long way to the overflow lot.

Halfway to Leo's truck, I finally said, "Look, we don't know any hard facts about your dad, so don't jump to any conclusions."

"Why would he leave the house without his phone?" Dutch asked.

"Why would he take you to the hospital to see Gigi and her family if he was involved?" I asked. "Give me the keys, and I can drop you off anywhere. I want to check on Leo and give him his truck back."

"I can go with you," Dutch said. "I don't want to go home, and Quinn is hanging with his girlfriend."

"Sure, I just want to stop at the condo first and put on some clothes that actually belong to me." I thought that was better than saying I needed a bra. I even threw in the diner-food collision story to break the bleak mood.

I texted Leo that we would be there in thirty but to let me know if someone had come and got him out but no immediate reply.

We got to the truck, and I spied the driver's-side door. I would have to spring step my way into the seat. I thought about driving the beast and decided it best to let the kid keep driving since he seemed comfortable behind the wheel.

It was unfortunate my need for a bra led to the next series of events. The truth can be hard to hear.

FORTY

The ride from the parking lot was the last dull moment of the afternoon. I texted Maz, asking for an update on Bo and said I was stopping at home before going to visit Leo in the hospital. Maz responded with *hospital* and a question mark. I guessed Bo had failed to fill Maz in about her afternoon.

Dutch parked Leo's truck on the street and followed me into the house.

His phone rang, and his eyes lit up. I motioned towards the den or patio for privacy. I saw *Mom* appear on his phone before he swiped to answer.

I ran upstairs and tossed items out of my duffle bag. Since I had packed in such a hurry, I really had no idea what I was going to find. I got lucky and found fresh clothes top to bottom.

I grabbed them and went to the bathroom for an airplane bath—a washcloth under the wings and through the cockpit. I applied some deodorant and slipped on a fresh pair of underwear, socks, and a bra, with clean jeans and a black long-sleeve thermal top that used to belong to my ex. If I was ever going to have a sex life again, I should probably stop wearing Joe's clothes.

I ran a brush through my hair and applied a little mascara. It wasn't an effort to make myself more appealing to either man, neither of which I should be attracted to, but it was an effort to look less like I was on a three-day bender.

Going down the stairs, I heard the patio furniture sliding across the deck and some shouting. I ran to the bottom of the stairs.

Van was shouting at Dutch. The round metal patio table was between them, and Van's hands clutched the back of one of the chairs. I couldn't understand what he was saying. He flexed his arms, raised the chair an inch, and slammed it down in frustration.

Dutch spied me watching and stepped into the corner of the deck. I was gobsmacked with what I'd witnessed. Torn between running inference for Dutch, hiding under the kitchen sink, or confronting Van, I was currently glued to the kitchen floor.

That only lasted a second because momma bear kicked in, and regardless of who was right, my instinct was to always protect the kids.

I marched past the Statler and Waldorf chairs and pushed the sliding glass door open. "Is everything ok?"

"I want to know what's going on!" Van shouted. "Why are you and my son hanging out, and he's refusing to call me back?" Why am I getting calls from my neighbor telling me people are in my house?"

"There's no need to shout." I had to stall until I figured out what to tell Van. Had we done anything wrong? We had been in his house, but really, what had we done? Only one person had gone to the hospital, and no damage had been done to the house.

Did I just say only one person went to the hospital like that was a positive thing? I may no longer look like I've been on a three-day bender, but I sure as hell am thinking like I did.

Van continued his rant at me. "Don't tell me to stop yelling. There are too many people coming at my family and you—"

"Dad! Stop!" Dutch pleaded.

"Come inside before Mrs. Bein calls the police," I said and

backed away from the doorway and stood near the kitchen entry. Dutch remained in the corner on the small deck until Van pointed inside. Dutch came in stood in the middle of us.

Van stepped just inside the doorway and continued his rant. "Let her call the police. They know who I am since I just spent the last hour with them. Answering questions on why Gigi had been hiding out in my house! While I was there, I get a call saying my son is at the house with a woman and a man."

"Gigi was at your house? She's awake? How is she?" How many questions could I fire off and reroute this conversation?

"The police wouldn't tell me. They asked me to come down there and answer some questions. Now answer some for me. What were you doing at my house?"

"Leo and I went for a walk. He actually fell, well, actually he really tripped and started bleeding. Dutch and his friend drove past and were kind enough to help."

Van's eyes darted between me and Dutch.

"After we got Leo taken care of, your son volunteered again. This time, he helped me find my car keys. You should be proud of the kid you raised."

Van said nothing, and then Dutch's phone beeped.

"Dad, I gotta pick up Mom."

Van went from shouting, to listening to me praise his son to completely stunned.

"She called when she exited the plane, and that was her texting. She has her bags and is at door three."

"She's in Milwaukee?" Van was stunned.

"Yeah, she flew in to surprise me and I guess you. She was supposed to be here yesterday, but got delayed. Can I go?"

Van only had a few options. "Of course. Take my car. It's gassed up." He walked over, handed Dutch the keys, and put a hand on his back, causing Dutch to flinch. "Don't drive like a speed monster."

"Don't worry, Dad," Dutch said, leaving through the kitchen door.

Van dropped into my father's chair and said, "Great, now I have to navigate this."

"Dutch seemed excited to see his mom."

"Of course, Charlotte is going to swoop in, give hugs, make false promises, and be gone before anything is resolved. Leaving me to clean it all up after I slept on the couch for the week."

I sat on the arm of the sofa and figured I had nothing to lose with some questions. My earlier story seemed to have worked about Leo and me being with Dutch. "What were the police questioning you about?"

He didn't answer right away. He got up and started pacing as he had done the other night. "They wanted to talk to both Dutch and me. I held off on bringing Dutch in until I knew what they wanted, and partially, it was because he wasn't answering his phone. We have nothing to hide. I think I know my son pretty well, but when he's asked to answer questions by the police, I get a little protective."

"I get that. We all worry about our kids. I used to track mine on my phone when they're with kids I didn't really care for. I trust my kids, but it's other people's kids I worry more about."

"Charlotte was crazy about that when we first got to London. Here, Dutch tells me where he is going. Maybe I'm a fool, but I believe him and he has never given me cause for concern. And until five days ago, he has never been in trouble. Actually, he isn't in trouble now, but the police want to question him more. Well, he'll have to tell me why he wasn't answering my calls."

I couldn't help but wonder why he hadn't tracked Dutch when he didn't answer his phone, especially when the police wanted to question him. Either he had tracked him and was keeping information from me—although he had no reason to share it with me—or he was playing me for information.

Do I really know there were no cameras in his house? How much did the neighbor see?

"Do you really think Dutch knew Gigi was at the house?" I asked.

One of these men was playing me, and I had to figure out who.

"I don't think so, but then again, I don't know how any of this happened."

"Can I ask a tough question?"

"I've just been with the police, so if you think you have a tough question, I think I can handle it," Van said.

"It isn't so much a tough question, but a hard reality. Do you think Dutch and Gigi are into some type of drugs?"

Van dropped onto the other end of the couch I was resting on. He looked past my parents' recliners out to the deck. After a long pause, he finally spoke, "Before today, I would have said absolutely not. Drinking, yes, and occasionally, pot, but it seems like I don't know him as well as I thought. He has never not answered my calls and has been so flippant towards me. When I handed him my car keys, he jumped three feet away. He couldn't get away fast enough."

It seemed like genuine emotion. I slid off the armrest and was two feet from Van. I could feel his angst pulsing through the air. I could almost reach out and push his blond hair back and hold his chin in my hands as he had mine just last night.

Did I say it had been several months since I'd had sex? And last night, I'd passed on two opportunities. My body had not let me forget it. I wanted to touch his hands, and our fingers to interlock, and have him pull me close.

"And you?" Van asked.

I was so caught up in my body that I lost Van's words. He was expecting an answer, so I started with "Well," faked a coughing spasm, and excused myself to the kitchen. It wasn't smooth, but at least I wasn't throwing and going like yesterday.

I played the coughing stint up and poured some water. I went to the freezer, and the cold air snapped my mind back to reality—I was really considering jumping into bed with a man that might be connected with Gigi and had his estranged wife en route to his condo.

Did I say it had been several months, and this man was my crush of old and new? I threw ice into two rocks glasses and threw my dream aside. I poured two Scotches and returned to Van. He raised his eyebrow but not his hand.

"I don't care that it's midafternoon. You have been questioned by the police and will be sleeping on the couch contemplating your parenting."

"When you put it that way, maybe you should have made it a double." He stood up, walked to me, leaving little room between us for me to breathe. When he reached for the glass, he let his fingers linger on mine.

"Cheers," he said without stepping back.

We clinked glasses, and I took a long sip.

Van continued, "Here's to you, being here this weekend. I think I need to thank your friend for getting sick. What is her name? I should call her and thank her for her misfortune of canceling your weekend."

Friend? Sick? What was he talking about? Oh, shit. I should have known by now to never lie, because it would probably burn me later. I'd told him I was on my way north to visit a friend, but her kids had gotten sick.

Who did I say it was?

"Oh, let the sick rest, and you just enjoy your Scotch," I said, removing myself from temptation, and threw myself onto Statler, my mother's recliner.

There was nothing less sexy than curling up in my mother's hand-knitted blanket and receiving a text from Maz insisting he see me immediately. Regardless of Van and Charlotte's relationship status, I was sure he would excuse himself when Dutch and Charlotte arrived, so I gave Maz my parents' address.

Our conversation lasted into exchanging funny stories about our kids between sips of calmness.

"So tomorrow you head back to Chicago," Van said. "I'm going to miss our Scotch time."

"My father will have a drink with you anytime. Although coming back from France, it might be all about the wine."

"Something tells me his visits will be very different." Van laughed.

The doorbell rang, interrupting what could have been a very troubling flirtation. I spied Maz through the window. His hands on his hips, he was pacing on the patio, looking like he was ready to explode.

I opened the door. "Maz, come in. Is everything ok with Bo?"

"No, not everything is ok. I just came from the hospital."

"Calm down. Tell me what's going on," I said.

Van stepped into the kitchen. "I'll just excuse myself, and let you two talk."

Maz looked like he'd seen a ghost. It took me a second to realize he may not have seen Van since high school. Even talking to Dutch and knowing the family is one thing, but to see Van and Dutch, it's like seeing twins decades apart.

"Oh man, hey, Maz." Van stuck out his hand. "It's been years. Decades probably since we've seen each other. My son told me how you came to his aid when the reporters were after him. I apologize for not saying thank you sooner."

Maz stepped forward, but instead of shaking Van's hand, he clocked him in the jaw with a solid right hook.

"*WORBY, DAMN.*" There was no whisper in my voice.

FORTY-ONE

"What the hell!" Van's head snapped sideways. He didn't advance on Maz. He righted himself and held his jaw.

"How could you? She's just a child!" Maz shouted.

It was a little pathetic how I tried to hold Maz back. A sneeze could have knocked me over.

"What are you talking about?" Van's voice was controlled but loud.

"Bo would do anything to protect those kids."

"Who the hell is Bo?"

"My wife."

"She's Hattie," I said.

Van kept his eyes on Maz, and I didn't think he had even heard my words.

I gestured to Maz. "The current Hattie is Bo, his wife."

"What does that have to do with me?"

"I just left her in the hospital. She was so worked up, her migraine became debilitating, and her medicine wasn't helping. They had to sedate her, but not before she tried telling me everything. She saw you and Gigi in your car."

"I don't have to stand for this. First the police and now you. Just leave me and my son alone. If you come near either of us again, it will not end well."

"You can't leave here until you tell me what you did." Maz moved towards the door.

"Why should I answer you? So you can throw more wild accusations at me. Should we get the press here so it's one-stop shopping for you?" Van said.

Neither man moved. I was trying to read Van's reaction. Does a guilty man swing back or take a punch without retaliating? My insides were screaming for Van to be innocent in all this.

With Charlotte arriving any minute, the chances of me getting some sex had dramatically dropped, but I could always return next weekend. My parents would be back, so that would take sex off the table.

Why, as a fifty-plus-year-old woman, did my parents' travel schedule affect my sex life? Why, when I looked at Van, my thoughts automatically went to sex. However, his long, lean body with bold arms that could move over my entire body in seconds just screamed at any woman this natural reaction. His kisses sent me to the edge of bliss so I couldn't imagine feeling all of him on top of me.

Van's anger snapped me back to reality. "I don't know what your wife saw. If she's talking about a week ago when my son forgot his laptop and Gigi opened the door and I handed it to her so she could . . . Forget it, I don't need to explain it to you or your wife."

Maz was inches behind me. His twitching leg hitting the doorjamb behind him.

"They found her a hundred yards from your house! You may have been able to fool the police once, but they'll get you. Once Bo is well enough, she's going to tell them everything."

"Great, go now, and they'll clear me and my son."

Maz pushed me aside, lunged for Van. "You arrogant son of a bitch."

Van deflected Maz's outstretched arms with a wide sweep of his right arm. Maz bounced off the doorway to the basement and returned to Van. The men collided into the stove, sent the pot of yesterday's leftover stew crashing to the floor and the clatter of the metal broke my screams. I didn't know if anyone had landed a punch. I screamed again when the bodies moved my way and crashed into the table and back into the center of the room.

When I didn't think it could get worse or more bizarre, a gunshot rang out over my shoulder, followed by Mrs. Bein shrieking. The sliding glass door in the living room spiderwebbed. Her chubby fingers clasped a pistol so small I could hardly see it. Her little yappy dog toddled alongside her.

"Men!"

I didn't know if my voice was screaming in my head or into the kitchen because my ears were ringing from the gunshot.

Mrs. Bein plowed her way past me but slipped on the stew that had spread across the floor. I watched her five-foot-tall frame wiggle for balance. She reached for the kitchen chair but missed. She dropped the pistol and held herself up with the edge of the table. Stew came flying through the front door, pushing me away, and I bowled into her.

Maz dropped his arms from Van's shoulders. Blood gathered on the sleeve of his forearm.

Barely audible, Mrs. Bein said, "Blood," before collapsing on the kitchen floor, her head hitting the tile.

Apparently, our gunslinger was tough as nails until the sight of blood. The dog curled up to Mrs. Bein and licked her face.

Stew dove for the gun.

I screamed, "*Stop!*"

He'd heard a gunshot and had seen the men fighting—he had no idea Mrs. Bein had shot the gun.

Stew slid across the floor, scooped up the gun, and pointed it at Maz and Van.

Blood continued to spread across Maz's sleeve. The little pistol's bullet had clipped Maz's arm before hitting the glass door to the patio.

Stew stood in the midst of the dance between Maz and Van, holding the gun. He looked at Maz's sleeve and then to Van. He repeated the motion again. He seemed to come to the conclusion that Van had shot Maz.

Maz abandoning his fight had caused Van to overcorrect his stance. He was still trying to right himself as they hurtled towards the open basement door.

The vein on Stew's neck was pulsing so hard I could see it across the room. His eyes held more rage than Maz's had just moments ago. Stew dropped the pistol on the counter to resume Maz's fight.

"Stop!" was my mantra on repeat.

Stew stepped into the melee of Maz and Van who was trying to remain upright. Somebody kicked the stew pot.

I thought I should throw myself into the mix, but I tripped on Mrs. Bein, who remained on the floor. It was surprising how my body weight was enough to hurl the three men four feet to the top of the stairs. Metal scraped on the floor. One of the boys had their foot caught on the lid of the pot.

Stew grabbed my shirt and flung me back. His arms shifted back as he was getting ready to push the men, so I jumped back into the fray and got caught up in the movement.

"Stop! You're going to kill them!" I yelled.

Maz was shouting something undecipherable.

Van shouted, "Son of a bitch!" on top of my yelling.

Mrs. Bein provided the only serenity in the room, having passed out on the floor.

Stew swung his arm forward as I hung onto his arm.

I repeated, "Someone is gonna get hurt!"

Would-be photographs—not a movie playing out in slow motion —flashed in my mind.

All three men plunging towards the open door.

Mrs. Bein on the floor.

Stew's rage.

Maz's blood.

Van swearing.

It was Van's anger that nearly drowned out Stew when he answered my cries to stop.

"You're going to kill 'em!" I said.

With a last shove, Stew hissed, "I've done it before."

FORTY-TWO

Stew's words echoed in my mind. *I've done it before.*

There was no humor or remorse in his whisper to me. The little weight I had contributed to the foursome dropped as Stew's confession hit me.

His final push sent the four of us tumbling down the basement steps in one giant pile. Maz's arm skidded along the white walls, leaving a streak of red. Van, still trying to control the group, tried pulling Maz upright, but they clunked heads before dropping to the bottom of the stairs with Stew and me landing on top of them.

I rolled sideways, and Stew rolled to the other side of the pile. I crawled around Van and Maz and leaned against the cinder-block wall. Maz and Van lay side by side, with little movement. No bones were sticking out, so I figured their heads knocking together on the way down the stairs was their major concern and, of course, Maz's gunshot wound.

Stew remained where he was. I kicked him in the leg until he dragged himself over.

"What was that all about?" I asked.

"I saved your ass. You could give me a thank-you."

"You're not gonna get a thank-you from me. The guys were not after me."

"There was a gunshot. I was sure he would shoot again."

"Maz nor Van shot anyone. It was Mrs. Bein with the pistol. Remember the lady you plowed into? Now answer my question. What did you mean when you said you did it before—"

Car doors slamming and muffled noises came from outside. Maz and Van started stirring and sat upright. No one spoke as the shouting outside got louder. Finally, police officers were at the top of the stairs. Two of the men descended the staircase with guns barely raised until they saw the blood on the walls.

"We're fine. No one's in danger. Might need a paramedic or two." I didn't know if Mrs. Bein was still on the floor or if she had waddled off somewhere.

The police walked around the unfinished basement, taking inventory of everyone and the injuries.

I couldn't help but think my father would have loved all this activity as long as no one trampled on his flower garden. My mother would have been a mix of emotion: mortified because of the drama, but also in her glory, having the inside scoop of knowing what the big story in the neighborhood was.

I reached for my phone in my back pocket. My arm was sore. Sometime during our four-person tumble down the stairs, I'd pulled a muscle in my upper back. I was fortunate that was all I'd injured.

Van retreated to a lawn chair my folks had stowed in the basement for the winter. Maz remained on the floor, touching his arm and moving like a slow-motion cartoon. I'm not sure he knew which way was up.

I finally got my phone out and texted Dutch. *We're fine. Regardless of how it looks outside, we're fine.*

I imagined Dutch driving up with his mom into this scene of police cars.

Two officers stood looking down at us. Officer Number One

said, "Anybody want to give us an explanation of what happened here?"

No one volunteered, so I finally spoke.

"Three of us were having a lively discussion in the kitchen when Mrs. Bein, the lady on the floor upstairs, entered and fired a shot. Immediately following the gunshot, Stew came running in, and in the commotion and with the slippery floor, we all ended up cascading down the stairs."

"Is that your story?" Officer Number One asked.

"Yes, sir," I said.

"I think we need to take separate statements," Officer Number One said.

"It's exactly as the lady reported," Van said.

"Didn't I just see you at the station a few hours ago?" Officer Number Two asked.

Van nodded.

The officer looked pointedly at Van. "This has nothing to do with that, now does it?"

I was done with this. The guys needed help. "We told you what happened. Now, can you get someone to check out his arm and maybe his head? I think it hit the pavement pretty good when we landed. Maybe check his ribs. They were used as a cushion mat for several of us."

I was in awe and yet still leery of Van's demeanor towards Maz. He was showing grace with no underlying anger and wasn't implicating that Maz was the instigator.

From upstairs came an "Oh shit," followed by a thud.

Officer Number Two looked up the stairs and shouted, "Farrell, how many times have I told you not to come running into a crime scene? Serves you right for ending up on your ass. Now get up and carefully walk down here. Bring your medical bag."

Farrell and a second paramedic came down the steps. I could easily identify Farrell because he had a wet mark leading from his shoe, up the leg, and around his butt. When he knelt next to Maz, there was a carrot smashed into the sole of his shoe.

The paramedics led Maz upstairs, followed by Van. The police took statements from us separately and were treating this rather casually. I understood why when Officer Number Two radioed in confirming it was just another Betty Bullet Bein incident.

We later learned this was the fourth time Mrs. Bein had fired her pistol. It wasn't clear if she had a permit or would face charges. My mother always left so much out when I came to visit. She had been so consumed with fixing me up that she didn't think to mention her pistol-packing neighbor.

Stew and I ascended the stairs together, and the police left shortly after. Everyone made it clear no one was pressing charges, but we were unsure what would happen to Mrs. Bein. She and her dog were gone by the time we got upstairs.

Dutch pulled into the driveway as his father was walking to the ambulance with paramedics. A tall slender blond stepped out of the vehicle wearing a cashmere sweater, black jeans, and knee-high boots. She looked as fresh and vibrant as if she had come from the salon and not an international flight. Her leather handbag and boots probably costed more than everything I had packed for the weekend.

I wanted to hate her, but her immediate reaction to seeing her husband being escorted to the ambulance was to run to her son. Together, they walked over to Van. Dutch caught my eye, and I mouthed *misunderstanding*. The three of them talked to the paramedics. After several minutes, Van stood up from the bumper of the ambulance and shook the fellow's hand before walking towards his condo.

Charlotte guided Van by the elbow towards their place, and Dutch ran to me.

"We're taking my dad to be checked out. He's too cheap to pay for the ambulance ride." He was bouncing left and right. I had seen this young man confused, mad, insightful, angry, and now showing genuine concern over the well-being of his father.

"I'll tell you everything later," I said. "It was a crazy misunderstanding, and your father handled it with more decency than expected or required. I know you two were arguing before you went to pick up your mom, but give him a break."

Dutch leaned over and gave me a quick hug. It was so unexpected that, later, I didn't remember if I had hugged him back or stood there like a stick. He ran across the street and jumped into the back seat. Charlotte got into the driver's seat and drove her family away.

Stew was sitting in the driver's seat of his wife's car, waiting for the last emergency vehicle to leave. I walked over, pulled open the door, and pulled him out by his ear.

I let go after ten seconds when I noticed the police laughing. "Stew, start talking now."

Stew walked inside, sat at the kitchen table, and bent down to retrieve my laptop, flicking off a piece of beef. I think he was tempted to eat it until he saw me watching him. Did I say where he had gotten his name?

Damn it. How much I loved working for public radio could not compete with my anger at having to pay for a new laptop. They have asked for it back yet, and if they do, could I return it broken?

I pulled the second chair away from the table, and it clanged against something metal. I reached down and grabbed the empty stew pot and tossed it in the sink from ten feet away. All my respect for this kitchen was slipping away fast.

"Stew, I'm only going to say this once. I want no bullshit from you. Tell me what you meant."

FORTY-THREE

When someone utters a confession of murder, you should be ready
for anything, but how do you prepare yourself to take on the weight
of someone's guilt?

He remained quiet and sat back in the chair.

"Don't pretend you don't know. Don't lay this all on me. We
carried this for years, and you're going to play dumb now."

There was no laughter or anger in his voice. A new streak of
sweat rolled down my back, and a lump rolled up in my throat.

"What are you talking about?"

Stew studied me before he answered. "You don't know, do you?
She never told you? She never made contact." He stood up and
retreated into the corner behind the table, rubbed his face, and then
finally lowered his hands on a kitchen chair, looking like he wanted
to snap it in half. I waited for him to speak.

"There was . . . remember . . . I . . ."

Stew was mumbling, and I was beginning to shake. My skin was
clammy, and my insides were boiling. I felt myself shrinking with
each tremor.

He sat back down in the chair and let it out. "I thought you knew. One morning you ran out the door early as usual, and Mom saw that you had forgotten your permission slip."

I held up my hand, and he paused. My temples started pounding. I curled up my knees to my chest and cocooned my body on the wooden kitchen chair. He had done this in high school.

"Go on," I said.

"Mom insisted I find you before school and hand it directly to you so you wouldn't freak out. She rushed me out the door. I saw you and Maz walking towards the library, and I figured I would see you there. I stopped at the gas station for a soda, and by the time I got to the library, your stuff was there, but I couldn't find you, so I tossed the paper on top of your notebook. I was going to take off, but Lulu was there and I was thinking about asking her to the prom. She was talking with Boss though, so I left. Still had not seen you at this point. I got back in the car and spilled my soda and was trying to clean it. I finally saw you leave the library but go back in. Two minutes later, you came out with Leo wearing a different jacket."

The narrative I had been living with for decades was changing with each word Stew spoke. My arms wrapped around my knees, allowing my body to sway ever so slightly, allowing my heart to beat instead of seizing up.

He continued, "The rain was pounding down. I ran into school, hoping to ask what was up, but I lost you in the crowd. I went to your locker, but you weren't there. After practice that day, I gave Shelby and Ace a ride home. I saw you walking on the other side of Pultz Road. Ace said that you were probably delivering Bo's project assignment from the class the three of you shared. He called you teacher's pet and said you probably volunteered to bring her the stuff from class since she was out. Ace was still bitter because you wouldn't help him on some assignment. He lived three doors down from Bo. I went into his house for a piss and walked over to Bo's.

"As I was walking down the driveway, I heard screaming. I didn't know what to do. There was a loud crash and a bang.

Someone was shouting, 'You're not leaving me. Not alive.' I backed away from the open doorway and spied through the kitchen window. I saw this lady raising some type of marble pyramid statue thing above her head. I don't know what came over me. I just grabbed a garden shovel that was lying on the ground. When I entered through the open doorway, the lady was using the marble statue as a battering ram on the door. I knew whoever was on the other side was in trouble."

Stew's blue eyes were dark, his face pale. He sat still, telling the story as if he was reading the telephone book. One line after the other, like there was no connection to the previous statement.

"She didn't see me come in. I picked up the shovel and swung it at her. It connected with the back of her head. As she fell to the floor, she hit her head on the counter, and I'm not sure, but she may have impaled herself with the marble pyramid, because at some point, there was blood. No idea how long or how short of a time I stood there. Something came over me, something like a flash of light or reality. I knew what I had done. I wiped down the handle of the shovel with my sweatshirt and walked back to my car."

His words hit me with such force my body rejected reality, and for the second time since being back in Dome, I rolled forward and hurled. The vomit hit the floor, spraying Stew's shoes.

FORTY-FOUR

After my hurling incident, we sat there, surrounded by silence, neither of us moving to clean up. The vomit was congealing with the stew fat on the floor.

"Well, I guess that's all that needs to be said about that." Stew finally kicked off his vomit soaked shoes, jumped around the wet mess and lumbered over to the broom closet. He scooped up the vomit and did a half-ass job of getting the stew off the rest of the kitchen floor. He tossed the mop head and his tennis shoes into the garbage bag and took the bag to the trash cans in the garage.

"I have never spoken those words out loud before," Stew said.

"It's a hard story to tell."

"I meant the words *I've done it before*. That was the closest I ever got to telling anyone. For a while, I was convinced you had seen me do it, because you were acting so strange for a few days. Bo never returned to school. Ace said his mom got the feeling Bo's family were like gypsies moving from place to place. The lady who owned the house could only get Bo's mom to sign a six-month lease and was already looking for new tenants. I pretended they just packed up and moved on. I always knew Bo's mom never moved on."

"Yvette."

"What?" Stew asked.

"Yvette. That was her name," I said.

Stew twitched.

Tit for tat. It was my time to tell Stew, but Maz, Leo, and I had made a promise that we would never break our word. Sure, we had told Dutch, but we'd thought he was one of us. I'd chose the pact the three of us made over any loyalty to my brother. It scared me how easy it was to start the story where Stew left off. Once again, Bo continued to teach me who I was as a person. This lie rolled out of me so easily it should have been a sign I needed help.

"You were right. I was headed to Bo's, but I didn't see you. When I got there, she was packing up the car saying they're moving on. Bo said her mother wanted to experience spring in the South, so I left without ever giving her the project assignment. I felt so bad for her. Always moving around. It was no wonder why she couldn't make friends, and the only people she thought to impress were teachers. I really didn't know her, but I felt sad for her."

"Did you go in the house?" Stew asked.

"You mean did I see Yvette?" I asked.

Stew nodded.

"Not really. Thinking back now, it could have been . . . it might have . . . I'm guessing that is was her in the trunk. I remember thinking the boxes and luggage were neatly stacked in the back seat, but there was a lump in the open trunk and I saw a pair of white sneakers. Bo had made an effort of saying something like 'My mom can't stand having our shoes stink up our clothes, so we put them back here and our clothes up front with us.' I always thought that was such an odd comment."

I could have stopped there. But Stew had lived with his secret for so long, I wanted him to have an end. To face the fact he killed someone. The unknown, no matter how much the possibilities were sugarcoated, it could still rot someone from the inside out.

Stew let out a few deep breaths and tilted his head up towards the heavens. "That's great. Now tell me the rest. Why were you wearing her coat that morning?"

"I was screwing around with her. She would not help me on an assignment, and I was mad. Later, I felt bad, and that was why I volunteered to bring her the homework."

I should have felt worse for the lies spilling out of me so easily.

"There's more." I wasn't sure if Stew had heard me. "Two days ago when we met for breakfast, you said something—you knew I was back because another girl had disappeared. You and I both know Bo didn't leave voluntarily. You think she left because she ran away from her dead mother and something *I* did? I took her raincoat during a thunderstorm. I appreciate you including me in the mix, but no thank you. Your imagination is crap."

Lies were just like the tulips in my father's garden. Just simmering under the dirt and ready to pop out anytime.

"I'm here to escape a crappy spring weekend in the city and, yes, to get the details firsthand of a missing girl. You know I love this stuff. Not so much the personal grief side of the story. Remember, during college and years afterwards, Jam and I would be on vacation and would always add to our tacky photo collection —us in front of the house that inspired *The Amityville Horror* and outside the house where the wife whacked off the guy's penis, Lizzy Borden's house. I also love the mystery. Like I said, not so much about the tragedy, a good real-life mystery. Since my computer is dead and I might get fired if I don't get working on a new one soon, maybe I'll go work for a private investigator. My secret but not-so-secret passion for wanting to solve real-life mysteries."

I needed to stop talking. When my kids were younger, the longer the story they told, the bigger the lie. Right now, my story was building into Mount Everest. Maybe it was nerves, but I had a diversion.

"What I said before about there being more to the story, well, there is. Bo is back. Did you know Bo is Hattie and is married to Maz?"

Stew pulled his body forward, looking away from the ceiling and at me for conformation. "No kidding. The lady with the black hair is Bo."

I nodded. "You got it."

"I've only seen her once. That is incredible." Stew laughed and then shrunk into himself like a frighten turtle. "How can I walk in there again?"

"What do you mean?"

"How can I see the person whose mother I . . . Did she see me? Does she want revenge or solace? Why come here?" Stew's thoughts were as jangled as my stomach.

"Did you know Yvette abused her, and she had such an unstable childhood? She was probably a frightened teenager who thought god sent an angel to rescue her. After you left and she packed, she seemed to be fine. Maybe she's a great actress or was in shock from seeing her mother dead. Shock can do terrible things to a person's mind. If that was Yvette in the trunk, that means Bo moved the body or somebody else did. Either way, no one called the police. Bo ran because that was all she knew to do in life. That was the life lesson Yvette had taught her.

"I don't think she's looking to exact revenge. Maz told me they reunited a few years ago. It was her idea to come back here and live the life the rest of us had while she had been living in terror. This place had brought her glimpses of a life she wanted."

"I don't know if I can process all that. Tell me what I walked into."

It had been about an hour ago but also a lifetime ago that, before my brother had confessed to murder, two men had been fighting in the kitchen and Mrs. Bein had tried saving the day.

"It started with Van and his son, Dutch, arguing on the back porch. Mrs. Bein probably heard that commotion since she hears and sees everything. A little while later, Dutch left. Maz comes in and gets angry at Van and charges at him. More shouting, this time some of it was from me trying to keep the peace. Mrs. Bein came in, probably thinking I'm in trouble and fires off a shot right as you came in, and you know the rest."

"Why was Maz upset at Van?"

"You won't believe it. Maz thinks Van had something to do with that girl's disappearance since they found her behind his house."

"Here? Across the street? I thought they found her in the parkway."

"They did. Van is renting the condo across the street while his house is being renovated. He bought his parents' house over in the constellation section. Gigi was found in the parkway behind the house."

"Why is it Maz's problem? I mean, good for him if Van is responsible, but why does Maz care?"

"I'm not sure if I know the whole story." Another easy lie—I knew more than the story. I *was* the story. "Bo knew something was troubling Gigi before she disappeared and tried helping her. When she went missing, Bo freaked out. Maz was just channeling Bo's anger."

Stew seemed to accept my answer.

So I asked, "What happened to Mrs. Bein?"

"When you were giving your statement to the police, I heard one cop talking to another one. Mrs. Bein will be charged for shooting her gun, and apparently, once a year, she does something stupid like this. She has a record for firing a gun. I know of one story last summer, the folks at the rear of the complex here were complaining about the coyotes howling at night. Mrs. Bein set herself up on a chair in the bushes in that green space between here and the industrial park. When the coyotes came near, she shot off warning shots. It didn't go over well with the police and some neighbors."

"I guess I'll not stop her tomorrow when she takes Pa's newspaper." My mind wondered back to the green space Mrs. Bein had rid of the coyotes and where Leo and I had walked.

Leo! I forgot I said I would pick him up.

I jumped up, ready to toss Stew to the curb, grab my purse and keys, but I ended up being another casualty.

FORTY-FIVE

Eager to rescue Leo from the hospital, I failed to see how badly the kitchen floor had been cleaned up. One step, and my foot kicked out from under me. My arms swung up and around like I was doing the backstroke. Stew reached out to help steady me, but my arm pushed his arm down towards my face. The hundred-pound metal watch on his wrist clipped my temple. Blood flowed down my cheek as my butt hit the floor.

"Who still wears chunky watches? You dork! Don't you have one of the latest slim techie watches?"

Stew extended his hand to help me up, and I brushed it away. I rolled over on my knees, grabbed the counter, and yanked myself up. Stew had not so much mopped up my vomit and leftover stew but glazed over it with soapy water.

"Get me a towel," I said.

Stew tossed me a hand towel from the countertop.

I tossed it back. "How about a fresh towel with less chance of infection."

"You might not want to hear this, but you might need stitches. Let me take you to the hospital."

"You need to clean this floor properly."

"It can wait until we get back. Let me get a pair of dads shoes."

Stew ran upstairs, and I grabbed my phone and purse and delicately made my way out the front door. I had my keys but not my car, so I walked over to Leo's truck and found the keys under the floor mat where Dutch had left them.

I left Stew behind but not his words. He had killed Yvette. From his story, Bo must have been trapped in a bathroom or bedroom and had not seen him. When I arrived a few minutes later standing in the open doorway, she had come from some other room. I didn't see what direction because I couldn't take my eyes off Yvette's lifeless form.

She assumed it was me, and I her.

Bo said, "This morning I escaped, but now I'm free." There was no emotion. There was no delight or dread in her voice, only fact.

Then and now, I thought it was shock.

"You still need to go," I said but was unsure if I was asking or telling her to go. "This will be a cleaner escape for you. You can be her, at least keep her active on paper. If she did taxes, you do taxes. You be you, and sometimes Yvette. *Sometimes 'Y.'* Move out like you always do. Where is Olsen's car?"

"Two blocks over in the grocery store lot," Bo answered.

I stood there in the open doorway for minutes, hours, days, years—my mind was a dull buzz. Later, I only remembered the bright fluorescent lights and the cold outside air.

She had intended to take only one bag with her and use Olsen's car to get her to the Greyhound bus station in Iowa. Now, she had to move out of the small rental duplex like they always had. Clothes were their only possessions. I stayed in the kitchen while Bo stuffed all the clothes into garbage bags, and I put them in the back seat. We worked in silence.

The last load we carried together—Yvette rolled up in a bed

quilt. We carried her out with all our strength and placed her in the trunk, her white Keds sticking out from under the quilt. We cleaned up the floor and tossed the rags in the trunk.

There was no thought of who could be watching or what the neighbors thought. The car was on the single driveway twenty feet from the door. Bo and Yvette had moved so much, it was easy for her.

She left the keys to the sad little apartment on the linoleum countertop and switched off the one remaining light.

I spoke first. "You don't have much time before—"

"I've survived everything. I can handle what I have to do next," Bo said. She handed me Olsen's key ring with the rook hanging from it.

"Why did you come back here? You were supposed to leave town right away this morning."

"I wanted her to know I won. Just one victory is all I wanted. I wanted to see her face when I walked out on her. Should have known better. She pushed me down and dragged me to the cellar steps and locked me in. She only let me out to tell me to make dinner to prove she always wins. She laughed in my face and told me I didn't have the guts to leave. When I headed for the door, she came after me, so I jumped into that bathroom."

Bo opened the driver's-side door and kept her back to me. She had fresh bruises on her neck. "Tell the boys thank you." She paused before she got in.

I didn't know if she said something else I couldn't hear or maybe I hoped she was too choked up to say something to me.

Now thirty-four years later, after Stew's confession, I realized she thought I had killed her mother. What do you say to the person who set you free but also killed your only family?

My body was trembling. Tears rolled down my face.

Shame. It was all I felt.

Earlier this afternoon, I'd thought that maybe Bo had used us, and she wasn't the victim but a killer and was playing us again. All the despair and sorrow I had come across in my life would never compare to the depth of shame I felt in that moment.

FORTY-SIX

I didn't remember how I'd gotten to the hospital. The speed bump in the parking lot woke me from my daze. I parked and just sat in the truck, holding the towel to my head.

Stew had sent a text: *Please get your eye fixed. Hope you call me later.*

He sent another text: *Hope I can call you.*

Stew was in our parents' kitchen cleaning up a mess I'd started. I had abandoned him after his greatest confession, and I was worried about myself. I hadn't thought about what he must have felt right then. I couldn't repeat the words he'd said, much less do what he had done. Fight-or-flight. He had blindly protected someone he'd barely known.

For years, I struggled with the fact that I had moved a dead body and let someone get away with murder. I just hadn't known it was Stew.

Ten minutes ago, I ran away from my guilt and left him empty.

There was one answer he would get from me: *ALWAYS.*

I left my emotions in the truck. Emotions and the load of lies, I left behind me. Walking into the emergency room, crying, with a bloody eye, would raise questions of whether I was living in a safe environment and if I needed help. While I might have needed assistance in some aspects of my life, I wanted to save those resources for those who truly needed it.

I tossed my insurance card and driver's license to the lady at the counter. They had my file from three years ago when I had come in with poison ivy, so paperwork was minimal.

My shame and guilt still hung with me and prevented me from lying about being able to breathe. If one ever wanted to jump a line at a hospital, they should tell the staff they can't breathe, and they would see a flood of people immediately. It would also cost them dearly in time spent inside the emergency room and the insurance bills would be outrageous, so they must be careful if they want a bed or a chair in the waiting room.

My wait was brief. The doctor seemed pleased his patient wasn't hacking the flu at him, there was no pus to be extracted, and that I could clearly verbalize my ailment. His pun-filled humor pulled me out of my funk. There wasn't one pun worth repeating, but he kept going until I cracked a smile. He worked on my cut and my mood, both of which would carry a scar, but my mood was lifting from the shallow.

I asked if he had worked on someone else with a similar wound to the temple but a deeper cut than mine. He changed the subject as a good doctor should to avoid talking about other patients. The doctor applied something called tissue adhesive instead of stitches. It wasn't as bad as I'd thought, but it was good I hadn't bandaged it at home.

On the way out of the room, the doctor said, "You'll have less scarring and a lot smaller headache."

Smaller than what, I wondered, but then I realized he was talking about Leo.

Leo had sent a text asking if I was close to picking him up. I told him I was probably closer than expected and asked him for his room number. He said the nurse would have to walk me back to the room. He couldn't leave without a ride, and they were holding him in his same emergency room since they were slow.

I told him to show me his room number, and I would show him mine. I sent a picture of my wound.

From the hallway came the nurse's voice, "Back to your room, sir. I'm not telling you again."

Leo replied, "But my ride is finally here."

"Really, sir. Do you see her?" she said with a laugh. "Do we need to send you back for a brain scan? No one in the front office has claimed you."

"He's looking for me," I yelled and walked out.

The nurse turned her attention back to Leo. "Good lord, what do you think—I'm a fool? You're trying to bribe patients into taking you home? You need someone to watch you."

"Nurse Rose, I'm not kidding," Leo begged. He was still in his jeans but was sporting a hospital gown that went to his knees and exposed his sweet butt.

"He isn't lying. I just got delayed." I did a double take when I saw Leo's face and suppressed a laugh. "The stitches make you look tough, but the black eyes make you look like you lost a fight."

She looked at my wound and then Leo's bandage. "Maybe you two belong together. Let me make sure you both don't need an escort."

The doctor walked by and freed us both.

Leo would need to rest for a few days, but would be fine. He was allowed to sleep, and I didn't have to wake him every few hours. I felt my face blush when the nurse read the instructions to me. It was suddenly so intimate to be given instructions on caring for someone.

The claw of the hammer had ripped about a two-inch gash into his temple. He had several stitches and a massive headache; however, all his tests had come back clear. His nose wasn't broken, but the black eyes would get worse before they got better. He said the pain pills were helping, and the throbbing was reduced to a rhythmic pulse.

"Do you want to put on your sweatshirt instead of walking out in a hospital gown?" I asked.

"The nurse cut it off because of the blood. She was overzealous and thought I had a chest wound." He did a simple curtsy, holding the gown, and that finally broke my mood and brought me to full laughter.

"I feel like I should put on a gown. We don't know how to be around each other without wearing matching clothes," I said.

"Well, I could take the gown off and you could take your top off, and we'll match."

"Not in my ER!" Nurse Rose interjected.

"You're just jealous I didn't ask you," he replied with a laugh.

He started to leave, and I paused. He was charming, cute, and made me laugh. I had lusted after Van, but it was Leo I felt at ease with. Not once had I thought to check my hair or wonder if the bandage made me look silly. I had genuine concern about how he was doing.

"What's wrong?" Leo asked.

"Just making sure I have everything with me."

We walked out of the emergency room and into the parking lot.

"Can we walk faster? People will think I escaped. Where is your car?" he said.

"Hattie's. I have your truck."

Leo stopped in his tracks.

I knew instantly what he would say. "Take it easy. It's in the last row, and when I left it, there were no other cars parked near your beast."

"Give me the keys."

"No way. Doctor's orders. You need a babysitter." It was my turn to stop in my tracks. *Why am I picking him up? Where is his wife? I could even call my ex, and he would drive up to help me. Is he that much of a cretin that his wife won't come get her husband from the hospital?*

"Let me drive," Leo begged.

I ignored him.

"One condition," he said, "you drive where I tell you and just listen when we get there."

"You're not in any condition to start giving out commands. Keep walking," I said.

"Just agree to that, or I'll walk back in and report my truck stolen."

"Whatever." That was the only response I could muster.

Leo headed to the driver's side and raised his hand for me to be quiet. "I'm just getting a sweatshirt from the back seat. As long as you can handle getting out of this parking lot without hitting anything, I might enjoy being chauffeured around by you."

I held the passenger-side door open for him, and he slowly pulled himself up into the cab, but not before I glimpsed his body when he tore off the hospital gown. I guess I could add lusting to Leo's list. It really didn't matter how long the pro column in favor of Leo got, he would always have that one in the negative column— wife.

The ride was as smooth as I could make it. I eased over the speed bumps, took the corners at a reasonable speed, and kept both hands on the wheel. It was for me as much as it was for Leo. My head was hurting, there was no food left in my stomach, and my nerves were shot.

He pointed out turns, and I filled him in on the last with Bo in the hospital for her headache, Dutch and me looking for my keys, Van answering police questions, Dutch leaving to get his mom, Maz and Van fighting, Mrs. Bein's escapades, and finally wrapping up the story of Stew sending all of us down the stairs.

I stopped short of telling him sometimes "*y*." I would never break the promise Maz, Leo, and I made, and I'll never betray Stew's confidence.

"You're probably gonna have to repeat that again for me. That is a lot to take in since I left Van's house."

"I'm sure before the day is over we'll have more to add to the story."

"Pull into the second driveway, and come with me please." Leo undid his seatbelt, opened the door, and waited while I just sat there. "Please come with me. I know there's a lot going on, but if I don't show you now, it might never happen. I don't expect anything from you, but just listen."

He stepped out of the truck and didn't look back. I had no idea what he was about to show me. There wasn't much more I could take. Bo and Stew had pretty much rocked my world. I had thrown up twice and shit my pants once since I'd been back. What could he tell me that would send my body and mind convulsing?

Was I prepared for this?

FORTY-SEVEN

Leo held open the side door of the house, and we walked into a living room under construction. Furniture had been pushed to the corner, and raw floorboards were exposed. The kitchen had recently been redone but was absent of a table and flooring.

"Excuse the mess. You can tell I'm redoing the floor. I had to fire the flooring company, and I'm left in a bind. It's been like this for several months. Please follow me."

We passed a half bath and went into a bedroom that had been converted into a den. Leo bent down, opened a filing cabinet drawer, and stayed still.

"Are you all right?" I stepped in and touched him on the shoulder.

He rolled onto his butt. "Yeah, my head is just hurting." He eased himself onto an old futon and pulled out two files and handed them to me. "Listen, I'm married."

My head was beginning to hurt more, but maybe it was my heart dropping a little. He'd never said he wasn't married, but a small piece of me always hoped it wasn't true.

"It isn't what you think. Please look at the files. You will see the divorce papers. The first one I signed over a year and a half ago.

You will find Gina signed them six months later. If you see the next folder it's the start of the medical bills. She finally signed the papers and was in her car when she had a stroke and crashed her vehicle. She requires pretty much 'round-the-clock care.'"

I lowered myself onto the futon. He had my full attention. The lawyer documents were a blur, and his words were hitting me like I was on the bottom of a ball pit, trying to find my way to the surface but more balls kept me from finding fresh air.

"I was still her emergency contact, although we had been living apart for nearly a year. The hospital called me when she was brought in by the ambulance. The nurse handed me her phone and purse with the signed documents. All I had to do was drop them in the mail. I could have done it at the hospital, but that would make her the responsibility of my daughter or Gina's mother, and I couldn't do that to either of them. Peggy, her mother, is old and will need help herself. Jenna has her whole life in front of her. She should not have to make these type of decisions or not go away to college.

"She's bedridden and living at Peggy's house. That's where I had to run to this afternoon. Peggy thought she messed up the medicine. Gina can speak, but there isn't much left of the person we knew. I'm fixing this house up to accommodate a hospital bed and all her medical needs, a room for Peggy and, soon, a full-time caretaker for both of them."

"I'm so sorry. Why didn't you say something?" I said.

"At what point would it have been right?"

I sank farther into the futon and tried to understand everything he was saying. "Again, I'm sorry you have—"

"That's just it. I don't want pity. Sure I probably should have said something at the food truck event. It's just that I'm done with the pity. I tell someone, and I get pity attention. The women get all Nurse Nightingale and think they can fix broken me. Never thought I was the broken one. Or, worse, they get all weird when I say I have to take Gina to a doctor's appointment, like they're jealous. I wanted something with a beautiful woman who wanted me for me and where I could leave that corner of my life out of it for a short time."

"I'm sorry." I held up my hand for him not to shun my apology. "Listen, I'm saying sorry for being such a bitch."

"I gave you plenty of reasons."

We exchanged half smiles.

"A million bucks, and I would not have guessed that was what I was gonna hear when I walked in. Thank you for sharing," I said.

"Thank you for listening and not driving off with my truck."

"Of course. Now I have an idea. Go take a shower and grab your toothbrush," I said. "Don't ask questions. Just go."

Leo did as he was told. He spent ten minutes showering and changing clothes and did one productive thing before I just about melted into the futon. It was easy being mad at Leo, but suddenly the dating door was wide-open. Wait, was it open? Maybe he just wanted one night of sex. I was so lost in my thoughts, I didn't notice him standing in the doorway.

Leo stood there in sweats, holding a toothbrush like a kid ready for his first day of summer camp. Crazy hair and all. He caught me staring. "I didn't wash my hair because I didn't want soap and water near the bandage."

"Is there anything else you need to do before we leave?" I asked.

"Just lock up the house, but to be honest, I don't know if I can contribute any more to solving the disappearance and reappearance of Gigi tonight."

"No more homework tonight. Just lock up and meet me at your truck."

I drove us to Zsoka's and picked a large pizza, several salads, breadsticks, noodle soup, and chicken parmesan. Leo looked at me like I was crazy when I came out carrying a box of food. "Dinner for us tonight and something for me to eat tomorrow."

"I was worried we were going to a party," Leo said.

"Just me—the babysitter—and you, the one who must do everything I say per doctor's orders."

"I don't think that is exactly what the doctor said."

"I think your head injury is worse than you think," I replied.

On the way to my parents' house, I asked about his renovation nightmare.

He said, "I got up in the middle of the night once, went into the kitchen for some water. Out the window, I saw some guy reaching under the tarp in the driveway that was covering building materials. I figured the guy was trying to steal equipment. I went back to my room for my phone, and by the time I got back, the guy was gone and the tarp was still covering the equipment.

"The next morning, I got up and went for a run, came back, and looked to see if anything was missing—mind you, I didn't know what was under the tarp to begin with. There ended up being a stash of pills and cash under there. I left it where it was, went to shower and get ready. One guy showed up at seven, and two other guys at seven thirty, unloading more equipment and ready to work with no complaints about some of their stuff missing.

"However, my neighbor, Mrs. Sissel, complained to me about the number of workers coming and going during the day."

I laughed. "Every neighborhood has a Mrs. Bein."

"I finally figured out what the deal was. The crew lead was dealing drugs during the day. It was kinda ingenious but stupid at the same time. Changing locations every few weeks. Keeping the stuff out of your possession allows for deniability. It was him that night getting some cash.

"This home was supposed to be for Gina and Peggy. I was doing some of the work myself. It's five blocks to my shop, so sometimes I crash there at night if Jenna is away at school. Once I realized what was going on, I fired them immediately. The owner of the company had a fit. I started to tell him about his crew, and he got even madder. He said his son isn't to blame and would not let me say anything, so I walked out.

"I only hired them because they're from Dome, and I figured I should use someone in the area. The owner was such an ass I went to the police and told them what I had observed. No idea if they did something or not, but I worried about the next house and who might be home when the wrong people showed up."

We were nearly at my parents' condo, and it hit me with a ton of bricks. I couldn't hear Leo talking or really notice the cars around.

"Lou . . . Lou . . . *Lou!*" Leo's arm came across my right shoulder.

A car honked behind us. I was doing twenty miles an hour when it should have been forty-five. I hit the gas pedal and tore into the mountain section. I slammed on the brakes in front of my parents' place.

"What's going on? Don't make me take you back to the hospital," Leo said.

"Help me grab the food while I send a text."

Leo didn't move.

"What is that look for?" I asked.

"I thought you were supposed to be taking care of me and not barking orders."

He had such a wide grin I couldn't help but laugh.

"Fine, sit there, and I'll do it *all* myself," I said.

Leo was out of the truck before me. He came around to open my door. I grabbed the box of food and gave him the keys to his truck.

Stew had left the front door unlocked, and we made it inside without incident. The floor was spotless and presumably safe to walk on. I shuffled myself in. I kicked the basement door shut and noticed Stew had wiped the blood off the stairwell wall. Maz had left a few marks when we'd all made our way down the stairs. Stew had also put duct tape over the hole in the sliding glass door sporting the perfect webbing.

Leo put the pizza on the table, and everything else in the fridge. "This is no salad night."

"Right on, but grab the breadsticks." I poured two waters.

"I could use a beer," Leo said.

"I could use about five beers, but we should probably keep you, the pain pills, and beer separated for a few days."

"It's disappointing. I thought you would be the fun babysitter. Now tell me what that episode in the truck was all about. You nearly got us rear-ended."

"What was the name of the drywall and flooring company you fired?"

He held the pizza slice midflight. "I thought we're not going to do any detective work tonight."

"You asked about where my mind went when I was driving, so either let me answer or stop asking questions."

"Fair point." He put his slice down and waited before he answered. He sat back in the chair, taking a deep breath. Watching him was like a camping lantern getting brighter as I pumped it full of fuel and then lit it. There would be a small glow of light, it would flicker, and eventually gets brighter. "The company is Dome Home Renovations."

"Do you know anything about them?"

"You mean besides that it's the same company Van was using?" Leo started eating the pizza as if his life depended on it.

The company website information page listed a profile for the owner, Robert Calraug Senior. He had grown up in a small town up north, had gone to college, met his college sweetheart, and had two daughters and one son who worked with him. The profile picture showed the family standing outside a church. I couldn't help think that the son, Bobby Junior, could have spent more time at church. I felt like I had seen him before.

Junior, aka Cal, was easy to find on social media. He had graduated from high school here in Dome five years ago. Long curly brown hair with deep-set brown eyes. A little too skinny but a smile as wide as a mile.

I showed my phone to Leo. "Is this your crew leader?"

"That's him. The boss's son leading three guys, all with more experience than that idiot."

"I could see Gigi falling for him."

"What is this theory of yours?" Leo asked.

"When I was in the bathroom at the diner, two girls came in. I didn't catch the whole thing, but I overheard she was dating someone older who they had never met. One of them alluded to getting some so-called vitamins before finals and wasn't sure what they were going to do without Gigi."

"Holy crap. Did we just figure this out?" Leo said.

"This is just a working theory: Gigi was getting some pills from Cal and selling them to her friends. She went with Cal, remember Dutch told us she was skipping first hour, and something must have happened."

"That is pretty incredible. I have to say that's some good thinking, but how does Bo fit into all of this?"

"I don't know if I have that figured out yet. Let's save that for tomorrow."

Leo agreed, and we cleaned up the kitchen easily, like an old married couple who had been doing it for years. When Leo took the pizza box to the garbage can in the garage, I texted Stew that I was fine and would call him tomorrow.

Leo and I made our way to the living room sofa and mindlessly watched college basketball. When that got old, I switched it to reruns of *Law and Order*. Leo would give me the entire plot and the jury verdict, then return it to a different college game.

We sat side by side, not cuddling, but we were absolutely sidling up next to each other. This could have been my first Netflix 'n' chill night, as the kids say, but all we did was chill like adults. At one point, I could feel us dozing off.

I made sure the doors were locked and lights were off. I didn't want Van knocking on the door this evening telling some half truths about his wife or soon-to-be ex-wife. There was no need for a false marital confession from him. I put on something that resembled pajamas, brushed my teeth, and went and got Leo.

Despite the early night, Leo was sleeping when I found him on the couch.

"Hey, wake up. If you stay here, your back will be as sore as your head tomorrow. Follow me. Where is your toothbrush?"

"I left it at the house. I thought you were kidding."

"Doctor's orders, I have to watch you. My mother keeps the free ones from the dentist in the top drawer for her grandkids." I walked into the bedroom, waiting for Leo. My heart skipped a beat when I saw the cinch bag and diary. I quickly tossed it under the bed in time before Leo walked in."

"A big comfy bed for me. That is so kind of you." Leo made a few steps towards me.

"Nice try. You get the bunk bed, and I get the big bed."

"You know I could wake up in the middle of the night confused to where I am and jump up and hit my head on the top bunk."

I flicked off the lights. "Then sleep on the top bunk."

The room was dark, and my eyes were adjusting to the moonlight. When Leo stepped towards the bunks, I pulled him back. Effortlessly, he stepped to me. We were so close I could smell his fresh, minty breath.

We lingered like that for a while. His hands found my hips, and mine found his. Our noses touched. I let his breath heat my cheek until I couldn't take it anymore. We kissed, and when I opened my eyes, his eyes were smiling at me. Then I saw his bandage.

I put my hand on his chest. "Ok, now, that needs to stop. No big activities for you."

Leo laughed. "I know, doctor's orders." He turned towards the bunk.

"We can share the comfy bed, just no funny business."

"If you think shaking the sheets is a laughing matter, then let me teach you a thing or two. Boy, have you been missing out."

"Shaking the sheets? What are you, an eighty-year-old grandma? Now, shut up. Get in and slide over," I said.

Leo left on his T-shirt and slipped off his sweats, leaving on his boxers. He got in and shifted to the window side, giving me plenty of space. I crawled in, lay on my back, and reached for his arm, interlocking our fingers and placing his arm across my belly.

With a soft voice, he spoke. "Thank you for listening. Just getting someone to hear what you have to say is nice."

It was silly nodding in the dark, but I don't think he needed a reply.

Leo was asleep within minutes, and my mind circled around to Gigi.

Had she gotten mixed up with Cal? That would make sense with what Leo said. What had Bo seen that made her so concerned for Gigi, and what had led her to Van's house?

There was something else ticking away in the back of my brain. I was dozing when it hit me, and I shot upright.

The red dirt.

How could the red dirt have ended up on the kitchen floor? The only place it could be found was in the parkway behind Van's house. Nallwhit Park was over several hundred acres, but getting red mud on one's shoes would have taken some effort. The landscaping debacle didn't cover the entire area, but it covered the area behind the house because Dutch had said he'd been covered in it when he fell.

Did someone know Gigi was in that house?

FORTY-EIGHT

I fell asleep with the mystery of the red dirt swirling in and out of my dreams. We had gone to bed out of exhaustion with stitches on our heads at nine. I woke up at five thirty. Leo was on his side in the same position as when he had first gone to bed. I guessed with stitches on his temple, there was only one side to sleep on.

A proper shower for the first time in two days felt good. I applied some light makeup, and with a wet head, I went downstairs and made some coffee.

Leo came down at six thirty. His hair was crazier than yesterday. I wanted to run my fingers through it, so to be safe I handed him some coffee.

"Morning. How do you feel?" I asked.

"A little stiff and groggy."

"Drink up, it'll help. There's no milk but sugar if you need it."

"I like it as it is. I have an idea that will make this better, but you should probably dry your hair," Leo said. "Don't look at me crazy, you will understand. Trust me."

Like an obedient kid, I ran up and dried my hair. Leo on the deck when I came back down, wrapped in the comforter from the bunk bed with the second comforter waiting for me. "I left your coffee inside so it wouldn't get cold."

The dawn was just breaking on the horizon. The spring clouds kept it from being a pretty sunrise, but the slow light was a perfect way to start the day.

"Were you able to solve any other mysteries while I was zonked out?" Leo asked.

"I wasn't far behind you catching sleep, but I was restless."

"What was still bothering you?"

"Bo—how did she know to go to Van's house?"

"How did *you* know to go there?" Leo asked. He held up a hand. "Wait, that came out harsh. I just meant, why do you think it was Van, or did you not trust the kid?"

"They found Gigi in Nallwhit Park close to their house, and I couldn't shake this feeling about either. I don't think Dutch has told us everything. He might not be lying, but he's holding back. I saw someone leave that condo Friday night. They didn't take their phone, or at least, they turned off their tracking app. Plus, I had no other ideas."

"So, when in doubt, you guess. Maybe you should go to Vegas. You hit the jackpot at Van's house."

"Do you think it's too early to call Maz?" I asked.

"You should wait until the sun is fully up."

"This fresh air feels good. Nice idea you had."

"I usually go running in the morning but didn't think that would be wise with the stitches still being fresh. I've been doing a lot of running lately. It helps clear my head."

"Are there good trails around here?"

"Depends where I am in the mornings. If I'm at my house, I run towards town square. If I'm at the place I'm renovating, I stick to Simool Road since the sidewalks are pretty good."

"I would think the traffic would be annoying. Why not the parkway?"

"I usually zone out the traffic, and the parkway has limited sidewalks. Predawn, I don't care to cross with the coyotes. I like leaving the house and just start running and not fooling around with driving. My distance isn't great, but just getting out and doing something for myself feels good in the mornings."

Did he know I was asking if he would have reason to bring red dirt into my house? I thought I had played that pretty smoothly.

We chatted about nonsense for a bit, and he offered to get us breakfast.

"Sure, that sounds nice," I said, then went inside, Leo following behind me.

"Are you good to drive?" I picked up his shoes he'd left by the door as ransom.

"I was fine last night but didn't want to argue with you in the parking lot wearing a hospital gown."

I wondered if he had noticed me checking out the soles of his shoes. The guy probably had multiple shoes, but I had to start somewhere. When I gave him back his shoes, he had a strange look on his face. Sweat poured down my back and, not surprisingly, my stomach flipped but held it together. Did I just spend the night with a man who is involved with Gigi? Was he part of the drug operation and had come up with the cover story?

He reached for his shoes, which I quickly released from my grasp. I was contemplating my options: running out the front door or—crap—I didn't have a second option.

Leo fumbled with his words twice before finally dropping his shoes and stepped closer to me. My fight-or-flight instincts were stuck fighting inside me. I was pleased my body was done throwing and going, but something had to be done.

He finally broke his hesitation. "Listen, this is crazy. Minus the whole missing girl, Bo coming back, and Maz's secrets, I had a great time with you this weekend. Friday night was the first time in a long time I've laughed, and sharing coffee with you this morning was a bonus reward after getting to spend time with you last night. Whatever happens with Bo, I want to keep seeing you."

My insides turned to mush, and my hands started to sweat. He stepped towards me and waited for me to accept his advance.

He leaned in to kiss me. Last night's kiss had been steamy. This one was slow and tender. Pretty sure I had never made out with a guy at seven thirty on a Sunday morning before.

When we finally took a moment, I said, "And I was worried you were going to take off in your truck and not come back."

"Only if I have to ride shotgun again and watch you nearly crash us."

Leo left to get us breakfast, and I dropped into the kitchen chair. Was that the sweetest thing I'd heard in a long time or Leo playing me? Simultaneously, I was flattered and skeptical about his motives. Regardless, I wanted to sleep with him.

A car door slammed. I kinda hoped it was Leo returning because he'd read my mind and wanted sex before I found the link making him guilty.

Nothing should have surprised me anymore this weekend, but seeing Gigi's parents, James and Patty, walking up Van's driveway carrying flowers caught me off guard.

Charlotte wearing all-black leisure wear, with bare feet and hair twirled in a lazy bun, looked like jet lag rolled off her with ease. I couldn't hear the exchange, but Charlotte embraced Patty and seemed to console her when they all entered the house.

Maz sent a text to me, Leo, and Dutch, asking if we could all meet as soon as possible. He suggested the kitchen at Hattie's at nine. I popped into the conversation before anyone else and said my house at any time.

I went upstairs, threw cold water on my face, and brushed my teeth. I wanted to remember the feeling of Leo's body pushed up against mine. But I needed a clear head for whatever Maz was going to drop on us now.

Again, nothing should have surprised me at this point, but I would never have guessed what I was about to hear.

FORTY-NINE

Maz was at my house in fifteen minutes, looking like hell. When I let him in, I noticed James and Patty were gone.

"Are you ok?" I asked.

"I guess. Not really. Have you heard from Leo? I want to say what I have to and get back as fast as I can."

"He should be here any minute. Do you want to sit?"

He paced around the kitchen.

And I tried again, "How is Bo? Can you tell me that much before Leo gets here?"

"She's been better. We'll get through this," Maz said.

"Through what?"

I got no response.

The knock on the door belonged to Dutch. He stepped inside and took one step back when he saw Maz looking like the bogeyman.

It didn't help when Maz lunged forward. He extended his arm, and Dutch slowly raised his to meet Maz's handshake.

Maz vigorously pulled him into the man hug, half handshake and half hug. "Oh, man, Dutch. Tell your father I'm sorry. It wasn't right of me. I appreciate you still coming here."

Dutch pulled out of the embrace rather fast. "It's ok. I think you guys are good. He said you made peace at the hospital last night."

"We did, but I still feel like I owe you an apology too," Maz said.

"Ok." What more could Dutch say in that moment? He moved closer to me and asked me, "What is going on?"

"We're waiting for Leo, who should be here any minute. What did you tell your parents?"

"They left for breakfast five minutes ago."

I put Dutch in the corner kitchen chair and cleared off the table. I didn't expect another fight, but I was protecting the kid and what was left of my resumes and laptop. Leo walked in a few minutes later, breaking the uncomfortable silence.

Whatever would become of us did not matter in that moment because, right now, he was carrying fresh coffee, pastries, and several breakfast sandwiches. The man was pure gold.

"Morning, everyone. I was in line when I got your message, so I brought stuff for everyone. Dutch, I didn't know if you like coffee, juice, or soda, so I got all three."

"Thanks, I'll take the Coke."

Leo turned to Maz. "Hey, you look like hell, man."

"Lou thought so too, but she chose to keep her opinion to herself. Try it sometime." Maz's laughter at his own joke broke any weirdness in the room. "You care to explain your black eyes and stitches?

"Not really," Leo replied.

We spent a few minutes eating when Maz finally shared with us what was going on.

"I feel responsible for not telling you guys sooner about me and Claire."

It would only make sense for Maz to call his wife by her name, but it sounded so foreign to me.

He went on. "We found each other later in life, and maybe I

wanted to preserve our happiness for a while before dragging in our past. It does not excuse my silence, but I want you to know it was just selfish and not spite."

"It's all right," Leo said.

I wasn't sure where I stood with those feelings.

"Last night, Bo told me everything. She and Gigi had gotten close over the last few months. One day, Bo saw a large amount of cash in Gigi's purse, and Gigi's behavior shifted. Claire put it together. Kids don't carry cash these days, or at least, not a big wad. She tried talking to Gigi but got nowhere. Claire knew Gigi was skipping school and followed her one morning. She had seen her talking to Van in the parking lot and later followed her to his house. Claire knows now she got that part wrong, the part about Van being involved. I guess the police are looking for someone else."

"It was a guy, Cal, that graduated a few years ago from Dome," Dutch said.

It surprised me that he had spoken up.

"This morning, Gigi's parents came over to apologize for attacking my dad yesterday and thanked me for trying to help the police on day one. Gigi's stepmom was a wreck. She was crying and wouldn't stop talking. I guess, at first, Gigi was talking when she came to yesterday but wasn't disclosing everything. The police threatened her with all sorts of charges like obstruction and false kidnapping, so she finally started talking. Tuesday morning, Cal was the one who picked her up and instead of going to our 4QB at the library. They went straight to my house because that's where the guy was working. I guess she tripped out on something, and Cal put her in one of the upstairs bedrooms until she came off whatever they were doing."

"Dammit," Leo said and got strange looks from Maz and Dutch. "I had the same idiot working at my house and fired him when I suspected of him dealing. The police did nothing with the information I gave them. Sorry, go on."

"Gigi didn't know where she was and was too freaked out to leave the bedroom, must have been a real bad trip. She stayed there all night. In the morning, when Cal came back, she was still there. I guess they thought it was a perfect hiding spot. The media attention made it harder for Gigi to go home. Gigi's stepmom is crying about kidnapping, but her dad wasn't owning that idea. Sometime Friday night, she had another bad trip and went running into the woods, and that's how they found her.

"Claire really wanted to help. After a few days of no leads, Claire got it in her head that she was at Van's house and wanted to help. She became obsessed with making someone pay for what happened to Gigi. Again, sorry, Dutch, Claire really thought it was your dad."

"Was she at the house Friday night?" I asked Maz but turned to Dutch for an answer. "Would you have not seen her?"

"You were in the house?" Maz blurted out.

"In the garage. We go through the parkway and hang out in the garage."

"Sorry to jump on you." Maz shook his head. "I'm full of apologies today. Sorry."

The three of us let out a little laugh, and Maz too, seconds later when he realized he had apologized for his apology.

Things were coming together for me. "When she saw you, Dutch, come into the house on Saturday, she thought you were your dad."

"That is exactly right," Maz said.

"So if she wasn't at the house, Hattie's, or home, where was she Friday night?"

Maz went rigid. The only movement were the tears welling up in the corner of his eyes. Leo, Dutch and I exchanged looks of confusion. Maz stepped out of the kitchen and came back, looking like a lost soul.

"She was in the hospital. For the past six months, she has been telling me she gets these migraines." He had to stop talking and regain his composure. "She couldn't tell me the truth. We were so happy, and she wanted that to last as long as possible. Claire has an inoperable brain tumor and only has a few months left. She was so desperate to pay it forward. She thought that was how she would finally be able to say thank you to us for helping her escape her crappy home life."

I got up and gave Maz a hug. He collapsed into my arms, sobbing. I walked him over to a chair and let him collect himself.

"She developed a good sense of when the migraines and other symptoms would present themselves. She had given a couple of employees time off that weekend and knew the others could not handle the store without her, so she closed it for the weekend. Saturday morning, she left the hospital and went to the house hoping to get a confession, or I don't know what. She's still in the hospital, and I don't know if or when she'll get out." Maz leaned over and put his head in his hands. You could practically see the exhaustion running off him.

"If you guys don't need me, I'm going back to the hospital. I just had to give you an update," Maz said.

"Of course, go. Tell her we wish her well, and let us know if we can do anything for you or her. I mean it. Heck, I would even run Hattie's for her."

All the boys laughed at my last comment, and that kinda stung.

Maz left a few minutes later. On the way out the door, he stopped and turned to Dutch. "She wants me to give you her quote for your school newspaper report: *My time in the classroom was brief, but your impact on me lasted a lifetime.*

I wasn't sure if he should be driving, but I didn't think anything would have stopped him from going to Claire. I wasn't sure if I'd ever said her real name other than to Dutch three days ago in room five. Then or now, I didn't know if I'd ever gotten to know the real Claire Cosworth, but she had taught me a lot about myself.

Leo had to leave too. He had promised Peggy he would sit with Gina while she went to have her hair done and then go play bunko with her friends.

Dutch was the last out the door and seemed to linger. He could have easily gone earlier. "I just want to say thank you for including me. You didn't have to do that."

"I'm just glad you made it over this morning."

"No, I meant on Thursday in room five. I didn't understand how much you were trying to help."

"That is all we were doing. Just like all those years ago, we just wanted to help Claire."

He turned towards the front door, and I stopped him, "I have to ask. I feel bad for asking, but why did you lie to me about Friday night?"

"I told you everything."

"I saw you leave. After all the lights in the condo were out I saw you leave."

He nodded his head, flipped his hair back, and leaned against the door. He took a moment before he said something, then shoved his hands into his pockets, almost turning into a frightened turtle. "It has nothing to do with any of this. I should not have implied it was my dad. I was mad because he might have been involved with Gigi, and it's something I didn't want people to know right now. There was so much attention because of Gigi that I just didn't want it to be more of an issue. I could only imagine what the rumors would be if everything got mixed together. That is part of the reason my mom came home. I told her but not my dad. She wanted to show her support. I met someone, and we started seeing each other."

"I didn't think your parents would be uptight about you dating someone—" Sometimes, I could be slow at figuring out things.

He practically had to hit me over the head.

"Do you have a boyfriend?"

He nodded.

"I'm a little tongue-tied. I never had someone come out directly to me before. Thank you for sharing your secret with me. I hope I didn't force you to tell me when you weren't ready."

"It's all right. I just felt like I should tell my dad first."

"Your secret is safe with me. I've a feeling your dad will be cool about it."

"Not too worried about it in that sense. He hates confrontation. It's the hundred questions and him overdoing trying to show his support that will get to be tiring."

"Well, that's our job as parents. We get to support, love, and embarrass our kids."

"Don't I know it? I just hope this Gigi stuff will finally stop, and everyone at school can put their focus on someone besides me."

"Good luck with that. Hey, is it Quinn? He's cute. Forget that I asked. You told me more than you ever needed to, and I appreciate that. That was just the parent in me. See, that was me overstepping. I'm sorry."

"It's not Quinn, but he is the only other person from Dome I told. Him and my mom are the only ones that know. That's really why she is coming back now. Somehow she thinks I need her support when I tell my dad."

"Thank you again for sharing. If you ever need anything, please let me know. A lot of what happened this weekend will hang on you for a while, but don't let it weigh you down."

Dutch was on the porch step when he turned back. "Hey, I still need your quote for the Quell, sorry, Mrs. Quell project."

It didn't take me long to figure it out. "How about this: *I may not have heard every word you said but I understood every lesson.*"

"Not bad," Dutch said.

I shut the door and dropped to the floor for the third time that weekend. Every word, every question, and every confession fell on me like a ton of bricks.

Later that week, I would learn Gigi and her family told the

narrative that she'd had a friend drop her off at her aunt's house. She was supposed to be taking care of the plants while the aunt was on vacation. She had collapsed in the basement and was recovering from some infection. The rumor at school was that she was in rehab. Gigi returned to school several weeks later. Dutch came out to his dad and let a few friends know and that led to everyone knowing. I was happy for Dutch and that it had been easy for him, since lots of teenagers still struggled with it these days.

Sunday night, I needed to myself. Leo wanted to get together, but I needed time. I also needed sex, but there was so much to understand I couldn't balance it all. We have been chatting and texting, and he'll visit in two weeks.

I had come back the following Saturday just for a few hours to finally get a chance to see Claire. She was at home with Maz in hospice care. She touched my arm like she had all those years ago, but this time I heard the words "Thank you."

The tumor progressed faster than the doctors had predicted. Claire passed away two weeks later. The following week, I received a certified letter from a lawyer's office. Claire had signed over ownership of Hattie's to me.

FIFTY

I couldn't say these words before—the final part of the saga. I wanted to hear it from Claire, but that hadn't ever gotten to happen. I only had his words, and they would haunt me forever.

That Sunday when Maz, Leo, Dutch, and I had gathered in the kitchen eating breakfast, Stew came over with a new sliding door for the patio. Apparently, the big-box hardware stores open early, even on weekends. Stew was all about fixing my parents' condo, as they had left it a few days ago.

While Leo and Stew were fitting the new slider in place, I saw what I had been looking for but had missed earlier. It was there in his shoe treads. Stew had red dirt in his shoes.

Bile backed up in my throat. I planted a smile on my face. I had to get through this morning.

I helped Stew carry out the old door. "Where did this truck come from?"

"It's Larry's. My neighbor. I still have Kay's car. She won't be home with my truck for a few hours, and I wanted to get this done." He hopped into the truck and started it. He rolled down the window. "I don't know what is going on in there with that group, but maybe

327

just have breakfast and send everyone home. I'm headed to Chicago for the Bulls-Bucks game. I don't have time for anything else."

"What do you mean?"

"I clean up the messes you always seem to be a part of."

"What are you talking about?" I asked again.

"You are not as slick as you think you are. Just because you don't share your side of the story with me does not mean I'm in the dark. I watched you pretend to be Bo that morning. I watched you carry out Yvette's body and say goodbye to Bo. I watched you drive Olsen's car to the mall parking lot with the Greyhound Bus substation."

My feet were tingling, my hands were numb, and the ringing in my ears was pulsing with my heart. I thought I might drop in my parents' driveway.

Stew kept talking. "But let's keep focus on this weekend. Who do you think found Gigi in the parkway and who led me there? I knew it was Bo the second I walked into Hattie's nine months ago. Who do you think she called to meet her at Hattie's on Friday? Before I drove her to the hospital Friday night, she told me to rescue Gigi and that she might be at Vans house. Bo didn't know about the kid. She thought it was Van. I found Cal and Gigi high on something and figured out it was him the whole time. It was never Van. Don't worry, they'll never find where I put Cal's body. I cleaned up this mess like I did with Yvette. Now, let's just stop lying to each other."

BOOK CLUB QUESTIONS

How far would you go to protect someone? Is going to the authorities the right first step?

If you learn someone has killed multiple times, how would your relationship change?

Should Lou turn her brother in to the authorities?

Vigilante justice—is there ever a right time for it?

Are you harboring any old feelings for a high school crush? Do you have a cool opening line ready if you accidentally run into them?

What is your favorite spot to return to when visiting your hometown?

DOMESTIC ABUSE SUPPORT

There is nothing funny about the abuse and mistreatment of others. It is often used as a storyline in books and television, but it is a serious problem. It is devastating to know it is so pervasive around the world.

Please reach out for help if you experience any abuse. You are worth it.

National Domestic Violence Hotline
1-800-799-6233

Report Abuse, Neglect, and Exploitation of Adults or Children
1-800-922-5330

ACKNOWLEDGMENTS

This book is fiction. Let me say it again—this is all make believe. Yes, I grew up in a suburb of Milwaukee very similar to this town, but that is where any similarity ends. There might be some references to my town—some intentional, some not. There are some private jokes that only certain readers might understand. If you think you recognize some reference or joke, let me know, and I might confirm it for you. I hope you all loved this book as much as I enjoyed writing it.

Just a few shout-outs:

Brian Van Kooster, thank you for answering my questions about libraries. I took many liberties with the inner workings of libraries, but you provided great insight. The mistakes and rule-breaking are all me.

I have to give credit to Will Arnett—yes, *that* Will Arnett of Hollywood and especially his podcast, *Smartless*, with two other Hollywood greats Sean Hayes and Jason Bateman. No they don't need a plug from me, but I have to give Mr. Arnett credit for the expression *throwing and going*. Will told a hilarious/mortifying story about getting sick—throwing and going. I'd never heard it explained that way before, and I love it.

My friend Shannon Caul taught me the other great expression— airplane bath. Under the wings and through the cockpit.

A thank-you to Robin Leduc for answering tedious questions on things unfamiliar to me.

Thank you to my beta readers for the feedback—Alexis, Molly, and Mel.

Thank you to my editor, Starr Baumann. The story and mistakes are mine, but Starr helped smooth out the rough edges.

Most of all, thank you to my husband, Brian, and son, Alex, for their love and support.

ABOUT THE AUTHOR

After graduating from the University of Wisconsin-Stout, TJ embarked on a career in the hospitality industry, which led to multiple moves across the country. An avid marathon runner, TJ turned to writing after her knee eventually gave out. The author lives in Kansas with her husband Brian, son Alex, and dog, Reba. When not writing, TJ can be found hiking our national parks or traveling with her book club.

GO